INTO THE DARK

INTO THE DARK

Andrew Jennings

Parallel Universe Publications

Prologue

Even in the ragged snatches of clear thinking of which he was still capable, the boy could no longer remember how long he had been here. The numbing weight of the heavy manacles had long since chaffed his wrists and ankles with sores.

It was weeks since he last saw daylight. In its place, in the harsh glare of the neon light fixed to the ceiling above his head, he had no way of knowing night from day. Both had long since disappeared from his thinking. All that mattered any more were the unpredictable periods of rest when his tormentors left him, to do whatever it was they did when they weren't here.

*Too late he wished he could undo everything that brought him to this place. But what else could he have done? His mum's latest boyfriend had threatened to beat 'six shades of shit' out of him with a baseball bat for borrowing a few twenties he'd found on the kitchen table. How was he expected to know that Wayne had put them there for a supply of heroin he was having delivered that morning? All he'd taken had been a couple of notes from the thick wad. Not enough to be noticed. But Wayne had noticed. Wayne noticed everything when it came to money - especially **his** money.*

The worst thing, though, was that Craig knew his mum would have done nothing to stop the bastard from beating him.

Craig sobbed to himself, as he had done so often after being brought here by the men who'd befriended him. At the railway station in Lancaster where they'd found him, pretending to be waiting for a train, they had looked like saviours, especially after they gave him his first hot meal in days. Now he would rather have had a thousand shades of shit beaten out of him by Wayne than have gone through what had happened here. Nothing he had ever seen or heard or dreamt about could have prepared him for what the bastards had done to him.

Nor would it end — not till he was dead.

Craig knew what was going on here. He wasn't naive. He was old enough at thirteen to know why they had lured him here. The dirty, stinking, filthy perverts!

They had cut him repeatedly, checking each wound and making notes, mumbling about how long it took to heal, as if they were doctors. That didn't fool him. Doctors didn't torture people, didn't cut them like this.

If he could have only gotten himself free of the manacles, he'd be out of here and straight to the cops and have the bastards sent down for good.

But the manacles were solid.

He knew there was no escape.

Not now.

Not ever.

1

It was growing dark early tonight.

Already shadows were beginning to fill what gaps there were between the cars parked in front of the office blocks.

Janice Burroughs feared the dark. Ever since adolescence she had feared it. Though as she grew older she had thought this phobia would fade, she now knew better. Especially on overcast days like this, when night seemed to fall so quickly it almost caught her out.

She glanced at her watch. It was nearly four. In another few minutes she could finally leave. And to Hell with how it would affect her flexitime. When the clocks changed back to British Summer Time she would make up for it. During spring and summer she never minded working late. And she would soon get her hours up to scratch. But for now, she'd leave early and make sure she got home not long after dark. As it was it would be well past five by the time her bus dropped her off at the end of Melmott Road.

'Going home early again?' Michelle looked round from her monitor as Janice reached for her handbag from under the desk, a faugh expression of disapproval on her face.

'And what if I am? What's that got to do with you?' Janice regretted her words as soon as she'd said them.

'What's got into you?' Michelle stopped typing on her keyboard. 'I thought you were in a good mood today.'

Janice shook her head. 'I'm sorry. I really am. It's just...' She glanced at the window; the sky loomed like an enormous grey shutter above the office blocks across the road, their anonymity unmitigated by the uniformity of the blinds drawn across their windows. 'It's just I hate gloomy days when it never seems to brighten up.'

'I know, I know: *you hate the dark.*' The two had worked together long enough for confidences to be common currency between them. 'Well, you'd better get going. It'll be four in another few minutes if you want to get home early.'

Janice gathered up her handbag. 'You know how it is,' she half apologised. 'Some of us have phobias about spiders and heights and things like that. With me it's the dark. I never could

7

stand it, even when I was a kid.'

'You've told me. You always had to go to sleep with a night light on in your bedroom.' Michelle laughed quietly. 'I'll see you tomorrow.'

As luck would have it her supervisor glanced across as she made her way between the rows of computer monitors. 'I expect you'll be in early tomorrow? To make up for lost time,' Bickerstaff added unnecessarily as she passed, gold-framed spectacles perched on the balding dome of his head. They reflected the neon lights above like spherical mirrors.

She paused.

'Of course, Mr Bickerstaff. I always am.' *In the winter,* she added to herself as she scooped up her coat from the stand by the door and left.

A chill pervaded the air outside; plumes of exhaust trailed the cars that made their way between the speed bumps along the road. Vapour trails straddled the glistening tarmac. More vapours hung between the upper windows of the buildings; they diffused the pale disk of the sun that hung like a bleached satsuma above the ugly expanse of the multi-storey car park at the end of the road.

Janice tightened the scarf around her neck as she crossed the road and headed for the bus stop. A queue had already started to form. Which was a good sign. The next bus couldn't be far away.

Another Body Found On the Common

shrieked the stark headline at a newspaper stand near the head of the queue. Opening her handbag, Janice picked out some coins and bought a copy from the man who crouched at the stand, a steaming mug of tea in one hand and a folded copy of *The Evening Standard* ready in the other.

Janice thought she would try to read the paper on her way home if the bus wasn't crowded. Though news of another murder was the last thing she felt like reading now. This time of year was bad enough without adding to her fears horror stories like this. If she wasn't careful she'd need sleeping pills or a good dose of vodka to get to sleep tonight.

'Nasty business.' A middle-aged woman with a dark red hat nodded at the headline in her paper. 'Makes you want to stay in and never come out, don't it?'

'Some of us have got to go out whether we like it or not,' Janice said, more defensively than she intended.

'Don't I know it?' The woman held up her hand to show her knobbly fingers. 'Thirty years of typing have done this to me,' she said.

Janice smiled and nodded her head as their bus pulled up with a spiteful hiss of pneumatic brakes.

For some reason the red-hatted secretary wanted to continue their conversation on the bus, depositing her bulk alongside Janice. Realising she would have little chance of looking at her paper unless the woman got off first, Janice rolled it up and pushed it into one of the pockets of her coat.

'Third death this month,' the woman went on remorselessly.

'I'm sorry?' Janice asked, though she knew perfectly well what the woman was talking about.

'The body, *dear* – the body they found on the common.' The woman shook her head as her eyes took in the back of the man in front of them, as if determined to label him a potential killer. His thin, bony, rounded shoulders and narrow head, fringed with what remained of his grey hair, seemed to belie this potential in Janice's eyes, but who knows? Crippen was an insignificant looking man and look what he did.

'I haven't had time to read about it,' Janice said.

'Neither have I,' the woman retorted. 'I listened to the midday news on the radio. I don't need to read about it too, for Christ's sake! The basic facts are bad enough, believe you me. Besides, the police have already said it's obviously the work of the same man, so you know the same things happened to this poor girl as happened to all the others. I hope they get the bastard soon. They should string him up by the balls.'

The man in front seemed to shrink into his overcoat as the woman's words bore down against his back.

'I don't suppose it'll take them long. Each time he kills he'll leave more clues for the police to work on.'

'Do you think so?' The woman laughed. 'I wouldn't care to take bets on that, dear. The police will still be knocking on doors when the next victim's found on some derelict patch of land. You watch if I'm not right.'

By the time the bus pulled up at her stop, Janice's head was already beginning to throb with what felt like the start of a migraine attack. Embarrassment at the non-stop grating of the woman's voice was only part of the cause.

Dark clouds already hid most of what remained of the sun, and the street lights were still too dim to give much illumination on the gloomy streets; more light came from passing cars and shop windows.

As Janice approached the Victorian villa in which she rented a first floor flat, she saw Jimmy Legg's old BMW and transit van. They were the only vehicles on the flagged garden in front. Fancying himself as a bit of a businessman, Jimmy had once told her he only lived here because his divorce had cost him his family home in the suburbs. He was always talking about how successful he was before 'that woman fucked up' his life. Janice hoped he wasn't waiting for her to get back home. She had become exasperated by the relentlessness of his attempts to flirt with her months ago. If she could have convinced herself he was doing it with more in mind than just getting inside her knickers, she might have been tempted to go out with him. But she knew his type too well to be deceived by his chat-up lines.

As quietly as she could she inserted her key in the front door and eased it open. The hallway was empty as she let herself in. Just as quietly, she hurried to the stairs, her feet barely touching the carpeted steps as she headed for her door. From the floor above she heard Jimmy's door start to open. *Too late, this time, you sad pathetic man,* she thought to herself with a surge of triumph as she unlocked her door, opened it, then nipped in and slammed it shut behind her. She leaned the back of her head against its solid panels for a few seconds as she caught her breath; for the first time since leaving work an hour ago she smiled. Jimmy never even started down the stairs. He knew she wouldn't answer her door once she was inside, that his only chance of trying out his attempts to date her lay in catching her on the stairs. *Poor sod,* she thought.

Shaking her head in disdain, Janice shrugged off her coat and headed for the kitchen. A caffeine-saturated, high-priced coffee for starters, then she'd think about what to eat.

As she passed the answer phone she noticed its red light blinking at her, a small demonic eye. 'Hello, Janice,' her mother's accusatory voice started to drone as soon as she pressed play.

'It's been so long since you last called me I thought I'd better ring to make sure you're still all right, though I don't suppose things are any different than they were the last time we spoke. Dad's chest hasn't got any better – if you're interested. The doctor's signed him off another month, so things aren't exactly flush at the moment. It's a pity you aren't still living with us; I never could see the sense in a single girl living by herself when your board would have made the world of difference to the way things are. But you wanted your freedom, whatever that's supposed to mean. Anyway, I can't stay on the phone any longer. The bill was big enough last month, what with VAT and the rental charge and all the rest. If you can spare the time, it would be nice to hear from you. Hope things are going well for you at work.'

Her mother's voice ended in a forlorn tone that Janice remembered all too well. It had been this, as much as anything else, that had persuaded her at twenty-one to apply for a job in London. That was two years ago. And still her mother hadn't given up hope of getting her back. What with *Rudolf Valentino* Legg upstairs and her mother's calls from 'home', she sometimes wondered how she managed to preserve what measure of freedom she had somehow miraculously gained for herself. She knew if she was just a little bit weaker, if her thirst for freedom, for her own chance to make decisions for herself, wasn't as intense as it was, she would have been hobbled to her mother's apron strings for the rest of her parents' lives. Or at least for as long as her mother's, which was probably the same. Of the two she was sure mother would long outlive her father, whose lungs had been wrecked by too many high-tar cigarettes. No more than a shadow of the man he once was, his change of heart over smoking had come too late to make up for years of ceaseless abuse, not helped by a lifelong love affair with whisky.

For all that, though, Janice still preserved a strong feeling of affection for her father. At least his foibles were honest-to-God normal ones. Not like her mother's, whose subtlety clashed with abrasiveness at the first sign of dissent.

Her mood marred by the message on her phone, Janice padded into the kitchen. Whatever else she was going to do tonight she was going to have a large mug of coffee first, then relax while she watched TV. As for her mother, maybe, *perhaps*

11

maybe sometime during the next few days (or weeks) (or months) she'd ring her back, probably when she had a full bottle of whisky on hand to seek refuge in afterwards. (Thank you, Father, she thought, for passing this on in my genes.)

Her kitchen, though small, was bright and airy, fitted with as many gadgets as her small salary had enabled her to buy. After the living room, with its TV, Hi-fi and CDs, it was her favourite room in the flat, looking out as it did on the shared garden at the back of the house. Bordered by rhododendron, the lawn stretched for twenty yards. As she gazed at it now, the shadows that filled it made her shudder. Night had drawn in fast. Too fast, she thought. In a few minutes she would be unable to make out anything at all except for what was lit by the afterglow from the downstairs windows. All the other gardens in the surrounding area were pitch-black already.

She pulled the cord on the blinds to cut out the night, then filled the kettle. When her coffee was ready she took it into the living room and switched on the television. The early evening news was on – which, she realised, was a mistake. It was mainly about the murder.

'So far police are unable to confirm the identity of the latest victim to the stalker whose activities have left residents in south west London fearful of venturing out at night. Police confirm that it was almost certainly the work of the same killer...'

The sooner he was caught the better, she thought. It was bad enough having something like this going on at the height of summer, when it was light until late, but now it was almost enough to tempt her into taking the train up north back to her parents. Almost but not quite. Not even the threat of the midnight stalker could drive her to that... *oh, no, not yet,* she thought, *please God, not yet!*

Amused at her attempt at humour, Janice settled even deeper into the armchair, feet curled beneath her as the heat from the gas fire soaked into her. She flicked channels with the remote till she found a repeat of *Friends* instead of the news.

Then the lights and the TV went off.

The insistent knocking at her door eventually forced its way through Janice's hysteria.

Unsure whether to answer it or not, Janice forced herself off the armchair, stifled her screams with an effort of will, that left her feeling drained, and began to feel her way towards the door. 'Who is it?' she called, her voice too sharp, too brittle.

'It's Jimmy. Jimmy Legg. I heard you upstairs. Are you all right?'

Janice gulped back a sob; her arms were beginning to shake as reaction set in.

'The lights went out. I can't see anything.'

'It's all right.' His voice sounded muffled, as if he was stood too close to the door. 'There's been another power cut. It's the third this week, though you were probably out at work when they happened before. If it's anything like the rest it'll be over in a few minutes.' When Janice failed to reply, Jimmy said: 'Would you like to let me in till the power comes on? If it would make you feel any better, perhaps...?'

Janice hesitated, unsure if she should let him in or not, though his presence would help dispel her phobia. For a while, at least.

'Just till the lights come on,' she said finally, unlocking the door.

Only the smell of his after-shave revealed his presence against the murkier darkness on the staircase.

Relieved that he would be unable to see her trembling, Janice led Jimmy through to the living room.

'The sofa's somewhere in front of you. If you stretch out your hands you'll feel it,' she said, though the glow from the gas fire was more than enough to make it out after the darkness of the landing. His face showed as a dull blur above the blackness of his clothes as he reached for the back of the sofa, then felt his way around it.

'I thought you must have hurt yourself when the lights went out,' he said when they were seated. 'You could have been carrying a pan of hot water or something,' he said. 'It happens.'

'Thanks for your concern.'

'That's what neighbours are for,' he said with what sounded like sincerity. Janice tried to make out his features in the gloom, to see if he was smiling or not after he said it. Getting inside her flat was something he had been working on for the past six months. The blackout could have seemed too good an opportunity too miss, she thought, though she tried to suppress her cynicism. If she wasn't careful she'd end up as bad as her mother, God help her, with what anyone did being open to the worst interpretations.

'It's nice to know there's someone prepared to help out,' she said as honestly as her lingering doubts would allow.

Jimmy chuckled.

'You don't trust me, do you?'

Janice felt her cheeks redden, glad for the darkness for once. 'What do you mean?'

The man sighed. 'I know what you think of me. Divorced, unattached male, on the look out for any bit of skirt he can get hold of. I can see it in your eyes. At least when there's light to see them in.'

'And..?' she asked.

'And *am I*, do you mean?'

'It's the impression you give, Mr Legg,' she said, conscious how stilted she sounded but unable to help it.

'Mr Legg! We're past that now, aren't we? We've been neighbours nearly a year. I hope I can call you Janice?'

After an instant's uncertainty, she said, 'Of course you can. I'm sorry. It's my upbringing. My parents – my mother, anyway – were sticklers for formality. Anyone other than my personal friends or younger relations had always to be addressed by their full title – or else.'

'Or else your mum would play hell with you?'

'And if you ever met my mum you'd know what being played hell with was like.' She felt her lips broaden into a smile. Smiling while stuck in the dark! That was a new one for her. Janice felt a sense of well being flow through her. Perhaps she'd misunderstood Jimmy. Perhaps he wasn't so bad after all. Few people were, she supposed. Only her... Shaking her head, she let the thought die before it finished. She'd allowed her feelings to grow too vehement against her mother over the past few years. Perhaps it was time to let them go. 'I'd offer you a coffee but,

14

apart from the fire, everything's electric.'

'That's all right. I've just had a brew. Perhaps, when the power's back on...?'

As if his words had a magical power of their own, the lights flickered on, dazzling bright, then the TV spluttered and burst into sound.

'Hooray!' Janice felt a sense of relief surge through her like a booster shot of adrenaline.

'I told you,' Jimmy said, his lean, Gypsy-like features brightening with one of the biggest, most genuinely friendly grins she had ever seen in her life. He brushed a callused hand through the unruly mop of his hair. Jet black and curly, it flopped foppishly against his forehead. 'Did someone say something about a brew?'

'On its way,' Janice said, jumping up and heading for the kitchen in time to control the grin that might have been broad enough to match his own.

Chief Inspector James Yates meticulously wiped his lips with a large white handkerchief as he left the morgue, Detective Sergeant McKenna close on his heels. Both men were tall, but Yates had the advantage by more than an inch and an extra couple of stones in weight, though he bore his bulk better. What was muscle on his ponderous, heavy-boned frame, was blatantly fat on his sergeant, who had let middle-age spread all but consume whatever pretensions to athleticism he might, at some remote period in time, have had. Puffing already in an attempt to keep pace with his boss, McKenna was red-faced and sweating by the time the chief inspector came to an abrupt halt in the corridor.

'Damnedest murder I've ever come across,' Yates complained, as if the killer had done it as a personal insult. He still felt traces of hot spit burn the back of his throat, though he was no stranger to autopsies; he'd seen the insides of more bodies than he cared to remember. But that never seemed to make it easier. He gazed at his sergeant as he waited for him to catch his breath, unable to avoid the thought that it was time Ian pulled himself together or he'd barely be fit to carry out his duties.

When his breath had subsided, McKenna shook his head. 'At least we know the same man killed her as the others, sir,' he said at last.

'That's true. For all the good that does us.' As abruptly as he had stopped, Yates started walking again, hands in his pockets, his leather-soled shoes clattering loudly on the marble floor. 'Where do we go from here? Repeat all the enquiries we've made three times already? Appeal to the public yet again for witnesses – witnesses, I'd lay good money, just aren't there? Or get in touch with *Crime Watch* and arrange a spot on TV, though I've a feeling they'll be contacting us soon enough if some of the facts about this case leak out?'

McKenna shrugged. 'Just keep plodding on, I suppose, and hope we get a break.'

Yates grunted his opinion on that. Which was all, he felt, deep inside, any of them could do at this stage. 'Maybe it's time we released more details. Shock tactics, perhaps, to jog someone's memory, though I doubt it. I doubt it very much, Ian.' He gazed at the floodlit car park outside. 'Let's go for a drink. Perhaps that'll help bring inspiration. Nothing else seems to do it.'

McKenna nodded.

'Chief Inspector!'

The high-pitched nasal twang brought both men to a halt once again. They turned as its owner climbed from one of the parked cars, a short, broad-shouldered man with a shaggy grey beard and an eclectic taste in clothes: brown suit, drab green shirt and a nondescript mustard-coloured tie.

'Still trying to ferret out bits of tittle-tattle for your rag?' Yates asked, his disdain for the journalist so well hidden only someone who had known him long enough could have detected the slightest trace in his voice.

'Not *The Standard*,' Steve Grant called as he strolled towards them, pale brown Hush Puppies silencing his footsteps. 'I'm writing a book. This crop of killings might have the makings of a best seller in them. Who knows? I'm sure there's enough to catch the imagination of the public once the facts are released.'

'And what facts are those, Mr Grant?' Yates could not help putting a head-masterly inflection in his voice.

'Ah now, there you undoubtedly have the advantage, Chief Inspector. Not that I haven't tried my best to find out.'

Yates turned to his sergeant. 'And he expects us to believe him.'

'Ple-ease! If I'd heard anything, d'you think I'd be hanging around in the hope – the desperate hope, I'm sure you'd agree – of finding something I shouldn't really know from you?'

'In one word: yes.' Yates unexpectedly laughed. It was a deep-throated laugh that echoed metallically in the hallway. 'We're on our way for a drink. Care to join us? Perhaps – just perhaps, mind you – there'll be something we could talk about.'

Grant's eyes sparkled. 'What are we hanging about this bloody mausoleum for? Let's get going!'

*

The Grapes was only a few hundred yards down the road but it seemed a different world altogether: from a place of grim death

17

to boisterous, almost riotous life, riotous being a word that certainly came uppermost in McKenna's mind as he forced his way through the throng of office workers and off-duty medical staff wedged in a scrum around the bar. One day, when he was a chief inspector himself (or even a lowly inspector, maybe), with a DC or DS under him, he would waltz into a place like this and take a comfortable seat well away from the hubbub while his underpaid, overworked underling struggled to get the drinks. Sweat was already beading his face when he glanced back at Yates. He was sat next to Grant at a corner table, patiently awaiting their drinks. Well, there was nothing else for it, McKenna thought, the twenty pound note Yates had given him growing damp in his hand, and that was use his weight.

*

'So what can you tell me?' Grant asked as Sergeant McKenna began his big push to the bar. He scratched his beard as he watched the chief inspector through gold-framed spectacles.

'I really don't know. Officially, that is.'

'I hope you're not going to go cold on me after dragging me here,' Grant said.

'I didn't exactly have to drag you.'

'Perhaps not. But you did dangle a tempting piece of bait before my eyes. Come on. We can help each other, you know. From what I can see, you're not getting any nearer catching whoever's been killing those girls. Three so far. How long till it's four? How long before the public's braying for something to be done and you have your bosses breathing down your neck?'

'How do you know they're not doing that already?' Yates glanced round as McKenna returned with three pints of bitter clenched in his hands. 'Good man,' Yates said with a genuine feeling of bonhomie as his sergeant laid the pints on the table with extreme care. 'I knew you wouldn't take long to get through that rabble.'

For the next few moments the men silently tasted their beers, then Grant, his impatience showing through the air of carefree affability that was his well known stock-in-trade, placed his pint on the table and leaned towards the chief inspector. 'Well?' he said.

Yates put down his half-emptied glass and sat back as far as he comfortably could. 'I don't want anything putting out officially at this stage. Just a hint as to one aspect of the crimes. Unconfirmed, of course.'

'Of course,' Grant said.

'I say 'of course', because some at the station wouldn't approve of this being leaked.'

'Not you?'

'Normally I would, but three deaths are three too many.' Yates breathed out slowly. 'Just let it be known that one bizarre aspect of the case, that sets it apart at the moment, is this: after the victims were strangled the flesh on their faces was sliced off, before they were daubed with theatrical make-up.'

'Skinned? Theatrical make-up?' Grant's face twisted into a frown. 'Grease paint? Is that what you mean?'

'Dollops of the stuff. Not applied with any kind of expertise, mind, so far as we can tell, unless that was a deliberate ruse to mislead us. Grotesquely, you might say. Layers of it.'

'Do you have any idea why?'

Yates shrugged. 'If we had, we wouldn't be as stumped as we are. Why someone would spend time doing this after having murdered the girls, we don't know. We'll probably only find that out when we've caught him.'

'It's definitely a 'he'?'

'*Probably* a 'he', not definitely,' Yates corrected. 'A woman could have killed them. But we think it more likely a man.'

'A man obsessed with disfiguration?'

'Or someone who's had connections with theatrical work of some kind. Or someone who, for whatever strange reasons of their own, derives some kind of satisfaction from disfiguring his victims this way. Other murderers use knifes to mutilate their victims. This bugger uses a knife *and* make-up, as if he wanted to cover up what he'd done.'

'A psycho?'

'Or someone clever enough to lead us to that conclusion.'

'A lot of 'maybes',' Grant said as he reached for his drink. 'Still, you've given me enough to get started.'

'From *unofficial* sources,' Yates added with a nod.

'Naturally, Chief Inspector. I wouldn't dream of saying anything else.'

4

Although nearly midday, the ground mist that lingered across the bleak stretches of the common was more than enough to keep the temperature well below freezing, despite the sunlight that had already succeeded in bringing a hint of spring to the rest of the area. Detective Sergeant Ian McKenna rubbed his hands against each other in a useless attempt to generate warmth into his numbed fingers; he knew how futile this was after two hours spent with the rest of the team, meticulously searching the frosted acres of grass for clues. Two days had passed since the body of Helen Parker was stumbled across by a retired bus-driver, exercising his greyhound with two of his friends. They had been timing the dog as it sprinted between them till it became distracted by a bundle of what at first they thought was a bundle of old clothes, half-hidden inside a clump of bushes.

Despite an intensive sweep of the area, nothing had so far been found that could lead to the girl's killer. After more than a month of frost, the ground was so incredibly hard there was not even so much as the hint of a footprint near the body. Only the daubs of greasepaint remained of the killer's presence, and it was certain he must have been wearing gloves, probably rubber ones, when he applied it.

They were wasting their time, and McKenna knew it.

He signalled to his second in command.

'I'm going to see the girl's parents,' McKenna said. 'I promised the governor I'd see them sometime today. Keep the men at it for one more sweep, then call it a day. If we've found nothing by then, there's nothing here.'

McKenna hunched his shoulders against the cold as he headed for his car. The dark Mondeo seemed even colder than the common as he climbed inside and searched for the keys in his overcoat pockets. Still, there would be a hot cup of tea soon enough when he reached the Parkers' house. They were that kind of people. However distressed they might be, they could never overlook the normal civilities they would automatically assume was expected of them. It would take even more than the murder of their youngest daughter to do that, he supposed, unsure whether he should envy their resilience or not. McKenna had only met them twice during the investigation, but this had impressed him about them. And shocked him, too, knowing how devastating an impact something like that must have had on them. God help him if anything ever happened to his kids; he dreaded to think how he would react. Or his wife.

McKenna glanced again at the rows of large houses that overlooked this side of the common, their ground floor windows hidden behind privets or rows of firs. So well protected was their privacy that no one had seen anything on the night of the murder. Or heard anything either, secure behind double-glazed windows that sealed them in from the outside world. Although it would have been bright enough on the road traversing this side of the common, the lampposts that provided most of the light would have done no more than throw the common, by contrast, into even greater darkness. McKenna shivered as he started his car and drove down the road. It was hard to imagine any girl venturing across it by herself at night. He assumed she was forced here or lured onto the common by someone she knew.

A few minutes later McKenna parked outside the Parkers' house, a large post-war semi in a quiet neighbourhood, walking distance from the nearest shops. McKenna imagined during the summer its garden would have been a blaze of colour. Now only the pruned stumps of the roses that filled its borders showed over its low brick wall. Ornate hooks for hanging baskets covered much of the red brickwork, especially around the door, their bowls removed for the winter, while a fishpond glistened in front of the bay window that overlooked the garden. It was a neat house; not exactly cosy – it was a shade too tidy for that, in McKenna's view – but definitely neat.

Unfastening his seat belt, McKenna lurched out of his car, his shirt crumpled around his midriff. One day he would have to make an effort at dieting again. The uncomfortable weight of his stomach drew him back as he swung the car door shut, before striding purposefully up the path towards the house.

'She won't be long with the tea,' Harold Parker said distractedly a few minutes later after ushering him into the living room. Parker rose from lighting the gas fire. 'We always have the central heating on this time of year but it does no good in this room. The window's too large. Lets more heat escape than the radiators give out, I'm sure.' Though in his late forties, Parker looked older. In the time since they last met a few days ago he seemed to have aged alarmingly. Even though he was on extended leave of absence from work, the man still wore a tie and the buttoned-up waistcoat of a serge suit, as if he was ready to go to the office at a moment's notice. McKenna noticed he had forgotten to shave, though, and grey patches of stubble covered his chin. Dark lines on either side of Parker's face and bags beneath his eyes revealed the amount of strain he had been under since his daughter's death. Taking this in as he waited for the tea to arrive, McKenna hoped the facade of normality the man was desperately trying to maintain wouldn't make him crack up. There was a worrying artificiality about both the girl's parents, as if they were incapable of letting their true emotions show through. Parker handed him a college photograph of his daughter. She had been a pretty girl, maybe not beautiful, but pretty without doubt, McKenna thought as he studied it. Dark brown hair, solemn eyes, with a long, high-bridged nose that could have been described as aristocratic (a gift evidently passed on from her father, whose nose was even more prominent than hers), and a warm and pleasing smile as she stared at the camera.

'This was a year ago.'

'She was a beautiful girl,' McKenna murmured, handing the picture back. 'It was a tragedy, Mr Parker. We won't stop till we find whoever was responsible for what happened to her.'

Parker nodded. 'I know you're doing everything you can, sergeant. Both my wife and I appreciate it.'

'I'm glad you think so, though I admit we're not much further towards finding out who it was than the last time we met.' He pulled out his note pad. 'Perhaps if we could go through your daughter's interests once more to see if there's anything that might help.'

'Perhaps,' Parker said as his wife bustled in with a tray of tea and biscuits. Again McKenna felt a sense of unreality about the couple, and he had the sudden urge to shout at them to stop it and cry, to do something that would help him appreciate the pain he was sure they were going through.

'Help yourself to some biscuits, sergeant,' Mrs Parker said as she placed the tray on the coffee table in front of him with hands that suddenly started to tremble.

'Thank you.' McKenna reached for one of the cups. 'Please sit down, both of you. I appreciate what you must be going through.'

Mrs Parker pulled a balled-up handkerchief from her apron pocket and dabbed her eyes.

'We are trying to keep going as best we can, sergeant,' Parker explained. 'It's not easy. I don't think either of us can take in what's happened, that we'll never see our little girl come walking through the door again, that the body we were shown at the hospital was really hers.' Parker shook his head, rubbing his chin with one hand. 'We know it was hers. We know that, sergeant. But we can't accept it. Not yet. Do you understand what I'm trying to say?'

McKenna nodded.

'We didn't expect her home before ten that night,' Mrs Parker said. 'She was stopping off at the gym. It was her night for aerobics. She was keen on keep fit. Three times a week she went without fail. Sometimes she'd stop for a drink with some friends before coming home. But we never worried about her. She'd been used to going out by herself for years.'

'We've checked with the gym,' McKenna said. 'She turned up that night but left around nine. By all accounts she was by herself. At least no one was seen to leave with her so far as we've been able to tell from others who were there at the time.'

'She could have arranged to meet someone,' Parker said.

'Do you have any idea who that might have been? It wasn't her boyfriend, Peter. We've spoken to him. He was out with friends at a five-a-side football match. They went for drinks afterwards and he was given a lift home at eleven. His parents confirm it. So do his friends.'

'You suspected Peter?' Mrs Parker looked alarmed and dismayed.

'We have to suspect everyone to start with,' McKenna said. 'We eliminate suspects, narrowing it down till, hopefully, we arrive at the culprit. In this case, though, it was more than likely a stranger.'

'Because of the other girls?'

McKenna nodded. 'I'm afraid so, Mrs Parker. It's more than probable your daughter was just unfortunate enough to be at the wrong place at the wrong time. As simple as that.' He glanced at his note pad again. 'There is just one thing. You wouldn't know if she ever had any connection with a theatrical group?'

'Theatrical group?' Mrs Parker frowned. 'I don't know. She liked going to the occasional play. She went to *Les Mis* a few months ago with some friends. But I don't think it was more than that.'

Her husband agreed with her. 'She never told me about any interest in the theatre, sergeant. Unless it was a recent thing.'

McKenna nodded. 'Well, if either of you do remember anything that might have a bearing on this, or if someone mentions something about theatres to you, let me know. It could be important.'

With reassurances that they would, McKenna paid his condolences once more, then said he would be on his way. 'I'll keep in touch,' he said, 'and let you know if there are any developments.'

'Thank you, sergeant. We'd appreciate that very much.'

5

'What do you make of them?' Chief Inspector Yates asked when McKenna returned to the station.

'The parents, sir?' McKenna shrugged as he sat down opposite his boss's desk, pivoting his chair against the line of filing cabinets behind him. 'A bit strained, but you'd expect that, wouldn't you? They're certainly not acting as they normally would, of course, but...'

'Yes?'

McKenna unbuttoned his jacket to relieve the pressure on his abdomen. 'I just hope their family doctor's keeping an eye on them, that's all. In my opinion they're trying too hard to contain their grief. I don't like the look of it. They could crack any time.'

'But not through guilt?'

'Not that, sir. No, I'm certain of that.'

'Which just about clears the immediate family and friends. And we're left with trying to find an unknown stranger who killed her and the other girls earlier this month. We've run all their friends, relations, work-mates, schoolmates, employers, et cetera through the computer again, but there are no connections between any of them.'

'So we're flying blind.'

'That just about sums it up.'

'And none of them had anything to do with any kind of theatre group, sir?'

Yates grunted. 'If, indeed, even their killer had any kind of connection with the theatre. For all we know he might have got hold of the grease paint for reasons of his own and never set foot on stage in his life.'

'Perhaps we should start to broaden our enquiries amongst theatrical groups, amateur and professional, as well as their suppliers, sir?'

'DC Watkins has been looking into their suppliers, especially of grease paint, though that could have been bought anywhere in the country. Still, he might turn something up, even if I'm not particularly hopeful.'

'I suppose that's the only thing we can do at the moment, sir, apart from keeping vigilant in case he strikes again.'

'Which is something I'm a damned sight more certain about.'

*

In the general office, McKenna spotted DC Watkins sat before a computer monitor, studiously scrolling through a series of files. Strolling over, McKenna perched on the edge of his desk.

'The Chief mentioned you've been looking into theatrical suppliers. Come up with anything?'

Watkins looked up, hair dishevelled about his forehead. His lack of expertise for using the computer network system was a joke amongst the rest of CID. Which just went to show, McKenna repeatedly told himself, being young didn't automatically mean you were adept at using a computer – and thankful for the rabid interest his kids had for PCs. What they'd managed to teach him had proven invaluable in the last few years as computers began to play a greater and greater role at the station.

'Nothing so far, sarge.'

Noting the faintest trace of hesitancy in the DC's voice, McKenna said: 'Would you like some help with this thing? My kids tell me I'm getting to be a dab hand, which from them is high praise indeed.'

Suppressing the look of relief that McKenna was sure would otherwise have passed across his face, Watkins said: 'You wouldn't mind, sarge? I'm not too hot.' He glanced at his hands, with their chewed up fingernails and ugly, swollen boxer's knuckles. 'I can't seem to hit the right keys half the time.'

'Move over. I'll see what I can do.'

McKenna glanced at the print outs piled by the keyboard. 'What are these?' He picked one up. 'Names of contacts of Helen Parker.'

McKenna moved his finger to one of the names listed on it: James Edward Legg.

'I arrested him a couple of years back – belted his wife for having an affair. Made a sorry mess of her face. He was lucky to get off with a suspended sentence.' McKenna tapped out a few details. Moments later Legg's name appeared on screen, complete with details. 'That's him all right. Five years, reduced to twelve months in view of the circumstances. I knew the old memory wouldn't let me down.'

'What connection did he have with the girl, sarge?'

McKenna glanced again at the sheet. 'He did some work for the family a few months ago. He's a plumber. Probably mended a leaky tap.'

'Doesn't make him a murderer. Beating up your wife isn't exactly something we could wholeheartedly condemn him for, could we, sarge? Any of us could find ourselves guilty of that, given the circumstances. I know I'd find it bloody hard to resist if I caught my wife having it off with someone else.'

McKenna glanced at Watkins. 'I'm sure you would, Tony. I'm sure you would. Though I'm far from certain I'd react the same way. Still, it's worth keeping an eye out for his name in case it crops up again. He could have a downer on women after what happened. Who knows? If I get the chance, I'll pop round and see him just to be sure. See what he's up to now.' He glanced again at the screen. 'Who knows?'

The boy looked down the over-bright room as the man he had grown to fear more than any of the others walked in. He was tall, with a straggly grey beard, wire-framed spectacles and the face of an executioner, with no trace of compassion on any of his features. Craig felt so weak after all that had happened to him he could barely stop from blubbering as soon as he caught sight of the man, knowing that pain always followed his presence.

The man barely acknowledged the boy. In one hand he held a syringe, which he began to fill from a dark phial.

Another man entered behind him. Craig knew his name. He was in charge of them all. The boss. He had heard him being talked about by the others. Cornel Pavlenco. For some reason the boy could not understand, they also sometimes referred to him as Conrad Phillips. Craig couldn't understand why the man had two names and wondered which was real. If either.

'How long before it starts to take effect?' Phillips/Pavlenco asked.

'A few hours for the first of the changes to be obvious. The metamorphosis in full will take several days, but the first, the most vigorous change takes only minutes. Which is essential for its success, of course.'

The men looked at Craig. He could feel their curiosity.

'His face will change soon,' the bearded man said.

'A good warning, eh? It'll make sure we keep away from his mouth. Wouldn't want to risk infection.'

Craig wanted to scream at them to stop whatever it was they were doing to him, to let him go, but there was a strip of adhesive tape fastened across his mouth and all he could do was make inarticulate gurgling sounds from the back of his throat as he watched the syringe being lowered to his stomach.

6

Janice stepped out of the office block with barely a glance at the long queues that had already formed at the bus stops. It was a happy feeling. As was the fact that she wasn't bothered it had gone six o'clock and street lights were starting to glow along the road. Strange how not having to return home by herself could alter her perspective on life, she thought as she watched the flow of traffic heading towards her. Any minute Jimmy's van would show up. At this time of night, it was unlikely he'd be driving the BMW. More likely he'd be coming straight from a job, the back of his van cluttered with copper tubing, plastic pipes and bags of plaster that had invariably been torn open down one side and spilled most of their contents over the floor, coating it with a layers of dust that would stain her clothes if she got anywhere near it. But she didn't mind risking even that. Anything was better than going home on the bus by herself with a ten-minute walk at the end down darkening streets – and her phobia more unbearable by the minute.

Spotting the transit van, Janice stepped to the edge of the pavement and waved her arms. Jimmy sounded a fanfare on the horn as he swerved towards her.

'Fancy something to eat before we go home?' he said as Janice fastened her seat belt. He swung into the flow of traffic with the ease of an experienced driver. 'I just completed a big job. Better still: they paid cash. No VAT to worry about.'

'Or tax, I expect,' Janice said with a grin.

'Or tax,' Jimmy agreed, returning her grin. 'So, what do you say? Chinese, Indian or haute cuisine?'

Janice laughed. 'Quite a choice! I don't know, Jimmy. How good a job was it?'

'Good enough, believe me. Good enough.' He turned right and headed along the dual carriageway. The cold spell had gone and rain drifted across the road ahead of them in a grey curtain. 'I know a high class restaurant we could go to. We could have a drink at the bar while I book a table.'

'In my work clothes!'

'Work clothes!' He laughed. 'You look okay to me.'

'And you? We should go back to change first if you're really serious about going somewhere posh. People would think we'd wandered in by mistake.'

Jimmy laughed again infectiously. 'As if we cared!'

'I'd care!'

Which made him laugh even louder.

'Come on, Jimmy, please be serious. If you want us to go somewhere like that let's at least get into our best clothes. It would only take a few minutes. And we'd enjoy the meal more if we were dressed in something smart.'

Janice flinched at the anger in Jimmy's eyes as he glanced at her. 'If you insist I suppose there's no alternative.' His jaw muscles clenched as if he was grinding his molars. 'It's a load of nonsense. You know that, don't you? It's only money that matters. So long as you've cash to pay for what you want, it doesn't matter a damn what you turn up in. But if you won't have it...'

Over the few weeks in which she'd started to get to know him better, Janice had realised that irrational quirks like this were an occasional but inseparable part of Jimmy's character. Sometimes it was as if he bore a king-sized chip on his shoulder about something that really irked him, which it only took an incident like this to bring out into the open. If she persisted in arguing she knew he would seethe all night, unable to let it alone.

'Okay. You win. We'll go as we are,' Janice made herself say as she tried to tell herself that perhaps, maybe, he was right after all. What did it matter what they were wearing if they had money?

Jimmy glanced at her, a lopsided, roguish grin on his face. 'Are you sure? Are you really sure? You'll go with me now, as we are, like a couple of scruffs?'

'Jimmy Legg, wearing work clothes or not, I am not and never have been a *scruff*. As for you, I suppose those jeans you're wearing probably cost more than most people spend on a suit.'

'Too true they did! A king's ransom.'

'I don't doubt it. I've seen the label. I wish I could afford to buy brands like that.'

'Then we're off. I know the very place.' A few minutes later he indicated left, before pulling off the dual carriage to head down a tree-lined avenue that Janice only vaguely recognised but which she knew would take them towards one of the wealthier suburbs. A half-mile later he pulled into the car park of a floodlit restaurant set back behind a wall of trees. A converted manor house, its name – La Petite Maison – was an obvious joke that had probably long since ceased to be funny.

As she watched it draw nearer Janice's first misgivings began to return. From the red-tinted ivy trailed around its walls to the expensive cars that were parked outside, everything spoke of money. Despite the lights that sparkled through its tall windows there was nothing inviting about it to her.

'You can tell this place has genuine quality,' Jimmy said as he parked between a Daimler Jag and an Alfa Romeo.

Janice glanced at him, her uncertainties revived by the cars alongside. 'And how's that?'

'No BMWs.' Jimmy laughed. 'It's probably a good job we came in the van.'

'Fool!' she retorted as he swung his door open and climbed out.

Hoping that no one had seen them arrive, Janice followed him as he sauntered towards the entrance with all the self-confidence of a millionaire. His mobile bounced in the back pocket of his jeans as he pulled out a thick wad of twenty pounds notes.

Inside the entrance to La Petite Maison, Janice's fears intensified and she began to regret having given in as easily as she had. The place was just too blatantly exclusive for her to feel comfortable in: the deep pile carpet in the reception area almost swallowed her feet as she walked across it, staring at the potted foliage that filled every nook and cranny between huge oil paintings on the walls. In contrast to her discomfiture, Jimmy seemed totally undaunted by the place as he swaggered towards the reception desk.

'I'd like to book a table for two,' he said to the tall, immaculately suited girl behind it as he thumbed through the notes still displayed in his hand like a deck of cards. Glancing at the cash with what Janice was sure was a well concealed look of disdain, the girl pursed her lips.

'I'm afraid we have a waiting list, sir. It wouldn't be till after eight before we could fit you in.'

Apparently unaware of her attitude towards him, Jimmy nodded his head. He glanced at the dimly lit restaurant area.

Precisely laid out cutlery gleamed on its otherwise empty tables. 'We don't start serving for half an hour,' the girl added, 'though the bar's open if you'd care to order drinks till there's a table free.'

'Okay. Eight o'clock will have to do. We'll just have to make our drinks last, won't we, Jan?' Jimmy turned to her with a wink.

Far from sure if she really wanted to spend the next hour and a half drinking on an empty stomach, Janice dumbly nodded her head.

There were only a few guests sat about the room when they stepped in. A solitary girl was busily cutting slices of fruit behind the bar. Again, Jimmy's impervious nonchalance impressed Janice, who fervently wished she could as easily brazen things out. She felt childishly unsure of herself, as if any moment someone would walk up to her and tell her she had no right to be here. Her clothes felt wrong. God knew, but Jimmy's clothes looked totally wrong here too, especially when she glanced at the few well-groomed couples sat around the sumptuously furnished room. Even if Jimmy had agreed to drive back first in order to change before coming here, she would have felt out of place. There was nothing in her wardrobe to match anything she could see on the women here. She accepted the gin and tonic Jimmy bought for her and meekly followed him to a couple of seats near one of the windows. Taking a sip of his glass of single malt whisky, Jimmy suddenly stretched his legs in front of him as if he felt at home in this place. Was he putting on an act for her benefit? A feeling of resentment bubbled its way through her discomfit and made her stare at him. Why was he forcing her to go through with this? Surely he must have known what it was like in here, that she would feel out of place, especially dressed in her drab office clothes?

'Not a bad drop of scotch,' Jimmy said, before taking another appreciative sip. 'Not bad at all.'

Janice sipped her drink, hoping its influence would help make her feel at ease. But the liquid seemed to stick in her throat and she had a sudden embarrassing urge to cough. She felt for a handkerchief in her handbag, the glaring cheapness of its imitation leather adding to her plight. Why couldn't he have been considerate enough to settle for a pub meal instead? There were plenty of places they could have gone where she would have felt at ease without coming somewhere like this. If he thought he was impressing her, he'd made a big mistake.

Angry and embarrassed, she put down her drink.

'I don't think we should have come here, Jimmy,' she said, her voice a steady monotone.

With what looked like a genuine expression of surprise, Jimmy said, 'Why, sweetheart? What's wrong with it?' He frowned. 'Not good enough?'

She wondered if that was sarcasm. Angrier than before, she said: 'Wrong with it? Nothing's wrong with it, you idiot. It's us who are wrong. It's me. My clothes, my handbag, the lot. You should have let me get changed or taken me somewhere it wouldn't have mattered, like I asked you to.'

'It doesn't matter, for Christ's sake, Jan. Can't you see that? I told you before. Money's all that matters in places like this.'

'Not when you look cheap, it doesn't. And I look cheap. That's what people see when they look at me here. It doesn't matter how big a wad you wave around in front of you, that can't change what people see when they look at your clothes. Even the girls working here are better dressed than me. You shouldn't have forced me to come here, Jimmy. It was wrong. You might be thick-skinned enough – or too bloody blind to see it – '

'Okay, okay.' His voice had become a harsh whisper as he interrupted her. 'Okay.' He placed his hand on hers. 'I can't say I fully understand what you're talking about, Janice. In fact, so far as I can see, you're being bloody stupid. But I won't force you to stay if you don't want us to. We'll leave. All right? Will that satisfy you? We'll go somewhere else.'

Again Janice saw the anger in his eyes, saw his jaw muscles tense as he put down his drink and stood up. Janice followed him, feeling suddenly guilty. 'I'm sorry, Jimmy. I didn't mean to spoil your treat. I appreciate you bringing me here.'

'It's okay, I told you. If you don't like it here we'll go somewhere else. It's no big deal.'

As he led her towards the entrance hall he stopped. 'What was that?' Jimmy glared at a couple in their mid-twenties who were laughing over a joke at a table near the bar.

Janice clasped a hand about Jimmy's tensed right arm. 'Leave them alone,' she said, alarmed at the intensity of his anger.

'Whatever you think they might have said, leave it. You'll only get yourself in trouble.'

Jimmy glared at Janice. His neck muscles stood out above his collar as he sought to exercise some sort of self-control.

Janice pulled at his arm. 'Come on,' she said to him. 'Let's get out of here.'

Jimmy grunted. 'Okay.' As he looked at the couple, though, his mouth moved into an ambiguous smirk. 'The company's crap in any case.'

Outside, Jimmy bustled Janice to the van.

As he drove onto the road again and headed with a roar of acceleration towards the dual carriageway, he burst out laughing.

'What were you up to back there?' Janice said.

'Does it matter?' He laughed again. It was a cold, hard, humourless laugh. 'Does it really matter? Those stuck-up bleeders are as bad as each other. Stuff 'em. Stuff the bleedin' lot of 'em!'

7

The Bell and Compasses was doing a roaring trade. It was darts night, and the home team were well on their way to their fifth consecutive win of the season. Landlord, Tom Howard, barely had time to see much of the match, though. He, his wife, Julie, and the three bar staff had had their work cut out pulling pints for the past two hours. Whether it was the match or the free platters of sandwiches which brought in the punters, he wasn't sure. Not that he was bothered. Trade was bad enough the rest of the week that nights like this were not to be questioned – or tampered with. If you've a winning formula, stick to it, he told himself as he wiped the sweat off his face with the back of his hand and turned to another customer, a ten-pound note held eagerly out across the bar to catch his eye.

Fiona Greenwood normally only got the chance to work in the pub during the week when there was a darts match on. Even weekends, though, were rarely as busy as this and she knew she'd be glad when Tom rang the bell for last orders and the final rush had passed. Though if her husband had been able to hold a decent job over the last few years it probably wouldn't have been necessary for her to work in the pub at all. Her wage from the electronics factory, where she worked on the assembly line, packaging, would have been enough. Sometimes she wondered if she'd known how hard she would have to graft after five years of marriage to a work-shy bastard like Barry, whether she would have married him. At twenty-three she was beginning to feel ten years older. Some days she was sure she looked it too. If it hadn't been for the kids they had in the first few years of marriage, she was certain she would have walked out on him long ago.

'Did you say you wanted dropping off on your way home to get a Chinese for hubby?' Samantha, one of the other barmaids, asked in a momentary lull. In contrast to Fiona's slim figure and elfin face, Sam was full-bodied, going on plump, with a carefree attitude that Fiona was sure went hand in hand with having ditched her own husband years ago. She lived in a flat only a few blocks from Fiona's council house, and they usually shared a taxi home.

'That's what he's asked for, the idle bugger. Can't be arsed to get up and walk to the Chinkie himself. Said it was easier for me to get out of the taxi at the Chinese and go the rest of the way by foot as it's only, in his *perceptive* words, a skip and a jump from our house. Though why he can't skip and friggin' well jump that far himself, God knows.' Fiona also knew that Barry would be asleep in front of the telly by the time she got home, beer cans littered about his feet. And about the only thing he'd be interested in didn't come in a polystyrene tray. But a Chinese was what the sod had asked for, and five years of marriage had taught her better than to argue about things like this.

'How come he can't drive to the Chinkie himself?' Sam said. 'Don't tell me he's too idle for that.'

'If the car was working.'

'Working? You're not telling me he can't even keep his own car on the road, and there he is trying to set himself up as a soddin' mechanic?' Sam had to stifle her laughter as she filled a glass with whisky from the optic.

Fiona pulled a wry grin, unable to avoid the irony, especially after Barry had turned their garden into a wasteland of tyres, brake pads, spark plugs and other less easily identifiable lumps of metal from his attempts to set himself up as a self-employed car repairer. Not only did he have little idea about cars, but some of their neighbours complained to the council about the noise and the mess and the cars propped up on unsteady piles of breeze blocks outside their house, claiming it was dangerous, that children could get hurt beneath the dodgily balanced cars and scraps of metal. This, and a visit from the local council's enforcement officers, soon put a stop to this venture, though Fiona didn't think Barry's enthusiasm for the motor trade would have lasted much longer. It had begun to look too much like hard work for him to persist past the summer, and there hadn't been anything like as much cash as he originally expected.

The girls were too busy after this to have chance to talk before the bell was rung for last orders. By the time Tom finally cajoled the last of his customers to go on home both girls were exhausted. As Fiona leaned against the shelves at the back of the bar for a moment's rest, Sam came up to her.

'Are you sure you want dropping off at the Chinkie? My feet are throbbing from heel to toe. Yours can't be any better. You look knackered.'

'I feel knackered too. But it's all right,' Fiona said. She made an effort to look less tired than she felt. 'The walk from Fu's will do me good. Help clear my head.'

'And hubby'll want his take-out, I suppose? And you can't let hubby down. Why d'you think I told mine to sling his hook. You ought to think about it. There's more to life than mollycoddling bone-idle buggers like them, take my word.'

Despite feeling that Sam's words had more than a smattering of truth in them, Fiona knew tonight wasn't the time to start anything. She felt too tired to have a row with Barry now. It was best to humour him, get him his take-away, and think about what Sam had said over the next few days. Perhaps she'd find time on Saturday when they were behind the bar again to have a longer, more meaningful talk, maybe get some tips on how to go about getting her life sorted. Despite the kids, she was sure she couldn't face many more years of this.

'You girls off for a night out clubbing?' Joe, their usual taxi driver, said with predictable humour when they climbed in his cab a short while later.

'Chance would be a fine thing,' Sam said as she settled next to Fiona.

'One day, Joe, one day we'll surprise you and do just that,' Fiona said.

Samantha laughed. 'If I thought you meant it, girl, I'd pay for both of us. Right now.'

'That's a dangerous promise the way I'm feeling tonight,' Fiona said, wishing she had the guts to do it.

'Sounds like there's trouble ahead for someone.' Joe cut in front of a bus, before speeding down the centre of the road.

'If my friend takes my advice there will be, Joe.'

'But in the meantime duty calls.' Fiona felt resentful that her friend could do as she pleased. 'Will you drop me at the Chinese on Market Road, the one before the railway bridge?'

'Will do, sweetheart. Make sure you don't linger on your way home, though. There're some bad bastards around the streets these days.'

'Don't I know it! I think we've served most of them tonight.'

'Just remember: take care. The police are still hunting that evil bastard who's been murdering those women.'

After passing through several sets of traffic lights in the

shopping centre, Joe skewed the taxi through the lanes of traffic, then pulled up outside Fu's Chinese Takeaway. 'Be sure to give Barry my kind regards when you see him,' Sam called with an ironic forefinger salute as the taxi set off.

Laughing, Fiona shouted back: 'I'll let you tell him next time you meet!' Though she knew the last thing either of them would risk with a short-tempered prick like Barry was to insult him to his face.

As the taxi disappeared into the fast-moving traffic, Fiona sighed. Alone now, the adrenaline that had kept her going for the past few hours seeped out of her, leaving her drained and even more tired than before. She looked through the plate-glass window of the Chinese. Though it was always busy after pub closing time, midweek there was usually not too long a queue. To her relief she saw there were only three customers lined up at the counter. One of them, a teenage girl in a black bomber jacket, was Kayleigh Bentley, whose mother used to work at the factory. She looked as if she was ready to leave from the look of the neatly wrapped cartons being packed into a brown paper bag by Mrs Fu.

'Hiya, Fiona,' Kayleigh called as she turned to leave, the parcel clutched in front of her.

'How's your mum?' Fiona asked, smiling back. 'It's ages since I saw her. Is she still at Pearce's?'

'Nah, she left them months ago. She's expecting again.'

'Again?'

'Dad's not feeling chuffed.' Wiping an unruly lock of hair from her face, the girl said: 'You'd have thought they'd have more sense at their age, wouldn't you?' She laughed as she left, picking open a packet of chips from the top of the bag.

'Chicken fried rice and a side order of chips,' Fiona said a few minutes later when it was her turn at the counter. She didn't feel like anything to eat herself. All she wanted was to kick off her shoes and slump on the armchair. The heat in the Chinese was starting to make her drowsy. In fact, it was a good job there weren't any seats in here or she'd fall asleep before her order was ready.

While she waited, Fiona leaned her back against the counter and stared through the window. The shiny, rain-blackened surface of the road was filled with reflections from the lights of the cars speeding along it, white and then red as they hissed through puddles. Few people were walking along the pavements now and the area looked lonely. Once she passed beneath the railway bridge and turned into the estate the final stretch home would be even quieter. That was the worst part about stopping off here. Normally she would have stayed in the taxi till it reached the gate at the end of their garden.

'Five pounds thirty,' the Chinese girl called in her singsong voice, interrupting her thoughts. 'Would you like some salt and vinegar on your chips, please?'

Fiona shook her head as she sorted out the money from her purse. She picked up the package; its warmth radiated through her gloves like a comforting balm as she stepped outside.

Before Market Road veered off to her right at the end of the block, she passed a dismal row of closed shops, hidden behind steel shutters, daubed with graffiti. Unlike during the day when they were open, there was an air of dereliction about them at night which never failed to unnerve Fiona, making her hurry as she walked past piles of bin bags huddled along the edge of the pavement like furtive squatters. On a large billboard beyond the shops, posters for one of last year's festivals flapped in the wind, making her flinch, while sodium lamps buzzed overhead as she approached the railway bridge. Its tunnel loomed in a huge shadow across the road when she turned the bend. As she always did at this spot, Fiona wished the Council would get their act together and put more lights beneath the bridge. In the distance she could barely make out the road that led to her estate. As she walked towards it she felt a deep-rooted need for the reassuring warmth of the cartons she hugged tight to her chest. Her footsteps echoed tauntingly like unseen companions. The heavy rush of traffic had gone now and she felt even lonelier as she walked close to the red brick wall. Stained by years of exhaust fumes, only posters that had been pasted along it created an impression of colour. Everything else, from the concrete paving stones to the cast iron railings by the road were darker shades of grey.

The atmosphere beneath the bridge was so oppressive Fiona felt an intense euphoria of relief when she reached the end and stepped out to where Market Road became Pitt Street, with its tower blocks and old Victorian houses, most of which had been converted to flats long before she was born. The entrance to Park Farm Estate lay to her right past a stretch of landscaped grassy knolls and a cluster of telephone boxes, most vandalised beyond repair. The pale brown bricks of the houses on the estate looked unreal, like ghosts in the streetlights. But she had passed the worst of her journey now. In a few minutes she could deposit her cartons before Barry's bleary, beer-reddened face and stagger upstairs to bed. The way she felt now she knew she would be asleep within minutes of her head touching the pillows, whether Barry liked it or not.

Increasing her pace towards the estate, Fiona's attention was caught by something moving on top of one of the knolls that planners must have thought would add an appealing look of rustic charm to the area. At the same time, she heard a panic-stricken scream, unmistakably female. Fiona looked around to see if there was anyone she could call to for help, but the streets were deserted. Even the nearest houses were in darkness, while others were too far away, even if anyone would be willing to open their doors at this time of night. On an impulse she started to run up the knoll towards where she thought the scream had come from. She knew she was being stupid. It would have been better to have gone to the telephones, hope she could find one still working and call the police, but all she could think of was that whatever was happening up the knoll couldn't wait for the police to arrive. She had to get there now and see what was going on. Perhaps it was the alcohol she'd drunk in the pub. Perhaps it was simply the fact that the cry had been that of a girl. She neither knew nor cared. All she could think of was that some poor bitch was in trouble.

Despite her urgency, her breath was wheezing down her throat by the time she scrambled to the top of the knoll where she could see down into the gloom on the other side, shielded from the street lights.

Her first impression was that a large animal was foraging through the rubbish that had been dumped in the hollow between this hillock and the next. As her eyes, though, adjusted to the gloom she realised she could see the back of a man's coat. He was kneeling on the ground. It was only then that Fiona realised she was watching a struggle. Beyond the man's back, sprawled on the grass, was the woman who had screamed.

'Stop that! Stop that now!'

The shout burst from Fiona's lips before she realised she was going to do it. At the same time, she started to run downhill. She hurled the cartons of Chinese food at the man with as much force as she could muster. 'Stop it, you bastard! Leave her alone!' Somehow her shouts seemed to bolster her courage. When the man turned, only the white blur of his eyes was visible as he stared up at her from between the slits of the balaclava that hid his face. The food cartons came apart in mid-air and showered him in chips and clotted rice and small pieces of chicken. Brushing them aside with his gloved hands, the man jumped to his feet. Only a few yards away from him now, Fiona suddenly felt vulnerable. Which was when she realised how stupid she had been to rush down the slope. There was no one to see them here. Or hear them either. And he could do what he liked to her.

The man moved towards her. With a scream, Fiona started to scramble away from him, but the slope was too steep and slippery, streaked with mud which her shoes could barely grip on now.

The man made to snatch at her feet, and Fiona only just managed to pull them back before his fingers could grab hold of them. *'No!'* Her hands and feet scrabbled at the grass. Again he reached for her, his own feet slipping. This time she kicked at his hands. One foot caught him on his forehead and she heard him grunt in pain.

'Bitch!'

His voice was forced between his teeth as he lunged at her.

Scrabbling at the grass, she felt a stone beneath her fingers. With a heave, she tugged it free and tried to throw it at the man, but his forearm came up to deflect her blow. He was close enough now to fall against her legs and pin her to the ground, but Fiona found a solid foothold and was able to push herself further up the slope before he could trap her. She kicked out again. This time she felt the heel of her foot hit his chest.

In the seconds of time in which the pain stalled him, Fiona turned and managed to pull herself further up the hill, scrambling on all fours till she reached its summit. Screaming constantly, she hurled herself down the far side towards the estate. In the distance she saw a house door open. A silhouetted figure stared towards her. 'Help me! Please help me! For God's sake help me!' Fiona cried as she tripped and fell down the hill, grazing herself on the grass.

'Hoy!' The man from the doorway, closely followed by a smaller figure, perhaps his son, ran towards her along the roadside. He was an elderly black man with grizzled white hair and a creased face. His sandals slapped through the puddles. Dressed only in baggy trousers and an old T-shirt, he looked as if he was ready for bed. 'What's going on?'

Fiona looked up as the smaller man, a youth in his teens, caught up. 'Back there,' she gasped as she climbed to her knees and pointed up the hillock. 'He was attacking me. He's already attacked someone else.'

The men looked uncertain for a moment, but it was obvious they knew they had to do something. 'Go back to the house and ring the police. Tell 'em to get here prompt,' the older man said. He clenched his fists as he stared up the slope, but there was no one in sight and the hill looked deserted.

'There's a woman up there. He was attacking her. We've got make sure he doesn't do anything to her,' Fiona said as she caught her breath.

The man's breath smelt of beer as he leaned down and took a firm grip on her arm. 'Here, let me give you a hand up first. We'll take a look, but he'll have scarpered now,' the man said, though this didn't seem to make him look any more enthusiastic about the prospect of climbing uphill to make sure.

'Come on,' Fiona insisted. 'We've got to look. She could be dead before the police get here.'

Nodding in agreement, the man reluctantly started up the hillock, his sandals clinging more firmly to the wet grass than her shoes. At the top he paused for a moment to stare down the other side. 'I can't see him. But I can see the woman.' More quickly now, he headed down the slope, Fiona behind him. 'Easy, now,' the man said reassuringly. He put his hands beneath the girl's head to cradle it. 'She's alive,' he said to Fiona, relieved, as he looked up at her.

Fiona leaned down beside him. For the first time she recognised the young girl's clothes, her black bomber jacket caked in mud.

8

McKenna sometimes wondered if his kids would one day look back on their childhood and to struggle to remember who their father was. If it wasn't for their shared interest in computer games, there would have been doubts in his mind as to whether either Tom or Susie would be able to put a face to him. As it was, their time together was sometimes so sparse as to be negligible, especially with the murder hunt going on now. Tonight, nearly a fortnight since the last body was found, was one of the first times he'd been able to spend a full evening with them, though that had been fraught enough with the new game they'd bought. It had more blood, guts and general mayhem than a whole series of Quentin Tarrantino movies rolled into one.

Now the kids had been tucked into bed, he could spend a few hours with Linda, his bare feet stretched to the fire as they watched a late night film over a couple of cans of beer. Although he knew he should get some sleep (it would be an early start tomorrow), it was a rare enough event that he wanted to make the most of it.

'Would you like another drink?' Linda asked a split second before the phone rang. Linda raised her eyebrows as she glanced at the clock. It was nearly one o'clock in the morning, and both of them knew there was only one place a call at this time of night could be coming from.

Ian groaned. 'Duty calls,' he said as he reached from his armchair for the phone. 'Hello,' he grunted as if he'd just been woken from sleep. 'Ah, ah.' He looked over at his wife, who pulled a sour face at him. 'Okay, I'll be there right away.'

'Another murder?' Linda asked when he put down the phone.

'Attempted.' Ian got up and rubbed his eyes. 'Looks as if this time the bastard was interrupted before he could finish the job.' He felt far from ready for what promised to be a gruelling, stress-filled night. 'Yates has already been told. He asked for me to be called in. Don't know whether I should be flattered or not.'

Minutes later as he sat in his car he felt cold and fuzzy headed from tiredness and not really sure whether he should be driving or not, though the two cans he'd drunk had not been full pints, he told himself as he started the ignition. Linda had given him a flask of coffee before he left, hastily brewed while he rummaged in his wardrobe for a clean shirt and his jacket and splashed cold water across his face in the bathroom sink.

By the time he reached Park Farm Estate the area around the landscaped knolls had already been cordoned off and several police cars, an incident van and a couple of unmarked cars, including Detective Chief Inspector Yates' dark green Rover, were parked nearby.

Emerging from a cluster of policemen between the vehicles, Yates strode towards him even before Ian had had time to get out of his car.

'Looks as if we might get some clues at last as to who he is,' Yates said.

'Witnesses, sir?'

'One got a look at him, though it was too dark for her to make out much. As for his intended victim, we've yet to find out. She's been rushed to hospital with injuries to her throat. By all accounts another few seconds and he would have finished the job off. It was only the intervention of the other woman that saved her life. So we've a heroine on our hands tonight, Ian.'

'Do you want me to talk to her, sir?'

'No, I'll handle that. I'd like you to go to the hospital and see what the victim can tell us. There's a WPC with her now, but I'd like you to handle it. The victim's in her teens and badly shocked. I thought perhaps, being a family man, with teenagers of your own, you would be the best man to handle it.' Yates paused for a moment, only a hint of tiredness showing through as he brushed a hand across his face. 'It's important we get as full a description as the girl can give. Let's see if we can get on his trail.'

Pausing only to drink a mug of coffee from the flask Linda had given him Ian arrived at the hospital less than quarter of an hour later. Feeling refreshed by the caffeine, he inquired where the victim was. A staff nurse led him down a tiled corridor to a side room.

Inside, the WPC who had arrived with the girl, was sat beside the bed. The girl was awake, lying propped on her pillows.

'She's been sedated to calm her nerves,' the nurse said, 'so she should be able to answer your questions. But her throat's very sore. She'll have to answer most of your questions through hand signals or writing.'

'I managed to get hold of a note pad,' the WPC said. She handed Ian a thick jotter and a pen. 'It was volunteered by one of the doctors,' she added.

Hitching his pants, Ian took a seat by the bed. 'Inter-service co-operation seems to be going well,' he said. 'I should congratulate you, constable.' He gazed at the girl in the bed. 'If you feel up to it,' he said to her, much as he would have talked to one of his kids, sick with some kind of bug, 'could you tell me what you can about the man who attacked you? It's Kayleigh, isn't it?'

The girl nodded, obviously nervous at hurting her neck. Her pinched face, topped by a fringe of curls, looked grey; dark rings circled her eyes, though Ian noticed purple bruises already starting to darken the skin below her ears and across her chin. The girl held her hands for the note pad and pen.

'Good,' Ian said. 'Perhaps you'd just note what you saw of him: his height, his hair colour, the colour of his skin, his age, anything that could give a clue as to who he is. If you recall anything distinctive about him, birth marks, scars or any tattoos, or if he has a distinctive odour, just jot it down. Take your time. Think about it. Then write whatever comes to you.'

The girl nodded again. And for the next few minutes she stared into space, before jotting down the first of her notes. Ian peeped at what she was writing, his face filled with concentration.

9

Janice's desk looked as if someone had deliberately held back her workload for the past few days, then suddenly dumped it on her in spite. Perhaps someone had. Though perhaps, more likely, she already felt so pissed off with things it looked it anyway. Irritably, Janice dropped her handbag on the floor and switched on her PC, ignoring the files piled on her in-tray.

'Bad night?' Michelle asked, arching her eyebrows.

Janice grimaced. What were workmates for if not to gripe about things? 'You wouldn't believe how bad it was,' Janice said, wishing for some reason she smoked, even though she never had.

Michelle leaned back in her chair. 'Go on, tell me. Get it off your chest, girl. It must be something to do with that new boyfriend of yours.' She glanced across the open plan office; it was gradually starting to fill up as other early birds came into work. 'It's all right. Bob's at a finance meeting. Something to do with budgets. He'll be gone for ages. So fire away. There's no chance of being interrupted for hours.'

Nibbling at one of her fingernails, Janice told her about the fiasco at the restaurant. 'You should have seen us,' she said finally. 'We looked like a pair of tramps who'd stumbled in off the street. I wouldn't have minded so much if I'd been able to have a shower after finishing work and a chance to put on some fresh make-up. But, no, we had to go straight away. He wouldn't take no for an answer, not him, not without some major sulks. So I allowed myself to go along with him, until I realised how exclusive a place it was. It was only then, feeling a complete fool, sitting in my work clothes while other women were dripping in designer labels and jewellery, I realised enough was enough. If he'd wanted to make me look a frump, he couldn't have done any better. When I realised I wasn't prepared to stand it any longer, I made him take me out.'

'What did you do? Go somewhere else?'

'If he'd had any bloody sense he would have done to calm me down and sort things out. A Bernie Inn or somewhere. Even a decent pub. I could have done with a stiff drink after that just to settle my nerves. But the bastard wouldn't. Instead he sat there seething, grinding his teeth – like he does sometimes – and staring through the windscreen. It was scary. I didn't know what he was going to do next, whether he was going to explode or do something stupid. He hardly said a word till we got back to the flats. Then all he said was Good Night in a cold voice as if I'd done something to annoy him, and drove off, leaving me stood on the doorstep like a gormless fool.'

'The bastard!'

'I'll second that. In fact, no, I'll propose it. I know the man. You can second it.'

Michelle laughed. 'At least you got home all right. He could have left you stranded.'

'If he had I'd have killed him.'

10

Jimmy Legg hated the old van that a severe cash shortage had reduced him to using for his business. The divorce had damn near bankrupted him, and it was only by selling off almost everything he had he'd been able to keep going. Negative equity on the property he and Alice bought on a hundred percent mortgage hadn't helped, nor had the overdraft he'd built up on the strength of an over-optimistic business plan drawn up in the early days. To clear his debts, he'd auctioned off most of his equipment, the lease on the land and the lockup he used as his business base, plus the top-of-the-range vans he'd bought to ferry the men he used to employ from job to job. Now all he had was this one, dirty second-hand van... and Toby.

For the umpteenth time this morning Jimmy looked at his watch. Where the frigging hell was that idle waster anyway? He might only be paying Toby the bare minimum but that didn't mean he was prepared to lose time waiting for him to prise himself out of bed to get here. After working for Jimmy for over six months, the acne-scarred youth was still a gangling strip of moronic muscle. If Jimmy could have found someone who would have been prepared to work for less, he might have sacked Toby months ago. But as a labourer, gofer and dogsbody, so long as Jimmy made his presence felt, Toby managed to be marginally useful most of the time. Jimmy sighed. Never a patient man, waiting for someone was something that infallibly put him in the worst of moods. Not that today had started with him being in what anyone would have called a good mood anyway. That sad bitch, Janice, had made sure of that, dragging him out of the restaurant after he had already booked a table. Women! He should have learned his lesson once and for all after Alice.

Parked on double yellow lines by a prominent row of shops, including a video rental shop he knew Toby regularly used, there was no way the idiot could have got lost getting here. So where the hell was he? Jimmy craned his neck over his shoulder to see if the lad might have stopped to wait for him further along the road, and to see if there were any traffic wardens anywhere about. Although he'd put his hazard warning lights on, he knew a couple of wardens in the area who wouldn't hesitate in slapping a parking fine on him even if he'd been slumped on his seat with a major coronary clogging up his arteries and foam flowing from his mouth.

At last, drifting along like a lost soul through the crowds of shoppers and office workers, he caught sight of Toby Cartmel, his thick mop of hair standing out. Jimmy sounded his horn to hurry the lad along.

'About fuckin' time,' Jimmy said as Toby tugged the door open and bobbed inside the van. 'What kept you? Forget to set your fuckin' alarm?'

'Sorry, Mr Legg. I overlaid. I don't have an alarm clock. I broke it by accident. I was up late last night.'

'Watching videos, I suppose? More sex and violence?'

Toby grinned. It was a grin Jimmy preferred not to linger over. Toby's teeth were the brownest, most disgusting set he'd seen on anyone outside cardboard city. It astonished him the lad didn't spend most of his time on a dentist's chair.

'Okay, Toby, now your excuses are out of the way, let's see about earning some money. We've a lot to get through and I don't want to be still at it tonight.'

11

It was an early night for Janice, back into her old winter months' routine of leaving work as soon as she could. No lift from Jimmy meant a bus journey home and a long walk from where it dropped off to the flat. Although the day had been bright for April, it was turning dark by the time she stepped off the bus. Shop windows glowed in the dullness, drawing her to their comforting nimbi as she hurried by. Disconcertingly, she felt herself glance at the road as if she half expected to see Jimmy's van draw up beside her. She hoped against hope he'd stay away. His anger had frightened her more than she cared to admit to her friend at work. Michelle would have wanted to go into it with the intrusive, probing scrutiny of a pathologist, turning over every last scrap of flesh. Instead she told Michelle as much and no more than she was prepared to admit. Her private feelings, her nervousness, her fears were too unsettling for her to talk about yet.

When the flats came in sight, Janice was relieved to see Jimmy's van wasn't parked alongside the BMW. Even more than before she wanted to avoid him now, whether he intended to apologise about last night or not. It wasn't just the restaurant that bothered her. Not that the stupidity of dragging her there as unprepared as she'd been didn't still annoy her. It did, and it would for a long time to come. She was a girl whose self-confidence was fragile already and it would take more than a few choice words to make her forget the deep-rooted humiliation she felt sat in that place in her office clothes. More than this were her doubts about Jimmy as well. That he was divorced was no secret. The reasons why he and his wife got divorced were something else. Jimmy claimed his wife had been having an affair. Had she? Janice wondered about this now. Or had it been his wife who had wanted to leave? In the brief time in which she had got to know him, Janice had quickly begun to realise what an inconsiderate and vicious temper Jimmy could sometimes have. Perhaps that had been what really led to the breakdown of their marriage. If it had, Janice could easily understand that now.

Hurrying inside the building as soon as she reached it, Janice went straight to her flat. She locked the door behind her, feeling nervousness shiver through her body. The darkness had been intensifying quickly during the last few minutes of her walk and had seemed even more threatening than before. She shut the curtains to cut out the sight of the darkened streets. She had read in the evening paper about the attack last night at Park Farm Estate, only a mile away from here. She found it difficult to understand why anyone, especially a fifteen-year old girl, would walk home alone at half past twelve at night. She wouldn't walk home at seven o'clock at this time of year, let alone after midnight. The consequences of what the girl had done didn't surprise her. It fulfilled her every expectation. In her mind, after dark the streets were filled with nightmares. They were a jungle within which any and every conceivable terror prowled and preyed, from which the only safety was to stay inside behind locked doors. She shivered again, before getting up to fetch a cardigan, though she knew it had nothing to do with the cold. She turned on every light, then the TV, though she avoided the news. Comedies, quiz shows, anything but the news and its possibilities of showing her more of what happened last night. What she had read in the evening paper had been enough. What she didn't want to see was any more footage of the actual area in which the attack took place. The familiarity of it would have been too much for her to take just now.

Unwilling to let her mind dwell on the attack, Janice concentrated instead on cooking a more time-consuming meal than she would normally have made mid-week. Instead of just warming up a few odds and ends of ready meals from the freezer, she set about defrosting a chicken, peeled some potatoes and set about preparing vegetables, a sauce and an impressive number of herbs and spices. Whether the end results turned out to be sumptuous or not, she was not bothered. It was the diversion she needed, not the food.

It was time for *Coronation Street* when she finally put the finishing touches to her meal, unscrewing a bottle of Lambrusco from the fridge and pouring herself a glass. Her plate, a side plate, cutlery and hot dishes were already laid out on the small, drop-leaf table, her chair positioned so she could watch the television while she ate. A time for relaxation, to forget about last night.

Which was when she heard Jimmy's footsteps on the stairs.

51

Heavy-footed, for all that he habitually wore trainers, his footsteps were unmistakable after all the months in which she'd heard them. He walked past her door. For a heartbeat she felt sure he was going to pause, turn and knock, perhaps call something to her. She stared at the back of her door, willing him to keep on walking past it. She knew she wouldn't be able to ignore him if he knocked. He'd know she was in, if for no other reason than he'd be able to see the light through the gap beneath her door or hear the TV. But a pause, if there was one, was so brief as to be non-existent as he started up the final flight of stairs to his rooms. Feeling sweat on her forehead, Janice released the pent up breath in her lungs, before sitting down at the table, what appetite she'd had only moments before now gone. Her nervousness at meeting him again seemed out of all proportion, she knew. Was this how things were going to be from now on, with her hiding from the man out of fear of seeing him, of having to face up to what happened last night? And what did happen? she asked herself as she drank the wine, its sweet, acidic taste making her feel nauseous. Nothing except that they had a disagreement. No hard words as such, no expressions of anger, no violence, only a tension, an atmosphere, perhaps, in which hatred and anger and even violence could have developed. Or was she being silly, she wondered, unable to explain to herself why she somehow felt that Jimmy Legg could have become violent towards her. What reasons did she have for thinking this? He had never behaved other than properly towards her, and the worst he had ever been was to be irritable towards her once or twice before the intensity of last night. Even that, for all that he drove off and left her at the flats, he had really said nothing for which she could reproach him. Janice put aside her wine and stared at the food going cold on the table. Perhaps she should make an attempt to apologise to him. She knew he had intended last night as a treat. That he'd misjudged it and forced her into a situation she had been unable to handle was not his fault. Not *wholly* his fault, she amended, unwilling to admit his stubborn determination to go ahead with his plans, for all her pleas to let her go home and change into something better than she was wearing at the time, hadn't contributed more than a bit to it.

Uncertain if she was letting her emotions control what she was going to do, Janice went to the door.

Outside on the landing she stared up the stairs to Jimmy's flat. Such a short way, yet the results of climbing those steps were so pregnant with possibilities she felt a twinge of panic tighten inside her. Could she do it? Was her reckless determination up to going through with it? Her feet had already taken her two steps up before her thoughts even resolved themselves into full-blown doubt. Then her hand was clenched into a fist. Racing up the remaining stairs, she reached out and rapped on Jimmy's door. Becalmed suddenly by what she had done, she stood and waited, her heart pounding.

A moment later she heard locks turn and the door swung open and Jimmy's face was staring at her, a look of surprise, of puzzlement, perhaps even of concern on his dark features.

'Janice?' He took a step back into the well-lit room. The door opened wider. 'I didn't expect to see you. Would you like to come in?'

Janice followed as he led her into his flat.

'I felt we had to talk, Jimmy, after last night.'

Jimmy waved to a huge well-worn sofa. 'Take a seat. Would you like a drink? Some whisky or lager...'

'No thanks, I don't think so.'

Jimmy followed her in, settling down on an old armchair that mismatched the sofa in every way. This was the first time Janice had set foot inside Jimmy's flat and she was surprised at the look of second-hand shabbiness, from the scratched 50's-style side-board, with a few, almost empty bottles and odd glasses grouped across it, to an writing bureau pushed against one wall. Evidently his 'office', the bureau was covered in receipts and a stack of lever-arch files, precariously heaped on top of it. A small television sat on a table by the gas fire.

Jimmy followed her gaze about the room. He shrugged when she turned her eyes to him. 'I've been putting most of my money back in the business, trying to build it up. It's a long job, though. And it doesn't leave much for luxuries.'

Janice shook her head, her eyes softening. 'But you still wanted to splash out on me last night when you got some money.'

Jimmy laughed self-mockingly. 'When you're in my position it doesn't matter a damn what your digs look like. There's only me to see them most of the time. That's why I spend money on

53

clothes. The next big investment is a decent car. The BMW can pass muster most of the time. Like an eccentricity. It impresses people who don't know better. They think I like it because it's a collector's piece.'

'When in fact it's the best you could afford at the time.'

'Three hundred quid, would you believe it? Complete with MOT, though I think that was fixed.'

'But you still wanted to splash out on me,' Janice repeated. 'Did I mean that much to you?'

Jimmy half looked away from her, a frown, perhaps a puzzled frown, creasing his forehead. He looked at her again. 'You still do, Janice. You still mean that much to me.'

12

Steve Grant worried at his beef and onion sandwich, demolishing it with as much finesse as a half-starved fox gnawing its way through the carcass of a chicken it had just slaughtered. Beside him on the highly polished pub table stood a pint of lager. Lunch for Grant in the unsteady, unreliable world of journalism was never much better than this, which probably explained why he had chronically bad stomach ache most days of the week and the kind of insomnia that made sleep sometimes seem like a fabled state of nirvana. With his untidy face, its bristly patches of beard and moist blue eyes above equally moist, pale blue bags, he looked far more harmless and ineffectual than he actually was.

Suppressing a belch, that rose from the depths of his stomach, Grant reached for his lager and drank half of it without coming up for air. Surfacing at last, he glanced at the clock above the bar. He had agreed to meet his latest informant at one. That was ten minutes ago. Though he wasn't surprised the guy was late. It was par for the course. The man had to let him know at just what level of importance he placed their meeting in order to up whatever he expected to be paid for his information. In which case Grant probably had at least another ten minutes to wait before he could expect him to turn up. Another ten minutes at least.

Grant stared morosely at his lager, as if contemplating his future in it. If he were, the dour expression on his face would have given anyone watching the impression nothing of any good could be seen in it. Sighing inwardly, the journalist finally raised the glass to his lips. This was his second pint this lunchtime and there would definitely be at least as many more before he finally left the pub. Unless, of course, his informant had something exceptionally juicy for him when he arrived. The last snippet of information supplied to him about the mutilations and the theatrical makeup used by the strangler had been good for starters, but that was weeks ago, and little more had been added since. Now, though, there had been another attack, and this time the intended victim had been lucky enough to survive thanks to the intervention of several members of the public. 'Girl saved from Strangler by Bar Maid' was the upcoming headline in today's evening paper. He'd seen that before leaving the editorial offices a short while ago. It would be nice if he could get something for tomorrow's edition that would catch the headline too, or provide him with some additional fodder for his book on the murders, but that was probably asking too much. Life was rarely that generous.

He drank some more lager, draining the glass in seconds. God, he was thirsty today. Either that or he was heading for another bender. It was months since he'd last felt so pissed off with things that all he wanted to do was drink.

Grant put down his glass. He'd wait for a refill till his informant turned up. However long that might be.

'Hey, Stevie, watcha up to?'

The sarcastic voice broke through his thoughts. He looked up to catch sight of a bushy-haired man with a full moustache and tinted spectacles perched on a stool at the bar amongst a group of others. Grant recognised them all.

'Nothing any worse than you're up to, Oscar.'

'Not ferreting after nuggets of info about this strangler? I saw your little piece in *The Gazette*. 'Unconfirmed sources' my arse! What little bird was it?'

'Don't know what you're talking about,' Grant said, getting up. 'If you boys can't take a bit of competition, of course...'

Oscar shook his head. His grin took in the men drinking with him. Like Oscar Trent, they worked for the nationals. 'Beavering away for the evening press is all very well, so far as it goes, but you're only as good as your sources.'

'Meaning what?' Grant tried to keep the edge out of his voice, though even he could tell he wasn't being all that successful.

'Meaning you've got to be able to supply something back in return. What do you supply?'

'Confidentiality,' Grant said. 'And bloody good writing when it's needed.' He headed for the door. However busy the pub might be, it wasn't busy enough to hold a private conversation with anyone now. Oscar Trent and his cronies would see to that. Grant thanked whatever guardian angels might have been looking after him today that his informant was late and that Trent had been unable to resist mouthing off. If not... Grant grimaced. He'd had little enough going for him lately. To lose out on what could be a useful link with the murders would have been too much for his jangled nerves to take right now. The taste of the alcohol he'd already drunk had been almost too tempting as it was.

Grant stepped out into the pub forecourt where he studied the cars already parked on the patch of tarmac. A badly dented, dark red car turned in from the road, sounding its horn as it ground to a halt. It sounded like a badly-tuned tractor. Recognising its driver, though, Grant waved as he ran towards the car. The stocky, dark haired man inside lowered his window. 'Anything the matter?' the man asked, his eyes twitching nervously.

'Not unless you're bothered about a few others ear-wigging what we're going to be talking about.'

'Friends of yours?'

'Hardly.'

The man nodded towards the passenger door. 'Hop in. We'll drive somewhere. Unless you're in your own car...?'

'Not after what I've drunk,' Grant said with a shocked tone of voice, and a grin.

'Thought not.'

They exited onto the main road, before heading out of the conurbation towards a more sparsely populated, more rural area, a mixture of common parkland, industrial estates and derelict factories, with the occasional stretch of water. Not exactly a pretty location at this time of year, beneath an overcast sky and the threat of rain, it was close enough – and quiet enough – for them to have a private conversation.

The man drew up on half an acre of tyre-tracked mud next to the corrugated iron fencing of a disused car lot. A crane towered against the sky beyond the fencing, squeaking loudly as it raised a battered Vauxhall Astra up from a pile of wrecks, ready to be crushed.

'I haven't much time,' the man said, grumbling. 'I have to be back at the house in half an hour.'

'That's all right,' Grant said, lighting a cigarette. 'When we met at the office you said it was your wife who saved the girl.'

'That's right. Fiona saw her being attacked when she was on her way home.'

'But you weren't with her, were you? She was by herself?

Coming back from working at a pub?'

Defensively, the man said, 'I couldn't meet her. I had the kids to look after. They were in bed. And you can't leave kids by themselves at night on our estate. You'd know that if you had to live in the dump.'

Grant shrugged. 'It's nothing to do with me what your marital arrangements are. Some other reporter might probe a bit for some kind of perverse sensationalism. That's not my scene. All I want is a good honest story.' Then I'll crucify you, you selfish bastard, later, when the murderer's been caught and sentenced and I can write my book. Grant smiled encouragingly. 'Go on.'

'Fiona's not keen on talking to the press. She says all she's got to say on the matter she's already told the police. She don't want no publicity.'

Grant nodded sympathetically. 'I can understand her feelings.'

'So can I, so can I,' the man said, with little conviction. 'Only I thought as how it'd be a shame for her to have done what she did and get nothing for it.'

'Like a reward, you mean?'

'That would've been nice. But anything, anything at all, would be better than nothing. So I thought as how why not get her to sell what she's got to say about it to the press. Why give it? You boys get paid for what you write, don't you?'

'So why shouldn't she?'

'Exactly. You're on my wavelength. It isn't as if we have much anyway. Any little would help the way things stand. Though, when I say 'little', I don't mean as how we'd like to sell ourselves cheap. Fiona saved that girl's life, after all. She pitched in and attacked the bastard, didn't she? Surely what she's got to say about that, about what happened, is worth something?'

'It is,' Grant said. 'Though I'd need it in her own words. It'd be no good second hand. I'd need to see her, hear what she's got to say. Could you persuade her to do it? She's refused to say anything to the press so far. I know. I've tried to get her to talk to me. Others have too.'

'From the red tops.'

'Yes, them too.'

'O' course, some of them might be prepared to pay more than

58

you.'

Grant studied the sly look in the man's eyes, weighing him up. 'You've contacted some of them, have you?'

'Maybe.'

'And what have they offered?'

The man smiled, faintly. 'That's for me to know and you to worry about.'

'I see.' Grant wondered; he wondered how far down the queue he stood. It was obvious that Fiona Greenwood's husband had been a busy man in the last twenty-four hours. If it wasn't that the book he had already started to write about the murders had received some favourable interest from a major publisher, there would have been no way he could have competed with offers from the national press. Even as it stood he could be struggling, unless he could sell whatever story he wrote to one of the better paying nationals himself. 'I think I can match any offer they've made. And promise you more in the future.' He mentioned the book he was working on. 'There could be a lot more in it later. There wouldn't be anything from the nationals once things have moved on. A month from now your wife's story will be old news.'

Barry Greenwood drummed his fingers on the steering wheel as he thought. 'I'll go home and have a word with her. I'll ring you later when it's fixed.'

'You sure?'

'I'm sure. If I tell her to see you, she will. You can rely on that.'

Grant studied the tattooed knuckles on the man's large hands. Distastefully, he knew that if Barry Greenwood told his wife to talk to him she would have no choice. Of that he was sure.

13

Janice didn't know whether she liked Toby Cartmel or not. Though, as Jimmy's gofer-cum-labourer, there was no real reason why she should have any feelings about him one way or the other. Simplistic, she supposed; too much so. The fact was that at times like tonight she had to share his company whether she liked him or not when Jimmy picked her up to take her home in his van, Toby perched on his haunches in the back as he peered over her shoulder with a large, knobbly, calloused hand clinging tight to the back of her seat.

What did she feel about him? She glanced at a corner of his face in the rear-view mirror. She couldn't say she liked him. His face was too pimply to feel anything even remotely like that. In many ways he repelled her, especially when she caught sight of him staring with a remote kind of concentration at her breasts. There was something about the single-mindedness of his stare that made a cold shudder creep up her spine. Perhaps she should feel sorry for him. He was too tall and gangly and unsightly to have much chance of having a girlfriend of his own.

'I'll drop you off at the flats, then I'll have to leave you,' Jimmy said, interrupting her thoughts as he swung the van with characteristic speed around a corner, almost rolling the van onto two wheels. 'We've a job to go to afterwards that's got to be finished today even if it means working late.'

'That's all right,' Janice said. 'It was good of you to pick me up.'

'That's the least I could do after the other night. Anyway, you hate the dark, don't you? This way you needn't worry about it. You'll be safely home in another few minutes. Perhaps we could nip out later for a drink if I get back in time?'

'If you like,' Janice said. 'That would be good.'

Jimmy watched her wave to him as he drove off a few minutes later. Toby climbed over into the front passenger seat, clicking the seat belt shut as he relaxed onto it. 'She's a bit of all right, Mr Legg.'

Jimmy glanced at him and nodded. 'She is, Toby. But a bit highly-strung. If you know what I mean.'

Toby's smirk made Jimmy feel unsure if the lad understood

what he meant, but he couldn't be bothered to explain it to him. That was one thing he'd learned already about Toby Cartmel. He might be willing, but there wasn't enough up there to make conversation.

Meanwhile, less than two miles away, Fiona Greenwood sat hunched on the edge of the sofa in her living room as Stephen Grant ('Call me Steve') explained what he would like her to tell him about events leading up to her attack on the murderer. Sat on an imitation leather armchair facing the TV (now, wondrously, switched off for once while they talked), her husband looked on, a can of beer in one hand. Surreptitiously, Fiona massaged the bruise on her ribs where Barry hit her when she told him she didn't want to speak to the reporter ('And you'll get more of that if you don't wise up,' he'd threatened her). Fiona had already run through what happened from when she bumped into Kayleigh at the takeaway up until the moment a short while later when she rescued her.

The reporter leaned back and stared at the notes he'd scribbled while she talked. He looked up finally and said, 'Now, to give this an extra edge, Fiona, how about giving me some more details about the attacker?'

Doubtfully, Fiona asked him what he meant. 'I've already told you everything I can remember about the man. He was tall and white. Most of his face, except for bits around his eyes and mouth, were covered in a balaclava. That's all I can tell you about him. I don't understand what you mean by more details. There aren't any more.'

Steve smiled. 'Perhaps not, but I'm sure, with a bit of prompting, you'll remember some. Think of all the victims he's suspected of having killed already. We owe it to them to give the public as clear a picture as we can of just what kind of cowardly, vicious animal we're dealing with. How about when you attacked him? Did he cry out? Did he show some kind of fear when the tables were turned? Try to remember. Didn't you feel you'd scared him, put the fear of God in him, perhaps, for just one moment? You said you threw the takeaway you'd bought at the Chinese at him. Did any of it hit him? Perhaps some of the hot food splashed his face and scalded him? Did it make him squeal? That would fit nicely. The animal that preyed on helpless victims squealing like a frightened pig as you bravely hurled scalding hot Chinese food in his face. Diminish him. Belittle him. Show the public the kind of worthless shit this man really is.' Steve smiled at her again. 'What do you think?'

Fiona shook her head, uncertain. 'I can't remember. It was dark. It happened so quick. I barely had time to think before it was over. All I remember was feeling scared he was going to attack me next, that he was going to do to me what he'd already tried to do to the girl. I can remember panicking as I scrambled up the hill away from him and screaming for help.'

'But before that,' Steve insisted, 'in those brief moments when you were attacking him, could what I've suggested have really happened? Could you say that they didn't? Could you honestly tell me that when you threw food at him some of it didn't splatter his face and make him cry out?'

'He did cry out once. I remember that. He made some sort of noise.' Fiona glanced at the window, the memory too raw for her to think about it objectively. Only the doctor's medication had enabled her to some sleep last night after what she'd gone through. And for much of today she'd felt ill.

Steve looked once more through his notes. 'I think we can safely say that much of what I've suggested happened. After all, let's face it, Fiona, the man must be a coward to murder young women. That's fair comment, isn't it? And you did succeed in scaring him off his latest victim before he could kill her. Perhaps you'll allow me a certain licence to make the story a bit more vivid.'

'More sellable,' Barry Greenwood said as he tugged the tab on another beer. Foam brimmed across it as he raised the can to his lips.

Steve nodded. 'Definitely more 'sellable', Barry. Immeasurably so.' He looked back at Fiona, eyebrows raised.

Fiona nodded. 'Perhaps...'

Smiling broadly, Steve ticked against his notes. 'That's a girl. I knew we'd be able to get to the core of it with a bit of persistence. Memories can play funny tricks. We don't always remember just how much happened. And there's modesty, of course. I'm sure you don't want to overplay your part in rescuing the girl. But we've to get to the truth. You owe it to yourself. You were brave, outstandingly brave, in standing up to him. You scared him off. Admit it. You faced up to him and showed the world what a cowardly bastard he really is.'

'Too true,' Barry said. 'Face up to it, girl, you're a hero.'

A hand still nursing the bruise on her ribs, Fiona looked at Barry. Somehow his praise seemed to hurt her more than his fists, and she wished that once, just once, she could face up to him with half the guts she'd faced the attacker last night.

Barry beamed back at her, his beer can extended in a mock salute that made her feel sick in her stomach.

14

As soon as Ian entered the station the desk sergeant told him the DCI wanted him 'prompt.'

After a fruitless day chasing up leads, Ian had intended going to the canteen for a coffee and doughnut, but that would have to go on the back burner, he thought ruefully as he headed down the corridor towards Detective Chief Inspector Yates' office, an excess of gravity weighing down his legs.

Yates waved him to a chair, then tossed a copy of the evening paper across the desk.

'Read that,' Yates said. 'That idiot, Grant, is up to his old tricks again. I thought a few titbits tossed to him would have helped to calm the bastard down. But no, he has to get hold of one of our prime witnesses and persuade her to elaborate her story to titillate his readers and move him a few yards further up the greasy pole to a job with the tabloids.'

''Barmaid Heroine Sent Mad-Dog Strangler Squealing in Terror?' That's a bit of a tortured headline even for *The Gazette*, sir.'

'Read on, read on. It gets better by the line. According to Grant's report the girl nearly had the strangler in tears before sending him fleeing for his life.' Yates sighed impatiently.

Ian put down the paper. 'What do you intend doing about it, sir? We can hardly prevent him from talking to Fiona Greenwood, or anyone else for that matter.'

'I don't know.' Yates pushed his chair back with one foot. 'I don't like it. The story has a nasty smell about it. It's provocative, distasteful, and blatantly untrue. There's no denying the woman's courage in rushing to the girl's help. There's no denying she risked her life doing it. But the rest of it, the way in which the man is alleged to have been scared off by her hurling her takeaway at him is a load of nonsense.'

Ian shrugged. 'Maybe so, but I don't see what we can do about it.'

'Probably nothing.' Yates stood up, strode to the window that occupied most of the outside wall of his office and stared down at the lamp lit streets below. 'I just hope that madman doesn't get ideas about setting the record straight. This kind of reporting could encourage him to strike again soon. It almost forces him to, if he's to maintain any kind of self-respect. Do you follow my gist?'

Ian nodded, the logic of his chief's deep-seated fears so obvious it didn't need more to be said about it. There was a rapport between the two that as often as not needed no more than the minimum of words. 'The only question is where he'll strike next, sir. If we knew that we could try and do something about it.'

'But he's struck over too wide an area for us to pin him down. I know what you mean. With a bit more time perhaps we could sift out some clues as to who he is. What we don't need is provocative stuff like the kind of trash Steve Grant's churning out. Mark my word, there'll be another strangling within days of this article. Within days.'

15

Market Road in Emlyn was as busy as usual. Midday, the shops were open and most of the few parking spaces available along the High Street were filled. It took Jimmy Legg nearly ten minutes to find a space for his van, and by that time what little patience he'd had, had been thoroughly exhausted. Grinding his teeth, he locked the van behind him, before heading down the pavement, hands in the pockets of his leather jacket as a cold wind whipped newspapers about his feet in clouds of grit. First things first, he thought. He was nearly out of cigarettes. With the jobs lined up for the rest of the day he needed a full pack at least, perhaps more. Singh's Newsagents was only a few shops away, close to the cafe he intended nipping in for some lunch. He rummaged through his jeans' pocket for some change.

'Hello, Mr Legg,' Singh greeted him as Jimmy pushed open the shop door. A large pile of lunchtime editions of the local newspaper dominated the counter. A middle-aged, grey-haired Indian, Singh was sorting the papers into smaller piles. 'And what can I do for you?'

Jimmy nodded at the cigarette display behind the newsagent. 'A couple of packets of B and H.' He glanced at *The Gazettes* on the counter. His lips drew into a restrained grimace as he read the headline. 'And I a copy of *The Gazette*.'

'Ah, yes, I was just reading it myself,' Singh said as he twisted round for the cigarettes. 'A very brave woman. She should be given an award for what she did to that monster. It's terrible that our streets should be terrorised by such a man, don't you think?'

Jimmy nodded as he counted out his change and pocketed his cigarettes.

'I hope they catch him soon,' Singh said. He leaned confidentially over the counter. 'My wife daren't even go out at night to visit her sister any more, and she only lives two streets away.'

Grunting sympathetically, Jimmy nodded Good Bye and strode out of the shop. Not bothering to read the newspaper yet, he headed for the café, where he secured a table by the window. It was a small establishment, pine-board walls and a plethora of dayglow signs for 'Bacon & Cheese Butties', 'Sausage & Chips', 'Burgers', 'All-day Breakfasts' and other tempting concoctions. Ordering a plate of sausage, bacon, fried bread, tomatoes, chips and gravy, with a side plate of bread and butter and a mug of coffee, Jimmy settled down to read *The Gazette*, laid across the Formica table.

*

As Jimmy read Fiona Greenwood's version of events at Park Farm Estate his jaws moved more and more furiously as he chewed his food, crimson darkening his weather-tanned face. Outside the cafe, looking in, Toby Cartmel's eyes lit up with relief when he spotted his boss. Late already, he had been expecting another of Jimmy Legg's bawlings out, but since his boss hadn't finished his lunch he was sure he had probably escaped that today.

Hurrying into the cafe, Toby ordered a mug of tea, then worked his way towards his boss.

Jimmy looked up as Toby reached for the back of the chair facing him. The youth felt his pulse quicken when he saw the deep anger in Jimmy's eyes.

'I'm sorry I'm late, Mr Legg. I missed my bus.'

Jimmy stared at him in silence, a puzzled look slowly emerging in his eyes. 'Late?' Jimmy reached for the newspaper, rolled it up and stuffed it in the back pocket of his jeans. 'Forget about it,' he said a few moments later, distractedly.

'Is anything wrong, Mr Legg?' Toby asked. He sat down and slopped a good portion of his tea across the table in front of him. Apologising, he started to wipe it up with the sleeve of his anorak till he realised how much of a mess he was making with his efforts.

'Wrong?' Ignoring the pool of tea, Jimmy seemed to make an effort to concentrate on what was being said to him. 'Nothing's wrong, Toby. Nothing at all.' He smiled, thinly. He looked down at the remains of his lunch and stabbed at what was left of one sausage with his fork.

'I just thought...' Toby faltered as he used a handkerchief to mop up the nearest pool that was heading towards his boss's plate. There was still that hard look of anger in Jimmy's eyes.

Always easily intimidated, Toby had grown to know Jimmy's moods too well. It would only take one word to get him going today. Just one small word.

So tense, in fact, was the afternoon that Toby could hardly believe it when it came time for Jimmy to pick up his girlfriend. Left to himself, Toby worked with a lighter heart, sure he had the best part of an hour in which he didn't need to watch his boss's face for the first warning glimmer of suppressed anger about to burst through. This had already happened this afternoon when Toby made a mistake in his work. He had grown so nervous after this that it had led to even more mistakes and a growing atmosphere of tension.

*

With an escape from work and the chance to express his feelings more openly on the road, driving with his foot pressed hard on the accelerator, swerving and roaring through the busy traffic like a man possessed, Jimmy's mood had lightened by the time he drew up near Janice's office. Catching sight of her, he sounded his horn.

He watched her hurry towards him with a wave of her hands. He waved back at her. The tension on his face relaxed slightly as Janice pulled open the passenger door and jumped in.

'My God, I'm glad to finish work today.' Janice buckled her seat belt with gusto. 'You're lucky you work for yourself.'

Jimmy smiled faintly. 'Being your own boss has its own problems,' he said. 'You don't have Toby Cartmel working for you.'

Janice laughed. 'That's true, I suppose.'

Jimmy drove off, swerving past queues of buses that seemed to appear from nowhere to block the road with their red bulks. The pavements were full to overflowing as office workers evacuated the tower blocks that surrounded them, while the cold drizzle that made everything look gloomy did little to dampen the energy with which people ran out across the road, regardless of traffic. Jimmy was forced to sound his horn again and again till they broke free from them. 'I'll have to drop you off again,' Jimmy said. 'I left Toby by himself at the last job we're doing. By now he'll have made a botch of it.'

'No time for a coffee before you set off?' Janice asked.

Jimmy shrugged. 'Maybe. But it would have to be quick. I daren't leave Toby for long.'

The sky was lightening by the time they reached the flats as the clouds slowly dispersed to the east. The grey slates of the Victorian house gleamed against it, still wet from the rain. Inside Janice's flat, Jimmy slumped on the sofa while she made them a drink in the kitchen. 'Everyone at the office was on about the latest attack of the strangler,' Janice called out to him while she worked in the kitchen.

Jimmy looked towards her. 'Yes?'

'It makes you feel better that a woman was able to do what she did to the bastard.'

Jimmy's eyes wandered to the framed copies of oil paintings Janice had hung about the walls of her living room, country scenes predominating. 'I suppose you're talking about that article in the paper?'

'That's right. She deserves a medal for what she did.'

'If she did it.'

'What do you mean?' Janice poked her head through the doorway while she waited for the kettle to boil. 'Don't you believe her?'

'Do you?'

'I don't know. I suppose so. Why shouldn't I? After all, she did save the girl he was trying to strangle. You can't deny that. It all makes sense, doesn't it?'

'That she went on to attack him and sent him running away like a scalded cat?' Jimmy laughed derisively. 'If that man and his son from the estate hadn't heard her screams and run to her aid, do you think she could have stopped him from dealing with her just as easily as he'd begun to deal with the girl? Do you think someone who has killed three women could be stopped so easily?'

Looking uncertain, Janice said, 'I don't know. I suppose it doesn't make sense if you look at it like that.'

'Of course it doesn't. The other victims will have fought back too. They would have fought back with everything they had to save themselves. They didn't succeed and he killed them. He would have killed her too if those guys hadn't heard her.'

'Then why did she say what she did?'

Jimmy snorted. 'It's like most of what you read in the papers, Janice, a pack of lies.'

Catching sight of her telephone, Janice swore.

'What's the matter?' Jimmy followed her gaze, and saw the light of the answer phone blinking.

'That'll be my mother again,' Janice said. 'She's rung me every day for the past two weeks asking me to ring her back. She never rings at night when she knows I'll be in. Always during the day when I'm at work, always whining on about how long it is since I last spoke to her, how tough things are and how much better off I'd be if I went back home instead of living in London by myself.' Janice's bitterness grew more intense as she spoke. 'What's your mother like, Jimmy? As bad as mine?'

For a moment there was an odd introspection on Jimmy's face. 'My mother's dead,' he said, flatly. 'She died four years ago.'

Crestfallen, Janice said, 'I'm sorry, Jimmy. I really am. If I'd known...'

Shrugging dismissively, he said, 'It doesn't matter. She wasn't much of a mother, truth be known. For the most part I was brought up by my father after she left, though he wasn't much use as a father himself once she'd gone, what with the booze and all. She destroyed him, body and soul. She was an actress. Not a successful one, mind. No one you'll have heard of. Most of her work was on the stage, minor rep companies up and down the country. She never stayed in one place long. Which was probably for the best, considering how she behaved.' He paused while Janice poured their coffee.

'Did you hate her?' Janice asked when she returned with two mugs steaming in her hands.

'Hate her?' Jimmy laughed. 'I despised, detested, abhorred her. It went beyond hate. It went *way* beyond hate. She killed my father, turned him into an alcoholic wreck. She left us when I was nine. By the time I was sixteen my father's liver was like a colander. Less than six months after I finished school he was in hospital. He never came out. He was dead before my seventeenth birthday. Ever since I've been by myself.'

'Except when you married,' Janice said.

Jimmy laughed again. 'Except then. And that was my mistake. Like my father, I married an actress. I should have

70

known better. All ego, no talent, she spent more time bed-hopping in the hope of better parts than any time spent on stage.'

'Your wife was an actress?'

'That's what she calls herself. Don't ask me what I'd call her.' Jimmy fell silent while he drank his coffee.

'So that's why you divorced her?' Janice said. 'She was having an affair?'

'By the time I realised what was going on, she'd had more than one.'

Which was probably why, Janice thought, rumour had it that Jimmy had been violent to his wife. If what he'd told her was true she couldn't blame him. Though she couldn't help wonder why he had been tempted to marry the same kind of woman as his father had. After what he had already been through, an actress should have been the last type of person he would have been tempted to marry.

She gazed at him. Silent now, there was a look of brooding on Jimmy's face, perhaps sparked off by her questions, Janice thought. She would have to make sure she avoided mentioning mothers and ex-wives again. With her own cross-patched relationship with her mother, Janice didn't think that would be much of a problem. The topic of mothers wasn't exactly top of her agenda either.

Draining his coffee, Jimmy placed his mug on the table before the fire. 'I'd better get back to see how Toby's doing.' He looked at her. 'I'm sorry if I got a bit strong about my mother.'

'And your ex-wife,' Janice added with a smile. 'Forget it. I won't mention either of them again. That's a promise.'

Jimmy smiled. 'That's a deal.'

*

On his way back to Toby Jimmy drove more carefully, more under control, his tension easing. Somehow Janice's easy temperament helped to cool his anger, letting him see things more clearly. It was hard sometimes to see things as they really were. Thoughts often tumbled through his mind with such repetitious force he felt unable to see what was in front of him, as if they could blind him, tunnelling his sight into a narrow channel. He sighed, at peace with himself for the first time today.

As the traffic built up ahead of him, he dropped into second gear. A newsagent's sign, propped against the side of the road, caught his eye.

'BAR MAID SAVAGES STRANGLER' was written across it in bold letters.

Jimmy's lips drew tight against his teeth.

16

'Do you think you should have come tonight?' Tom asked. 'We could always get someone else in. You look terrible. You look as if you haven't slept in days. Which I don't suppose you have after what you went through, girl.'

Fiona smiled as bravely as she could, knowing the landlord was no doubt right. But anything was better than another night at home with Barry, still obsessed with how much money they could make out of her story. He had been against her working tonight as well till she pointed out that backing out of her job might spoil things for them and give the impression she wasn't as tough as the newspapers made her out to be. The hypocrisy of what she said made her feel sick, especially when Barry's face lit up at the suggestion. He'd even gone so far as to volunteer to drive her to the pub. Her nerves still fragile after what she had been through, she readily accepted his offer, even when their Capri gratingly roared its way through the traffic in a cloud of exhaust fumes as black as soot.

'I'll be all right,' Fiona insisted finally to Tom.

'Nonsense. I'm not having our customers see you stood behind the bar in that state. What do you think they'd think of me? You take it easy. Don't worry, I'll pay you anyway, but you're going to be on the other side of the bar for once. And the drinks are on me. After what you did for that poor girl that's the least I could do for you, Fi. I'll arrange for Debra and Audrey to come in. My wife can have the night off too so she can keep you company. And don't say no. You're doing us a favour being here. After all, girl, you're a celebrity now and don't forget it. When word gets round, do you think your presence will do any harm for custom?' Tom laughed loudly. 'Come on. We'll start off as we mean to go. Get yourself perched on a stool round there and I'll send Julie with a couple of Bacardies.'

Unsure though she was as to Tom's motives, other than show her off as a kind of celebrity, Fiona felt relieved at not having to stand behind the bar. Even though she had insisted on coming in, she wasn't sure if she was up to it.

'Here you are,' she heard Julie call a few minutes later, handing her a drink while she seated herself on a stool beside her. Only just gone seven the pub was still quiet for a Friday night with only a few of the regulars in. Someone put a pound in the jukebox and the atmosphere was improved by the booming sounds of Meat Loaf promising 'anything but that'. Fiona sipped her drink, wondering why everything felt tarnished and full of lies. She did not know whether she could fully accept all the praise people kept insisting on giving her for what she did. In the hours that followed the strain was eased by the drinks Julie provided her with, one after another, growing more fulsome in her praise for Fiona as more of their customers came over, shaking her by the hand or kissing her or patting her on the back. Sober, Fiona would have run a mile. But by the time she'd drunk several Bacardies, a roseate glow had settled around her so that she began, in a detached kind of way, to enjoy the attention, basking in it.

Entering the pub at half past nine, Jimmy Legg made his way to the bar. Dressed soberly in a dull sports jacket and slacks, he looked almost drab compared to most of the drinkers pressed around the bar as he called for a bitter shandy. He didn't need to search for long to catch sight of Fiona Greenwood. The group she and the landlady were in the middle of would have been difficult to miss anywhere. Recognising her, he was surprised she was here tonight – he had only come on the off chance she might turn up for work or he would find out something about her from the regulars, bragging about their 'hero'. Jimmy took his drink to a quiet seat by the wall. Looking on as he sipped it he felt a growing resentment build inside him, knowing how little truth there was to the woman's claims. If those milling around her could have seen the terror that filled her face, the unashamed, whimpering, abject fear that had made her scramble in witless panic as her nails dug deep into the mud and grass of the artificial hill... Jimmy finished his shandy before he realised how little there was left of it. The drink left a fizzy, over sweet taste in his mouth. Although he felt like he needed something stronger, he knew better than to fall for that temptation, going back to the bar for another shandy instead. This time he would make it last.

Two older women, dressed in what would at one time have been called their 'Sunday best', sat at a nearby table, where they were making remarkably short work of their rounds of gin and tonic while they munched through a succession of bags of crisps.

The shorter, stouter of the two looked at Jimmy as he carefully pressed his way to his seat. Her left eyebrow arced inquisitively as she leaned towards him. 'Have you seen our celebrity?' she asked when he'd sat down.

'Celebrity?'

The woman tilted her head towards Fiona Greenwood, whose reddish-brown hair was visible between the heads of the chattering crowd of what Jimmy had already described to himself as sycophants that had gathered about her. Jimmy suppressed the sneer he felt pull at his lips and feigned ignorance. 'Who is she?' he asked. 'Someone famous?'

The women laughed contentedly, obviously pleased at the opportunity to show off their local knowledge. 'That's Fiona Greenwood, the woman who chased off that strangler who's killed three women already, and would have killed his fourth if it hadn't been for her. She works behind the bar normally. Though I suppose that's probably beneath her now.' Pride and resentment jostled for pre-eminence in the woman's voice. 'I always thought she was a quiet sort myself. Timid. You never hear her say anything back to that husband of hers. Now *him –*' The woman tutted as her friend nodded in agreement. 'Idle drunkard, that's her husband. Never done an honest day's work in his life. Made out to be a car mechanic once, God help us. Spent more time in the pub than doing repairs.'

'And he beats her,' the other woman chipped in, razor-sharp wrinkles radiating from her lips as she pursed her mouth in disapproval. 'I've seen her with bruises beneath her makeup. She thinks you can't see them but they're there, as clear as daylight to those that can see.'

'That's right, Annie. A right old knocking about he gave her a month ago.'

Jimmy shook his head. 'It makes it hard to credit she could have done what they said in the paper,' he said.

Annie nodded. 'That's just what me and Nancy were saying. Which just goes to show you can't always tell. There's more to some people than you think. Isn't there?'

'Perhaps she'll turn round and give that husband of hers a good hiding,' Nancy suggested.

'It'd not be before time,' Annie said. 'If I were her I'd have left him years ago. At least my old man never raised his hand against

75

me.'

'He'd never have dared, Annie. You'd have killed him first.'

'I'd have hit him on the head with the teapot. I'd have bust it or bust his head,' she said with a derisory laugh. 'Poor sod. He's been dead ten years.'

Jimmy smiled indulgently. 'Could I buy you two ladies a drink?' he said. He stood up, his own glass drained.

The women smiled up at him. 'That would be nice, young man. But we're drinking gins,' she added.

'That's all right,' Jimmy said. 'Two gin and tonics.'

When he returned to the women they became even more talkative than before, as if he had become an old friend. For the next twenty minutes he let them prattle on, ignoring their repetitions and lapses into reminiscences that only now and then made sense to him. He found he could let his mind wander while they talked, as his eyes half watched the glimpses he got now and then of Fiona Greenwood. Several more trips to the bar soon brought them to closing time, when his newfound friends decided they had better leave.

'We don't like to stay out late,' Annie said as they gathered their handbags and coats. 'That maniac's still out there. We feel safer going home while there are plenty of folk about. You never know, do you?'

Smiling faintly, Jimmy told them they were very wise. 'It never pays to be careless,' he said. 'In fact,' he added, standing up, 'I think I'll be on my way as well. I've to be up early in the morning for work.'

With only one glance at Fiona Greenwood as they headed for the door, he walked out with them. Still surrounded by her admirers, it was obvious it would be some time yet before Fiona left, no doubt by taxi, he thought. Outside, he waved Good Bye to the women, then headed down the narrow street alongside the pub to where he'd parked his car. His last few shandies had been made with alcohol-free beer, so he knew he was still under the limit. He had no fears of being stopped by the police tonight as he parked across from the pub where he could watch its doors. By the time a taxi drew up some time later, Jimmy's hands had become so numbed by the cold his fingers fumbled as he felt for the keys to restart his car. Waved on her way by the landlady, Fiona Greenwood emerged from the pub and climbed into the taxi. As it drove off, Jimmy followed.

Keeping a safe distance between them, he hardly noticed the cold any more. A familiar, tingling, anticipatory tension overrode any sense of physical discomfort. Jimmy's mind felt channelled, purposeful, so geared-up it seemed as if there was nothing he couldn't do any more, as if every nerve and muscle in his body was under irresistible control.

In the quiet traffic at this time of night it was easy for him to keep the taxi in sight as it drove through the centre of Emlyn, then out towards Park Farm Estate. Only as they entered the estate did Jimmy lengthen the distance between them in case it became too obvious he was following. In the event, ascertaining which house the taxi pulled up at was no problem. The open planning of the estate made it easy to see. Nor did he feel he would have any difficulty remembering which house it was. The piles of rusting car parts scattered about its squalid garden made it distinctive enough.

Satisfied, Jimmy drove back to his flat as a calm feeling of determination settled through him.

17

Normally on Saturday Janice caught the bus into town to do her weekly shopping. But today Jimmy Legg knocked on her door at nine with the offer to take her.

'I've to nip out first to sort a few things on a job I'm doing with Toby, but I should be back by eleven. I could take you then. I've to go into town for something myself, so I could drop you off, then meet you later for lunch.'

After making sure that Jimmy's idea of 'lunch' wouldn't be anywhere so exclusive as the place he took her to before, Janice agreed. Saturdays could be boring, and it was always hard work carrying her shopping back on the bus.

Smiling at having got her to agree, Jimmy hurried to his van.

Janice watched him drive off, then went into her bathroom for a shower. Her hair still smelt too much of the office. And, although she didn't rush, enjoying the heat of the shower and pampering herself afterwards as she dried off, it soon dawned on her that eleven o'clock had not only come, it had well and truly gone, and still Jimmy hadn't returned. By half eleven she was starting to become impatient. She had a lot of shopping to do today and always hated the town centre on Saturday afternoons, when it became claustrophobically busy. Again and again she looked out of the window, hoping to catch sight of the van. If he didn't return soon she would have to set off without him. She couldn't wait all day. Never the most patient of people, there was a set routine for jobs like this that had to be adhered to otherwise she would start to panic she would run out of time to get it done.

Janice pulled out a writing pad and scribbled a note.

'Dear Jimmy, I couldn't wait any longer. Many of the things I need will be sold out if I don't go into town soon. If you're still serious about lunch meet me outside Woolworth's at half one, when I should have finished. Hope you've had no serious problems this morning, Janice.'

Folding it into a neat square, she opened her door and went upstairs to Jimmy's flat. As she bent to push the paper beneath his door, she noticed he had left it ajar. Perhaps he had come back after all and for some reason had left his van elsewhere. Why he hadn't bothered to let her know she couldn't imagine. She tapped on the door and called his name as she pushed it fully open and stepped inside.

There was no one there. Curious, Janice was struck by the extreme tidiness of Jimmy's living room. Unlike her own, with its magazines and newspapers and half-read books scattered over the furniture and floor, not to mention the disgraceful number of mugs and plates that had still to be taken into the kitchen to be washed, his place was meticulous, despite the familiar shabbiness of its furnishings.

Still curious, Janice went towards the bedroom. Why not? In for a penny, in for a pound and all that rot, she thought. Smiling bemusedly, Janice opened the bedroom door, not surprised at the sight of the military-style neatness of the double bed inside. Other than that and a chest of drawers, the only other furniture was a wardrobe. Not a single item of clothing had been left out apart from a towel dressing gown hung behind the door. Uncertain whether she should admire it or be wary of such surgical neatness, Janice decided to say nothing about having looked inside the flat to him. Somehow she didn't feel he would take kindly to the intrusion. Just why she felt this Janice wasn't sure. Perhaps it was the obsessive neatness. Or perhaps it was something else, something she couldn't explain to herself. In fact, Janice couldn't be clear in her own mind about any of this.

Dropping her note on the floor behind the door as if she'd pushed it underneath, Janice returned to her flat. Collecting her coat, she decided she had waited long enough. If she were lucky a bus would be along soon and she could be in town in time to get all her shopping done before she'd promised to meet Jimmy. If, Janice added to herself as she ran along the road a few minutes later to the bus stop, he turned up at all.

*

Janice had barely caught her bus when Jimmy drove up to the house. Unaware she had already set off for town he raced to her flat and knocked on the door. His disappointment at discovering she had gone without him made him clench his fists in frustration. Only their plans to go out together had helped him keep his temper that morning as he finished off a major plumbing job at a nursing home with Toby. The lad's clumsiness seemed to get worse by the day. Swearing beneath his breath,

Jimmy turned abruptly and carried on up the stairs. As he reached his door, he suddenly remembered he had forgotten to lock it. He slammed his fist into the palm of his hand as it came back to him. He'd set out in a rush this morning, nipping down to Janice's first on an impulse, with the intention of returning to his flat before setting out. But their conversation had distracted him and he had clean forgotten to return before he left. Stupid!

Jimmy pushed open his door, the folded notepaper on the floor inside catching his attention. Warily, he picked it up. When he'd read it, he glanced around his living room, his suspicions aroused. Although the note looked as if it had been pushed under the door, Jimmy was knew that didn't mean Janice might not have entered his room. Still wary, he approached the door to his bedroom. He knelt beside it and peered at a small strip of Sellotape attached to one edge. When he saw part of it had become trapped inside the doorjamb his face darkened. Standing up, he opened the door and strode to the wardrobe. A second strip of Sellotape was still secured across the gap between the wardrobe door and its frame. Pent up for the past few seconds, he released his breath with a sigh of relief, then opened the wardrobe and looked inside. On the floor, hidden under a pile of pullovers he hadn't worn in months, he pulled out a metal box. He pushed his fingers through the handles on either side and picked it up. Carefully, he lowered it onto his bed. He took out a key from his jeans pocket. Again, he saw that the strip of Sellotape, unobtrusively stuck to the edge of the lid, was undisturbed. If Janice had come into the flat, she'd obviously resisted her curiosity. Jimmy smiled. Maybe he'd judged her well. Maybe not all women were as bad as each other. Maybe some could be trusted. Maybe... Shaking his head, Jimmy opened the box. Inside, he picked up a heavy object wrapped in an oil-soaked linen cloth. Handling it with reverential care, he unfolded the cloth, then gazed at the gun. It looked old and, despite the fact he had tried his best to improve its condition in the few months since he found it hidden in a cardboard box between the floorboards of a house he was working on, there were still patches of rust. Toby was the first to spot it. Alarmed it might go off in his hands, the youth had called to Jimmy. Unlike Toby, though, Jimmy's immediate reaction was an impulse to keep it. Inside the box were a couple of dozen rounds of ammunition.

Whether the gun or its accompanying shells still worked, he did not know. It had probably lain hidden inside the floorboards since the Second World War. It was an army revolver, an officer's. Reference to a couple of books in the library had confirmed this. By then he'd told Toby he had taken the gun to the Police. Not given to questioning anything his boss said, the lad accepted his word readily. The gun had frightened him, and Toby had been too glad to see the back of it. Wrapping it inside the cloth again, Jimmy placed the gun on his bed, before reaching into the box once more to pull out a second, smaller box. Made of tin, it was scratched and dented from years of use. Though heavier than it looked, it was small enough to fit inside the deep pockets of his combat jacket. The familiar smell of grease paint greeted him as he pulled it open to feel the dirty jars inside. A peaceful kind of calm settled on Jimmy's face as the smell brought memories back to him. But it was a deceitful calm. If calm it was.

Narrowing his eyes as the scent of grease paint filled his lungs, Jimmy reached alongside the jars for the knife.

The shining, well-honed, *special* knife.

As sharp as a razor, with a curved blade that could lift off skin and muscles with ease...

18

Fiona awoke with a start.

Conscious that Barry's side of the bed was empty, she looked at the chair he normally hung his clothes on. It was empty too. 'Shit!' Fiona muttered beneath her breath as she flung the sweat-damp duvet back and climbed out of bed. Barry had been in a foul enough mood as it was last night by the time she got home without him having to get up and make his own breakfast. 'And who were you drinking with?' he'd asked sarcastically when she got in, smelling her breath. 'Must have been some well off ponce to have afforded all those rums I can stink on you.' Despite her denials, she'd been lucky to get away with a few verbal threats about what would happen if he ever caught her with someone else. That he didn't want to risk marking her now was the only reason he'd not hit her. But that would pass. It wouldn't be long before he realised there was no more money to be squeezed out of what had happened. Then it would start again.

Fiona made her way into the bathroom, tripping over towels and dirty clothes. Her eyes were too sore to open yet and her head felt ready to burst. Whether last night was worth it she wasn't sure. Most of it remained in her memory now as little more than a blur.

Ten minutes later, her head still aching so bad she was close to tears, Fiona plodded downstairs. 'Where's your dad?' she asked the older of her sons.

Jason, at five, had a prematurely grave look on his face, as if the responsibility of being big brother to Carl, who was only three, weighed heavily on his narrow shoulders. 'He went out,' Jason said. Both boys were sat on the beat-up sofa in front of the television, watching cartoons. The crashes, screeches, yells and general mayhem did nothing to help Fiona's head, but she didn't feel up to the arguments that would follow any attempt to switch it off.

Stumbling to the kitchen, she pulled open a packet of paracetamols and poured out three, which she swilled down with a cup of water from the tap. Shuddering as she swallowed them, she trudged back into the living room.

'Did your dad say anything before he went out?' she asked as she slumped on the armchair, her fingers automatically feeling for the holes scorched in its arms where Barry had left his cigarettes burning. One day he'd fall asleep and set it on fire and kill them all. But it was no good warning him. She knew too well to try that anymore.

'Dad said he'd be out all day. He's work to do,' Jason said, his serious grey eyes taking stock of his mother with a mature look of concern.

'Work-tu-doo,' echoed Carl, red lips covered in melted chocolate and dribbled snot.

Fiona sighed. The only work Barry ever had to do was reach in his pocket to pay for his next pint. Gone eleven, she knew he'd be in the Royal Oak with his cronies. He'd not come home till tea, if then. If he had enough money he'd go somewhere for a takeaway and start another round of drinking till he'd got so steamed he had to be helped home later. If she were lucky, he'd be too drunk to do anything but collapse on their bed and sleep till the morning.

Lighting a cigarette, Fiona stared at the television set. She could feel her headache start to lift as either the pills or Barry's absence started to have their effect. Carl waddled towards her.

Reaching down for a paper handkerchief, she wiped his face, then gave him a hug. 'Just the three of us today, boys. Isn't that fun?'

Jason mirrored her smile with a bigger, more serious, worried smile of his own. Poor mite, she thought as she hugged him to her. How did he come from a father like Barry? Or had Barry, too, been like this at his age?

19

DS McKenna struggled from his car, self-conscious even more than usual about his weight. There'd been another warning, of course, from his doctor, which hadn't helped ease his mind about the occasional aches and pains in his chest, even though his cholesterol level was only slightly over the acceptable limit. But he couldn't deny the strain on his chest when he exerted himself. Even walking at more than a casual pace was an exertion now.

Puffing already only a few yards away from his car, Ian stopped to wipe his face with a handkerchief. The high street was hard enough to walk along at the best of times. Saturdays were so much worse he wished he'd never bothered. But his son and daughter had clubbed together to save up for a new game and had asked him if he would nip into the computer games shop to get it for them when he went through town this afternoon.

Emlyn's main shopping street was packed with stalls perched against the kerb. A cabbage tumbled into the road from one of them. Before it had rolled more than a couple of feet a hand reached out, retrieving it. Somewhere, nearby, he heard a guitar being plucked as someone sang a mournful song that sounded folkish. His good humour restored at the sound of it, Ian chuckled to himself as he wondered if there had ever been anything but a mournful tune for folk singers. Pressing on, he wove through the crowds of shoppers towards Games Attack. A broad-fronted shop between Boots and a cut-price clothes shop, its poster-filled windows beckoned him, unable to resist the allure. Admit it, he told himself as he pushed through the groups of teenagers who, for the most part, could only ogle the games sold here, you're as struck on this kind of stuff as your kids. If the truth were known, he sometimes felt he was addicted to them even more than they were. If not for his commitments at work he knew he'd spend more time than he did bent over the computer, joystick in hand. Though at least it was a cleaner kind of thing than he had to live with at work. Frustration at the lack of progress in tracking down the strangler had much to do with it. All the hours spent slogging about town, hunting for clues, had been so much wasted time so far. They were no nearer tracking down whoever he was than when they started, apart from the fact they now knew the man was white. And maybe, just maybe, he might have been wearing some kind of after-shave when he attacked the last girl, though she hadn't even been a hundred percent sure about this. Her only other pieces of description added up to vague generalities: he'd been wearing dark clothes that might have been black, he'd worn a balaclava, and had spoken in a rough voice, though the few words he grunted were in circumstances that could have made any man's voice sound rough.

Finally arriving at the shelves he'd been looking for, Ian reached for the empty box displayed of the game his kids wanted and took it to the counter.

'A very good game,' the young, smartly dressed Asian who was the sales assistant told him as he reached for the disk to go inside the box. 'I've played it myself.'

Ian smiled as he paid, wondering how often the man had said this today. It seemed every time he came in for a game this phrase cropped up with less convincing regularity. One day, perhaps, he'd test the assistants' knowledge of the games they professed so much to admire to see just how unfair his cynicism was.

Outside, Ian looked down the street to where he'd parked his car, loosening his collar. After days of wet weather, the sky had cleared to denim blue. The heat was building up fast, whether from the stronger sunlight or the crowds he wasn't sure. Sweating again, Ian started on his way, pocketing the game in case a traffic warden had already reached his car. With any luck he knew he could convince most of them he'd left it parked on police business.

No more than forty yards away, Janice was waiting by the roadside, watching for Jimmy's van to turn up. It seemed as if these days she never did anything but stand about waiting for him to arrive, though she couldn't complain. At least her flexitime at the office had begun to improve now that she wasn't bothered about getting home early. For all his occasional abrasiveness, she didn't suppose Jimmy was all that bad, though whether she wanted their relationship to go any further she wasn't sure. Unlike Jimmy, she had never been engaged, much less married, though she once dated a boy for a couple of years when she was with her parents. If she'd stayed they might have tied the knot by now, but she doubted it. Lee had been too deeply involved with amateur football and Friday nights out with his mates to be a serious contender for marriage for a good few years yet. Nor was Janice really sure if she was either. Her parents weren't an inspiring example of wedded bliss. If their relationship was anything to go by, she could do without marriage for a long time to come. Even though she knew all marriages didn't end like that, Janice knew of too many awful ones from stories she'd heard at work, where problems with spouses of either gender were a common topic of conversation.

Inching along the road behind a delivery truck, Jimmy's van came into sight. Janice waved as Jimmy leaned out of his window and shouted to her, his words lost in the sounds of shoppers packed on the pavement. Running out behind the truck, Janice waited while Jimmy opened the passenger door and reached for her bags. As he heaved them into the back of the van, she jumped onto the seat beside him.

He smiled at her. 'I'm sorry I missed you this morning,' he said, changing gears to follow the delivery truck as it picked up speed through a gap in the traffic ahead of them. 'Toby made a bigger mess of the job than I expected even an idiot like him to be capable of doing. It took hours to put things right.'

Janice said it didn't matter. 'It's only getting back afterwards that's a struggle on the bus,' she said.

Jimmy nodded. 'Judging by the weight of the bags you handed me, I can understand. Anyway, we don't need to go back straight away. We can grab a pub lunch if you like.'

As if making up for the disaster earlier in the week, their meal this time was easy and relaxed. Parking outside a family-style pub, with 'Meals served all day' cheerfully sign-posted on a menu held by a hardboard chef by the doorway, they spent the afternoon in the relaxed atmosphere inside, where they consumed their steak and chips and halves of lager, before setting out on the more arduous task of finishing off portions of what the pub called 'Death by Chocolate'. Janice had never seen Jimmy more relaxed nor anything like so cheerful as today, as if any worries he might have had had all been settled and laid to rest. The simple pleasures of their meal made the time seem to flash by, and Janice was surprised how late it was when they had finished.

Driving back to the flats afterwards, Janice felt her affection for Jimmy increase. Perhaps her apprehensions about him had been misplaced? More than that, she wondered if she had allowed her own feelings of doubt to darken them for her. Mellowed by the food and the lagers, Janice asked if he would like a coffee when they got back.

Jimmy glanced at her with a faint, almost boyish smile. 'That would be nice,' he said.

20

Fiona's expectations had proved more accurate than even she had expected. By half past nine that night, Barry was stood on the doorstep, propped between two of his cronies from the pub. Blood drying on his lips, she was apologetically told by Billy Maguire, the soberer of the two, that Barry had bumped himself when he tripped in the toilets and fell against one of the sinks. Knowing Barry's belligerence after too much drink, Fiona thought it more than likely he'd gotten himself into a fight with someone who could handle themselves better than him, though by the state he was in, as he was half-carried, half-dragged into the living room, she didn't think it would have taken all that much.

'Shall we take him upstairs?' Billy asked. He sheepishly looked at Fiona's sons who were watching from in front of the TV set.

Fiona folded her arms in disapproval. Nodding towards the open-plan staircase, she said, 'Dump him on the bed. He'll sleep till morning now.' She looked at her sons as they stared on in worried silence. 'It's all right,' she said. 'Daddy's just tired.' Though she knew that Jason had seen his father like this often enough to know better; there'd be hell to pay in the morning when Barry woke up with a hangover. Tonight, though, they would have some peace. 'Come on,' she told them. 'Let's put on a DVD.' It was late but she knew they could sleep on tomorrow as long as they liked. Besides, it was a treat for her to have the kids to herself like this. And she felt like she needed their comforting bodies next to hers, snuggled together on the sofa. Even though she knew if she had never had them she would have walked out on Barry by now, Janice would have missed her sons more than anything else in her life. In many ways they were the only good things she had.

After Billy and his friend had gone, muttering their apologies for Barry's state as if it was their fault, Fiona gathered her sons to her. At least she didn't need to worry about going to the Bell and Compasses for another week. Julie had given her the week off, and paid her too, though Fiona hadn't told Barry; he would have wanted some of the money she'd been given if she had.

'What shall we watch?' she asked.

Jason shrugged. 'Can we put *Jungle Book* on?' The cartoon had been a present from Fiona parents for Christmas, and Jason must have watched it a dozen times already.

Fiona smiled. 'Why not?'

Happily, Jason jumped off the sofa and hurried to the stack of DVDs piled by the TV. 'I'll do it,' he said, expertly placing the disk onto the tray. He looked at his mother with satisfaction on his small, round face. 'See?'

*

It had been dark for hours by the time Jimmy left his flat. The afternoon with Janice had left him with a warm glow of satisfaction. Marred only by doubts that no amount of stubborn determination on his part could ever quite manage to suppress, it was the nearest he had come to feeling this way for longer than he could remember. There must have been a few occasions during the early days of his marriage to Steph, but he couldn't be sure any more. Memories of his marriage were tinged by jealousy, rage, betrayal and pain. He could no longer be certain he'd ever felt anything good about it, even from the start. And before that, before he was somehow fooled into feeling he could rely on Steph, before there had only been his mother. And look how she had betrayed him, her true self showing through all the lies her acting skills had made her so good at fooling him with? He hunched his shoulders inside the black combat jacket, the heavy objects he'd placed in its pockets jogging against him as he walked towards his car, constant reminders of what he had to do tonight. He looked up at the sky. Almost cloudless, the stars that blazed across it, where the afterglow of the city's lights didn't obscure them, seemed to emphasise the cold that struck into him as he unlocked his car. And for a moment he wondered whether he should go ahead with his plans. It would be easier to stay in, to see Janice, perhaps. If he knocked on her door he was sure she wouldn't say no to going with him to the pub. The temptation was there. But did he know her well enough to place so much trust in her? As he sat inside his car he felt a well of anger flow through him at his lack of decisiveness. Why should he put aside his plans because of a few pleasant moments in her company when she might so easily turn out to be as worthless as all the other women he'd met? Why should he allow the insults already published in the press to go unanswered when action now could put this straight, could show anyone who might be tempted to dismiss him because of a few lies, that he was not someone to treat with contempt? Too many people had done that to him in the past and got away with it. Steph had been the last. The very last. And one day soon she'd learn to regret the tricks she'd played on him. He'd tried to show her once already. If it hadn't been for the neighbours who heard her screams the day he found out about her affair with Simon Worsley, if not for them phoning the police, he would have taught her then. Even now it caused a shudder of hatred to pass through him when he remembered the undignified way in which he was manhandled by the policemen who broke the front door in and pulled him off, handcuffing his hands behind his back, before dragging him to the police station. Stephanie had already left their family home to stay with her parents by the time he was released on bail, though the police had warned him not to go anywhere near her. With the help of her father, Stephanie had brought an injunction against him. Jimmy started his car, pressed hard on the accelerator as he remembered his trial, where he was arraigned with photographs of what his wife looked like when she was taken to hospital. These were more than enough for the judge to fine him the maximum he could. On top of all that, the divorce costs lost him his house, his car and his business as well, whilst the publicity proved more than enough justification in their eyes at least to lose him what few friends he'd had. By the time it was over he had nothing but a scant few pounds in the bank and his skills as a plumber. Still feeling the rage that burned inside him when he thought about the injustice of it all, Jimmy's face set hard. Even before their divorce came through Stephanie had moved away. When he tried to find out where she was, one of the few false friends still talking to him had only been prepared to say he thought she might have gone to stay with her parents, who had a house in Spain. Whether this was true or not, Jimmy was uncertain. One day he knew he would have to find out. Perhaps he could hire a private detective to search for her. Very soon he'd have enough money to afford the fees. Jimmy smiled at the thought as he drove down the road. Till then he would have to make sure he never forgot his hatred. Nor his anger. Almost incandescent in their purity, these interwoven emotions were so intense they could fill him with a feeling that approached so close to absolute pleasure they were better than sex. So much purer than sex. So much brighter, transcendental, as if they drew him to a higher state of being.

The busy, car-filled road ahead, with its flashing headlights, became a blur as his mind settled deeper into his thoughts.

*

Fiona had only just finished putting her boys to bed less than quarter of an hour earlier when the telephone rang. Hardly needing to glance at the clock to realise just how late it was, her first thoughts were that it had to be her mother and that her father had had another heart attack. The last time she received a call like this late at night it had been from the hospital where her father had been admitted into Intensive Care and she'd had to cajole Barry into looking after the kids while she booked a taxi to take her there. A feeling of panic hit her in the pit of her stomach as she picked up the phone.

'Is that Fiona Greenwood?' It was a man's voice, polite, inquisitive, seemingly genuine. But who can tell, she wondered, as she cautiously answered that it was, her relief at finding that her fears for her father were unjustified tempered with apprehension. 'Who's speaking?' she asked.

'Sean Westwood. I'm a journalist with *The People*. I apologise for ringing so late but my editor wanted an interview with you for tomorrow's edition. If I don't speak to you now it'll be too late. Would it be possible to see you tonight?'

Unsure about letting a journalist into the house so late, Fiona asked if it wasn't possible to do the interview over the phone.

'I wish it was so simple,' the man told her regretfully. 'But we'd need a photo to go with the story. It'd be no good without one.'

'I see.' Fiona shut her eyes, wishing no one had ever found out about what she did on Tuesday night. She was sick and tired of all the publicity. But what could she do? If Barry found out she'd turned down the chance for another story he'd go into hysterics, especially with a national newspaper. 'Would your paper be prepared to pay for the interview?' she asked, dutifully following the lead her husband had drummed into her over the past few days.

The man laughed gently. 'Of course it would. That goes without saying. Heroism is all very well but it doesn't pay the bills.'

Taking a deep breath, Fiona said, 'All right, I'll see you. But please will you try to keep it brief? It's late and I'm tired.'

'No problem. No problem at all.' The man paused a moment, then added as an afterthought, 'Would your husband be available as well?'

Fiona glanced towards the stairs. 'No,' she said, 'I'm afraid not. He's out.'

Unsure if she could detect relief in the man's reply, the journalist said that was okay. 'We'll have to manage without him, won't we? I'll see you shortly.'

Fiona replaced the phone and stared at it for several seconds. She hated interviews. She felt so false trying to remember what Steve Grant had made her twist her tale into the other day. Now that his story had appeared in *The Gazette* she was stuck with it. What really happened was irrelevant now. She had to repeat what she'd already been credited with saying or make herself look the liar she was. Sighing, Fiona went to the bathroom to wash her face and brush her hair into some kind of shape. If the journalist was going to take a photograph for tomorrow's edition she might as well look her best.

Before returning to the living room she glanced in the bedroom at Barry. His snoring, upturned face was a featureless blur in the gloom. For once wishing that he would be with her, she hurried downstairs as the door chimes sounded. 'Coming, coming,' Fiona whispered to herself, her thoughts still jumbled. A man's head was silhouetted against the frosted glass, framed inside the top half of the door. 'Well, here goes,' she muttered nervously, steeling herself, and feeling far from ready for the interview to come.

With one last pat at her hair, Fiona reached for the Yale lock. Hardly had she turned it when the door was suddenly pushed towards her. Propelled into her by the man's shoulder as he forced his way in, the edge of the door hit her in the face. Recoiling, Fiona fell against the sofa. Her protest caught in her throat, unvoiced, when she saw the balaclava that hid the man's face. Dazed, she watched him reach for her. His gloved hands grasped her arm in a grip so fierce it made Fiona squeal as his fingers dug into the soft flesh of her biceps. The next instant, grunting, he pushed her so viciously across the room she fell on the floor. Using the sole of his foot to slam the front door shut behind him, the relentless speed of the man's attack left her no time in which to think. All Fiona could do as he bore down on her was try to fend his hands from her throat, but his strength was too much, her own strength sapped by a terrible sense of panic that seemed to paralyse her every effort. Even her legs seemed unable to move as he fastened his hands about her neck and started to squeeze. Feebly, Fiona tried to kick him, but it was like trying to move her legs through mud. She wanted to scream, to call for help, but his grip was too tight, and she could feel blood pounding through her head as she fought for her breath, her tongue feeling too large for her mouth. One of his knees forced its way between her legs as he thrust down at her. The thumb of one hand probed hard into the side of Fiona's windpipe as he released his other hand from her throat to reach towards the hem of her skirt. She could feel his fingers grasp her underwear, which was when she realised he was going to rape her. God, no, please, Fiona thought, using every last ounce of strength she could muster to pry his fingers from her throat.

'What the fuckin' hell d'you think you're doing?'

Almost lost in the deafening, drum-like pounding of the pulse inside her head, Fiona could only hear her husband's shout as if from a distance. 'Get off her, you bastard! Get off her now!'

Her attacker's body shifted to one side. Fiona glimpsed Barry's hand on the man's shoulder as he dragged him backwards. His drink-reddened face loomed over the man.

'Gerroff her, you fuckin' bastard!'

Although he was unsteady from the beer he'd drunk earlier, Barry's anger was more than enough to give him the strength to haul her attacker back across the floor. His hands grasped so tight on the collar of the man's jacket that his knuckles stood out like bone-hard nodules. Fiona watched Barry clench his fist, bringing it down on her attacker's head. Ducking sideways, the blow glanced off, but Fiona could sense her attacker's panic. Too angry to pause, Barry pounced on top of him. 'You fuckin' bastard,' Barry shouted again and again as his fists came down on the balaclava. The man writhed over and swung his fist in a wild blow at Barry's face. Blood spurted from Barry's nose as the gloved fist hit him. Staggering back, he snorted in pain. Freed for a moment, the man rolled over, then scrambled across the carpet. Wiping blood from beneath his nose, Barry jumped at him, stumbling and falling so that his arms came down across the man's legs, pinning him to the floor. The man tried to kick himself free, but Barry was too heavy. Unable to get away from him, the man twisted around. Fiona saw the eyes through the slits in his balaclava staring at her. They looked wild and frightening. What was somehow even worse, they looked angry too. Fiona watched him struggle to free his legs from Barry's arms, but her husband had no intention of letting go as he remorselessly dragged himself along the man's body to hit him in the groin.

With one hand the man rummaged through his combat jacket. Wriggling to free himself, he gave a sigh. It was then Fiona saw the gun he was holding in his fist. To her startled, disbelieving eyes, it looked enormous, for one terrible moment cringing as the black hole at the end of its barrel swung towards her. The next moment the man aimed at Barry's head. Sobered by the sight of the gun that was pointed at him, Barry stared back at it. 'You're fuckin' mad.' His voice a hoarse, incredulous whisper, he let go, pushing himself away from the gun and climbing to his feet, his bloodied hands held placatingly in front of him as if he thought even now he could somehow calm things down. 'What's all this about? What are you doing?'

The man stared at Barry as he pushed himself into a crouch, then rose.

'Come on,' Barry said, a quiver in his voice. 'You don't want to do it.'

The shot seemed to explode like a grenade inside Fiona's head. Her scream at the intensity of the pain was drowned out as she clamped her hands to her ears. The piercing pain was so bad it was as if she'd been punched inside each ear.

Barry slumped to his knees. His mouth hung open as if he wanted to protest at what had happened. He stared in apparent disbelief at the gun. It was only then that Fiona realised there was blood on his T-shirt. It spread with incredible speed till his clothes were awash and it dripped on the floor. Barry uttered a moan, then fell to one side. The man strode past him. There was a relentless urgency to his sudden movements that made Fiona cry out as he pushed the gun inside his coat. He looked straight at Fiona, all the panic gone from his staring eyes as he moved towards her.

21

'Da-ad!' It was a familiar moan as his two teenagers looked on at the score building up on the monitor. Though at fourteen, a year older than his sister, Peter was almost two inches shorter, his face mirroring his father's tendency to overweight. Thankfully, Patricia took after her mother, with fair hair and a face that would one day look classical. Ian McKenna pressed the pause button on hearing his wife call up the stairs.

'Phone, Ian! It's the station. They want you.'

'Looks as if you two are in luck,' Ian told his siblings as he rose with an effort from the swivel chair. 'I'll have to compete against you tomorrow.'

Peter exchanged looks with his sister. 'We reckon you should go thirds on this game, Dad. You've spent more time on it than us.'

'That, my son,' Ian said, patting him lightly on one shoulder in mock condescension, 'is because I am that much better than you.'

He smiled in good humour as he waddled triumphantly away from their outraged moans. Linda was waiting for him at the foot of the stairs, telephone in hand. Her eyebrows raised in warning, she whispered, 'Sounds serious,' as she handed him the phone. His good humour fading, Ian took hold of it and said, 'DS McKenna speaking.'

'Can you get over to Park Farm Estate as fast as you can, sarge? All hell's let loose. There's been a shooting.' He recognised DC Barnes' laconic voice. 'I'm on my way now. So is the Chief.'

'I'll be with you in ten minutes.' Ian put down the phone. 'Don't expect me back till late,' he told his wife as he tugged his jacket and coat off the rack in the hallway.

Linda shrugged. She had become used to this recently. Ever since the stranglings began it had been rare for him to be home before late. And now this.

In a little under the ten minutes he'd forecast, Ian pulled up at the crime scene. The area had already been cordoned off while forensic were going over the inside of the floodlit house where the shooting took place. Outside, Ian caught sight of Barnes, stood with several other officers. Heading towards him, Ian asked, 'Any details?'

His hair dishevelled as if he had only just climbed out of bed, Barnes said, 'Someone broke into the house to attack the woman inside it. Her husband was upstairs asleep but was woken by the noise and got up to see what was going on. In the struggle the intruder produced a gun and shot him.'

'Is he dead?'

'Killed instantly. The bullet took him in the heart.'

Chief Inspector Yates' car drew up alongside. Lowering his window, Yates told Ian he wanted him to talk to their main witness. 'Fiona Greenwood,' he said heavily. 'You'll recall the name. She was responsible for stopping the strangler from killing his last intended victim.'

Ian looked across at where a woman, her shoulders draped in a red blanket, stood beside an ambulance. 'She's two small children, hasn't she?'

'They're with one of the neighbours,' Barnes said.

Ian nodded. 'Okay, chief. I'll get on with it straight away. Do you want DC Barnes to assist?'

Yates affirmed that he did. 'Find out all you can. If the strangler was responsible we might get our first clues as to who he is. It looks as if his plans ended in fiasco, which must mean he's either getting careless or going off the rails.'

A mug of hot tea held between her fingers, Fiona Greenwood was sat in a private room at the hospital a short while later, Ian and DC Barnes with her. She had already been seen by a doctor who confirmed her injuries were not too serious for her to answer questions, though Ian could see the bruises already starting to swell about her cheekbones. She looked ill as she took sips of tea.

Looking at Ian, Fiona said, 'He tried to save me, didn't he?' Her voice sounded strained as she felt at her throat; dark finger marks were starting to show against her skin like ink stains.

'Your husband?' Ian asked unnecessarily.

Fiona nodded. 'I thought I was a gonner till he jumped in and pulled the bastard off. That's what he called him,' she said. 'Barry. He called him 'you fucking bastard'.'

Ian nodded sympathetically.

'He wasn't a good husband,' Fiona went on in a toneless voice. 'He'd a vicious temper, believe me. Downright evil at times. But when he saw that bastard trying to...' She took a deeper, pain-filled gulp of tea, hesitating to go on. She looked at Ian, her eyes meeting his in a steady gaze as if she was trying to search his soul. 'When that bastard was about to rape me, Barry dragged him off. If he hadn't, he'd never have got shot, would he?'

'And you would have been strangled,' Ian said, aware of her feelings of guilt.

Fiona nodded. 'I know.'

'What made him stop?' Barnes asked. 'After he shot your husband, did he panic and run away?'

Shaking her head, Fiona said, 'He was going to finish what he'd started. I thought: 'This is it,' as he came towards me. There was nothing I could do.' She sobbed, and Ian heaved himself forwards to pass her a handkerchief. Burying her face in it, she blew her nose. 'It was the kids,' she said.

'Do you mean your children?'

Fiona nodded. 'They're only little. Jason – he's the elder – is only five, while Carl's just three. They must have been woken by the noise, by the gun going off, I suppose. It was loud enough to wake the estate. It deafened me. It was like a bomb going off. It was so loud I knew he'd have to finish me off as quick as he could before someone called the police. That's why I was certain I was done for. Till the kids called me. They were halfway down the stairs. Still in their pyjamas. They looked so small, so fragile, standing there. I remember crying out for them to get away. I thought 'He'll kill them too if he sees them.' But Jason wouldn't stop. He must have seen his dad on the floor. And seen the man who was after me. He screamed, 'Mummy! Mummy! Mummy!' again and again. The man turned to look at them.' Fiona gazed into her mug of tea. 'He stared at them for what seemed like hours, though it could have only been for a minute at most. I wanted to jump up and scratch his eyes or something, anything to stop him from harming the kids. But he didn't do anything. He looked confused. I don't know why. It was strange. He didn't say anything. He just stared at them looking at him from the stairs. Then he grunted something, God knows what, and made for the door.'

'And that's the last you saw of him?'

Fiona nodded. 'The next moment Jason was clinging to me.

Then someone looked through the door. It was Barbara, our next-door neighbour. When she saw Barry, she cried out for her husband and he phoned the police.'

Sympathetically, Ian thanked her. 'Was it definitely the same man who attacked the girl?' he asked.

Fiona said, 'I'm certain. There couldn't be two like him. I recognised the balaclava and his combat jacket. They were the same. He said on the phone he was Sean Westwood, that he worked for *The People*. He was supposed to be interviewing me.' Sobbing once more, she looked at Ian, eyes red with tears. 'If Barry hadn't got me to say what they printed in the paper none of this would have happened, would it? If I hadn't bragged about scaring him off...'

'You don't know that,' Ian reassured her sympathetically, though he knew she was probably right. 'He could have wanted to get you because you saved the girl from him. If anyone's at fault it was us for not thinking he'd be capable of doing something like this and providing protection for you.' He felt Barnes' discomfort at this admission.

'He must be a nutter,' Fiona murmured, turning her attention once more to her tea, as if somehow the mug held comfort for her.

Ian nodded. He glanced at Barnes. 'We'll leave you to get some rest.'

Fiona looked at him. 'Do you think you'll catch him?' There was anxiety in her voice. After what she had been through, Ian was not surprised.

'I'm certain of it,' he told her as convincingly as he could. 'In the meantime, there'll be a policeman outside your room to make sure he never gets another chance to attack you.'

'And when I'm home?' she asked.

'When you're home as well. Though, perhaps, you'd prefer to stay with some members of your family or with friends for a while? I'm sure the council would be more than willing to arrange to have another house made available rather than go back there. It would be better for the children. Somewhere with no memories attached to it,' he said, remembering the blood-stained floor.

Back in the incident room at the station, Ian reported to his chief. 'Whoever he is, sir, he'll have more than a few bruises to show for tonight's escapade,' Ian said. 'Perhaps we should circulate an appeal for anyone seen looking as if they've been in a fight.'

Yates stood before a board covered in details of the strangler's victims. For a moment the chief inspector stared at it, his heavy-framed body straining the shoulders of his suit as he stood motionless, hands in his pockets. 'Good idea, Ian. Get onto it straight away. And make sure we get forensic to try and identify that bullet.' Turning, he added, 'It seems we have a few more clues as well. Three people saw a man running from the estate in dark clothes. Two confirm he was wearing a combat jacket. And one,' Yates continued, a hard smile creasing the muscular contours of his face, 'one of them,' he repeated, 'saw him climb into a car and drive off. The description, together with tyre marks left at the scene, confirm it was an old style BMW. The witness thinks it could have been red.'

Ian nodded. 'Looks as if this is what we've been waiting for.'

Yates agreed. 'Make sure everyone gets this information. And check with garages for anyone who owns an old BMW. Then follow up any leads you get with visits. We'll get him soon. It's just a matter of time.'

22

The night seemed filled with confusion as Jimmy Legg drove his car northwards towards the Thames, crossing it at Westminster Bridge. Streetlights flashed across his retinas like so many meteors. How he managed to avoid crashing into any of the cars and buses and cabs around him was seemingly miraculous. His hands gripped the steering wheel harder than any aerial acrobat ever gripped a trapeze. His fingers ached, but his conscious mind, such as it was while he drove, was unaware of any physical discomfort. He was unaware of almost everything apart from the rage and self-contempt that seethed inside him. It was only when he'd circled the inner city twice that he eventually began to regain some sort of self-control. Realising that he was low on petrol, he drove into an all-night garage on his way towards Kilburn. He bought a packet of headache tablets. The bruising on his face was starting to make itself felt. Fortunately, the young Asian behind the security screen in the kiosk barely raised his head to look at him. The bruising felt like a beacon on his face as Jimmy passed the cash through the slot and collected his tablets, stopping at a drinks dispenser on his way out. Back in his car he swallowed three of the pills with a mouthful of coke. Only now did his pulse begin to slow down again.

Back in his car Jimmy stared at the road. Even now, almost two in the morning, it was busy. Jimmy sighed. He felt sick as he thought how everything had gone wrong. All his planning and cool determination had been for nothing. How could he have known the bitch would lie about her husband being in the house? When the man attacked him that had been the nearest he'd felt to fear for longer than he could remember. He shut his eyes as memories of his childhood in Peckham came back to him, of the flat he'd shared with his parents until his father's death, of the lodgings he and his mother moved to up and around the country as she tried to scratch a living on stage with third-rate theatre companies. The obscene falsity of their life from then on, her gross pretensions and constant lies, made him physically ill remembering them now. She'd once been beautiful. Photographs of her in her youth that were always pinned to the walls in whatever fleapit they stayed were testimony to this. But years of drink, poor food, late hours and a loose lifestyle soon made the thick makeup she came to apply more regularly to her face an essential part of her facade. Without it she looked old and ill. Even worse were the men. Everywhere they stayed there was always some clapped out actor who was taken in by her false looks. He still trembled at the memory, not long after his thirteenth birthday, when they were staying in some cheap accommodation in Torquay. Even today he could remember the smell of the place, of boiled cabbage and vinegary wine and old, mildewed paper. It had been an evil combination, though nowhere near as bad as the combination of his mother and Hector Blandish, her new boyfriend. Boyfriend! The absurdity of the word to describe the ageing 'Thespian', with his fashionably long, greying hair, drooping moustache and trendy sideburns, would have made him laugh if other memories of the man didn't overlay this image, especially that night, that awful night that finished him once and for all with his mother. Jimmy clenched his fists as he stared at the road, clasped by the remembrance. Both Hector and his mother had been out drinking after finishing the last performance of the farce they were in. By the time they arrived back they were already legless. But that didn't stop them from opening a bottle of gin.

Jimmy wanted to go to bed, but his mother insisted he stay up 'to keep them company'. The way she laughed made him fear for the worst. He had already come to dread her bizarre sense of humour, especially when she was hopelessly drunk. He'd been the butt of her jokes ever since his father's death had freed that poor, befuddled man from them. She needed someone to use like this. It was almost obsessive. Perhaps it was. Perhaps she could no more help what she did than he could now. But that didn't – that *couldn't* excuse her. Nothing could ever do that.

Despite his pleas to go to bed she insisted that he stayed with them. She even tried to get him to drink some gin, but the smell made him want to be sick and, for all her protestations, he couldn't make himself swallow it. It gagged in his throat whenever she bullied him into trying to take a sip. Finally boring of this game, his mother and Hector contrived a new one to amuse themselves with. They still had traces of stage makeup on their faces, and his mother, consumed with jealousy for a younger actress in the company, said even Jimmy would look better than 'that doll-faced trollop'. Hector protested that Jimmy wouldn't. His lack of seriousness, though, was obvious to Jimmy. And he knew they were in it together, that this joke was something they had planned to play on him. Only a few minutes later they were covering Jimmy's face in grease paint. Despite all his pleas, threats and protestations, they went on with it. When they'd finally finished they paraded him in front of the mirror in his mother's bedroom. There, beside her unmade bed, the very folds of its stained sheets suggestive of the tempestuous bouts of sex she'd indulged in on it, he saw the grotesque makeup that covered his face, his lips rouged into a hideous pout against whitened cheeks and garishly coloured eyes. It was a sickening joke, which the two of them fell about laughing at. His mother's hoots of hysterical laughter still rang in his ears even now.

But worse was to come.

Not satisfied by their own amusement, Hector suggested showing him off to their friends as well. Most of the touring company were staying in the same building and could easily be called together. Pushing Jimmy out onto the landing, Hector bellowed downstairs for everyone to 'come out and see'.

Tears welled in the corners of Jimmy's eyes when he thought of the shame that filled him then. Taking his arm, Hector dragged him to the top of the stairs.

'We've discovered a replacement for Maggie,' Hector shouted to those who'd come out of their rooms to see what was going on.

Twisting himself free from Hector's grip, Jimmy tried to get back into their apartment. When Hector grabbed hold of him again, Jimmy kicked at his legs. 'Stupid little bugger,' Hector grated in a vicious snarl, bereft of any amusement now. But Jimmy was behind him then and using the actor's body to shield himself from the gawping stares of those downstairs.

'Go on,' he recalled his mother shout from the doorway, urging the actor on. 'Push the little bugger out. Don't let him hide.' Her laughter was even louder than Hector's shouts when the actor tried to grapple with him. It was then that Jimmy gave him the push – the push that caught his tormentor unawares. Hector's face still came back to him with astonishing vividness when he thought of that night, as realisation dawned on the thespian that his feet had moved beyond the edge of the landing.

For a brief instant Hector tried to regain his balance, swinging his arms in what absurdly looked like a mad attempt at semaphore, but the momentum of Jimmy's thrust was too much for any amount of arm-swinging to counterbalance now. Even before he'd tumbled halfway down the flight of stairs it was obvious that Hector's neck had been broken. After that, even though the coroner's verdict was death by misadventure, Jimmy's mother would never look at him again. Rejecting her son as a 'vicious, nasty little beast', he spent most of the next few years of his life in various orphanages or fostered out. Not till he was informed of his mother's death four years ago did he see her again. And by then what looks she'd ever had, had completely gone. The mortician tried his best, but nothing could hide the ravages of dissipation that had turned her face into an ugly mask of mental, moral and physical decay.

Noticing the curious stare of the cashier from his office in the service station, Jimmy started his car and drove onto the road. His mother's face faded from his mind as he headed towards the ring road, intending to keep on driving till he could sort out his confusion. He needed time in which to think, in which to work out what to do next.

The shock that had shaken him most tonight had not been Fiona Greenwood's husband dragging him across the room. Near though he'd come to being beaten senseless by the drunken bastard, he'd known all along the gun in his pocket would be more than enough to deal with threats like that. What had really, thoroughly shaken him, though, shaken him so much that he couldn't go on, were the kids. One minute longer and he knew he would have killed the interfering slag he'd gone there for. She was helpless before him. What fight the woman might have had, had gone, and it would have taken only the briefest of seconds to force her back onto the floor and finish her off the way she deserved. The grease paint in his jacket pocket would only take a few minutes to apply after he sliced that lying face from her skull. But when he saw those kids (*her kids*, he now realised) that had been it. There was no way he could have done it, not with their eyes transfixed on him, one of them shouting, 'Mummy! Mummy! Mummy!'

As he stared at the lights of the car ahead of him, gleaming in the dark like demoniacal eyes, he wondered what there was for him now. The police would be looking for anyone with heavy bruises covering their face. That much was obvious. It wouldn't take a genius to realise that whoever killed the bitch's husband must have taken a hell of a lot of hard knocks. The state of the dead man's fists would be proof of this. Jimmy felt at his face. Swelling by the minute, he knew he would look an ugly mess by the time it finished. The only thing he could do was to get away somewhere no one would think to connect him with what happened tonight. If he didn't, the police wouldn't need to look far to become suspicious. He couldn't risk it. There was too much to lose. It was imperative he distanced himself as far as possible and hide somewhere long enough for the bruises to heal.

23

'I'll have to see you early this morning. It's urgent. I have to be away before ten. I can't tell you why. It's personal. But, believe me, Toby, it's important. I wouldn't ask if it wasn't.'

Toby Cartmel scratched the back of his head as he leaned against the faded flowery wallpaper in the hallway, trying to listen through the noise from the Parkins' flat further along the passage, their radio competing with the screams of their kids and the ongoing row that Rachel and Robbie Parkin would probably be hammering away at when he got back home tonight. 'Yes, Mr Legg. I suppose I understand. I can meet you any time you like… Half eight, Mr Legg?' Toby automatically nodded his head, then added, 'Of course, Mr Legg. I'll be there.'

He returned to his bed-sit, the smell of stale food, washing and cats making the atmosphere along the landing unbreathable. Immediately below the roof, the ceiling in his room had odd angles like an avant-garde set from an old German silent movie. Only a glimmer of light came through the window, and most of the time he had to rely on the electric light. Called away only a few minutes before by the call from downstairs that his boss was on the phone, his bacon and eggs were unappetizingly cold as he gazed at them now. Thanks, Mr Legg, he thought to himself. Thanks a bunch.

Putting on a scuffed bomber jacket, he shovelled his food into his mouth with a grimace of disgust, before trudging down the flights of stairs once more. Outside, Toby set off for the cafe Jimmy Legg used as a makeshift office. Talk about a Mickey Mouse outfit! It was laughable. Or would have been if Toby had felt in a lighter mood. Before he reached the cafe, though, he was stopped by a shout. Turning, he saw Jimmy's van draw up alongside the kerb. Leaning out of its passenger window, Jimmy told him to climb in. 'We'll talk on the way.'

Nodding his head, Toby pulled himself into the van. Before he even had time to fasten his seat belt, Jimmy set off.

'Is something wrong, Mr Legg?' Toby asked as he struggled with his belt; it was old and frayed and the material jammed when he moved the buckle. 'You look as if someone took a poke at you.' He gazed curiously at the bruise that covered the whole of the side of Jimmy's face. Not only that, Toby was shocked to see most of the flesh around his boss's eye on the other side of his head looked black.

Jimmy shrugged impatiently. 'Some bloody fools, with too much beer inside them for their own and anyone's good, started a scrap last night when I was in a pub. It got out of hand, that's all. One idiot took a swing at me before I floored him. Nothing to worry about.'

Sure he would have taken a different view if his own face had been battered as badly as Jimmy's, Toby shrugged, surprised for once that his boss's temper seemed under control. Normally questions nettled him. Jimmy Legg seemed more subdued than Toby could ever remember him. Perhaps the fight had done some good: knocked some of the cockiness out of the bastard. There'd been more than enough to knock out, Toby thought, smiling to himself as Jimmy suddenly pulled the van to the kerb outside an old Victorian house, a *For Sale* sign fixed above its boarded-up basement.

'We've to start on this Monday,' Jimmy said. 'But I won't be here. I'll have to show you what to do to get the job underway.' He handed Toby a manila envelope. 'There's four hundred quid in there. And a list of materials you'll need buy. You know where to get them. When you've bought everything, attach the bills and put whatever cash is left in the envelope and seal it up.'

'How long will you be gone, Mr Legg?' Toby looked at the house, a worried expression filling his face. 'I've never worked by myself before.'

'A week. No more. It's only a case of getting started. You'll have no problems.'

Unsure if Jimmy's optimism was misplaced or not, Toby asked about his wages.

'Take them out of what money's left. Okay?'

Toby pocketed the envelope. 'I suppose so, Mr Legg. Only, don't blame me if you're not satisfied with what I manage to do. I said I've never worked by myself before.'

Suppressing a sigh of exasperation, Jimmy patted him on the shoulder. 'You'll manage. After I've shown you what needs doing, I'll take you back to my place. I'll have to lend you a spare set of keys for the van. You'll need it while I'm away.'

24

It was only when Janice stepped out of the flats to go to the corner shop for some milk for her breakfast that she realised what must have woken her up half an hour ago. Surprisingly for this early on a Sunday morning Jimmy's van had gone from its usual space. When he dropped her off last night, he was going to go on to meet up with some friends who, he said, might have information about a big job for him. He hadn't mentioned anything about having to work this morning. In fact, he'd dropped hints of taking her somewhere for lunch if she was interested. Which just went to show how unreliable he could be. Unless, of course, she added to herself more generously, he came back soon.

A blustery wind whipped the leaves that had managed to linger around the beech trees on the edge of the pavement. Fastening her coat against the gusts, she pressed on, deciding she'd get a Sunday newspaper as well to pass an hour while she had her breakfast before she got on with washing her clothes. Not her favourite chore, her weekly wash was something she preferred to put off for as long as possible. At the best of times it took at least three mugs of coffee and a lingering breakfast of toast and marmalade, then still more toast, usually topped by a poached egg at lunch before she felt ready. Which was stupid, she knew, since there really wasn't all that much to do. If she started watching TV, though, things would get even worse. Then she'd linger till late afternoon before starting and feel thoroughly fed up by evening when she had to start ironing.

Determined that today, waking up as early as she had, she'd make an effort to get things done straight away (once she'd had some coffee, of course), she marched down the road, its early-morning freshness invigorating her. Even though it was later than she usually got up for work, there was something about this time in the morning on Sunday, when most people were still in bed. It was like being on holiday. Even the air smelt different. Cleaner, somehow, despite the whiff of fried cooking from basement flats.

'Good morning, Janice. You're up early today,' Mrs Lovell greeted her cheerily when she reached the newsagents. Janice reached for one of the cartons of milk in the refrigerated display by the counter. 'I'll have one of these, please,' she said. She casually scanned the newspapers piled on the counter. 'And something to read.' She fingered through the various tabloids as she tried to decide which had the juiciest scandals.

'Have you heard about last night's murder?' Mrs Lovell asked as Janice picked up a copy of *The People*. A small woman, with bleached blonde hair and pince-nez glasses, she was almost as good a source of news as any of the papers she and her husband sold.

'Another strangling?' Janice asked, looking up.

Mrs Lovell shook her head as she counted out Janice's change. 'A shooting,' she said in a stage whisper as if she didn't want her husband in the back of the shop to hear her. 'They think it's the same man, though. A young policeman came in this morning almost as soon as we opened up with a handbill to post somewhere in the shop.' She showed Janice a photocopied A4 sheet, with block letters on it. 'I asked the officer what had happened,' Mrs Lovell went on before Janice had time to read the notice. 'It seems whoever's been doing all those horrible murders tried to get that woman – you know who I mean? – the one who saved that girl from him last week – and tried to kill her. The police think it was probably revenge.' Mrs Lovell shuddered. 'He must be a madman to do what he did. He went to her house last night and would have strangled her if her husband hadn't come back in time and tried to save her. The poor man didn't know the killer had a gun. He was shot dead in their living room in front of their two young boys, poor things.'

Janice said something about how terrible that was. She had given up trying to read the handbill. There was little chance of that once Mrs Lovell had started. Besides, she'd find out more from her than anything written on the leaflet.

'The police are looking for anyone with a badly bruised face. The woman's husband managed to grapple with the killer before he was shot. Beat him something savage, he did, by all accounts.'

Janice looked at the handbill. Sure enough there were the details. The killer was white, male, five feet ten to six feet tall, with severe bruising to the face. Anyone seeing someone who fitted this description was asked to ring Emlyn Police on the number given at the foot of the sheet. All calls would be treated confidentially.

'Perhaps they'll catch him at last,' Janice said. 'It's the first time they've had anything to go off.'

'That's just what me and my husband said when we saw it,' Mrs Lovell agreed. 'You hardly feel safe to go out at night with that beast roaming. Even your own home isn't safe any more after what he tried to do.'

Janice thought about her fear of the dark. The inside of her flat had always felt secure till now, unlike the streets once the sun had set. Now nothing seemed safe any more. 'I hope someone sees him and rings the police,' she said as she picked up her newspaper and carton of milk. 'Someone like that deserves locking up.'

'They should get a lot more than that if you ask my opinion,' Mrs Lovell added. 'Though that's another story, I suppose.'

When she arrived back at the flats, Janice was surprised that Jimmy was sat in his van with Toby Cartmel. Parked on the roadside, the two of them were in deep conversation and didn't seem to notice her as she walked past. As far as she knew Jimmy never worked on Sundays except when he made the occasional visit to a prospective job, for which he wouldn't have needed Toby. Making her more curious, Jimmy then climbed out of the van as Toby shuffled to the driver's side and started the engine.

Too intrigued to go into her flat, she watched as Toby drove off, rasping the gears. Then Jimmy turned round to go into the flats, and Janice gasped with surprise at the sight of the bruises on his face. They were so severe it was almost as if he was wearing a mask. Janice immediately remembered what she'd read in the newsagents: roughly five feet ten to six feet tall, with severe bruising to the face. Janice tried to control her reactions but she knew, as Jimmy's eyes met hers, that he could tell she'd realised something was wrong. There was no way he could fail to notice the shock on her face. Janice tried to think of something to say, any excuse or another that would give her a chance to get into her rooms, but her throat wouldn't function. Jimmy stared at her for a drawn out moment that seemed to go on for an eternity before he suddenly took a hold of her arm. 'Come here,' he said. 'You're looking faint.'

There was concern in his voice. It was so unexpected, and at the same time sounded so genuine, it almost disarmed her suspicions. Her head buzzing, she could do nothing to stop him from leading her up the stairs to her door. He took her key from her hand, unlocked the door and let them in. As he shut the door behind them, he took the carton of milk and her folded newspaper and laid them on a table.

'You look like you could do with a drink of water. Sit down and lean your head forwards while I find a glass.'

Too confused to resist, Janice did as he said while he hurried to the kitchen.

He returned seconds later and pressed a tumbler into her hand. Dutifully, she took a sip from it.

'Feeling better?' Jimmy asked.

Janice nodded her head. The faintness began to recede as she looked up at him. His marred face was filled with concern. But the hideously dark bruises that covered his swollen, disfigured features stood out even more in the brightness of her living room.

'What happened to you?' Janice asked. Her voice sounded weak.

Touching his cheeks as if he'd all but forgotten the bruises, Jimmy said, 'Do you mean these?'

Janice nodded, studying his expression as it changed from concern to doubt to a look of scorn. 'It's nothing,' he said, dismissively. 'There was a fight in the pub last night. Some louts got out of hand. They'd been drinking more than they could handle. It was my bad luck to end up in the middle. This is the result.' He shrugged as if it was the kind of thing that could happen any day of the week.

'Did the police catch them?' Janice asked, before taking another sip of the water.

Jimmy shook his head. 'As soon as the landlord came over to sort them out they scarpered. I don't think they'd ever been there before.' He laughed. 'I doubt they'll go there again either.'

Janice put down the water. Her head felt better as the feeling of shock receded under Jimmy's soothingly rational explanation. 'Where's Toby gone in your van? Have you lent it to him?'

'I have to go away for a couple of days. He needed it to start work on a job we have this week.'

'You're going away?'

'Till Wednesday, Thursday. No longer. There's the chance of

a big job out of town. It'll require me being away to sort things out.'

Janice nodded, though the glibness of his words disturbed her. Even though what he said sounded plausible, there was something about it that didn't seem right. As if sensing her lack of conviction, Jimmy asked if anything was wrong. 'You look worried about something.'

'No.'

Janice tried to think but all that would come into her head were the words of Mrs Lovell: 'The killer was white, male, roughly five feet ten to six feet tall, with bruising about the face.' Janice realised that Jimmy was staring at her, and she suddenly felt as if he was trying to read her thoughts, to detect any doubts that were flashing through them. Disconcerted, she turned away from him and said, 'I think I should rest. I got up too early this morning. I'm feeling tired again now.'

Jimmy held onto her arm. 'There's something wrong, isn't there? What is it, Janice? You can tell me.'

Afraid she would give away her feelings, Janice looked at his face. Jimmy seemed so utterly, sincerely open she could not have explained why she didn't feel convinced by him. 'I don't know,' she said. 'I'm confused.'

'Did something happen this morning? Where did you go?'

'To the newsagents.'

'What happened there? What did you hear?'

'Hear?'

Frowning, he said, 'You heard something, didn't you? What was it?'

Feeling frightened again as his voice hardened, Janice shook her head, saying, 'I heard nothing, Jimmy. Nothing at all. I don't know what you're talking about.'

'But you do,' he insisted. Holding both of her arms, he forced her to face him. 'Come on, Janice, there's something you're not telling me. What is it? You can speak freely. You know you can. What did you hear?'

Unwilling to meet his eyes, Janice said, 'The police are looking for a man with bruises on his face.'

'What man?' Jimmy tightened his grip on her arms, making her wince as his thumbs probed tight into her muscles. 'What man is that, Janice?'

'The strangler, Jimmy. The one who's been murdering all those women. He shot a man last night and killed him. They think he was bruised.' She looked up at his face.

'And you think these bruises mean I might be him?' Jimmy asked.

Janice stared back at him, unable to speak, her thoughts confused. She was frightened as she felt the strength of his fingers gripping her arms, knowing how helpless she was in his hands. If he was the strangler he could murder her now and there was nothing she could do to defend herself.

'I don't know,' she confessed. 'I don't know what to think.'

Startling her, Jimmy released her arms and stood up. 'You don't understand,' he told her. 'There's more to all this than you know.'

Puzzled, Janice asked what he meant. Jimmy shook his head. He stared away from her at the window, his shoulders drooping as he stepped towards it. 'You wouldn't understand.'

Feeling drawn by his vulnerability, Janice said, 'I'd like to, Jimmy. I'd like to understand.'

He turned. His face looked sad, defeated. 'You would?'

Janice nodded. 'Of course I would.'

Again Jimmy shook his head. 'I don't know. Perhaps it's too soon.' For a few moments more Jimmy studied her face. 'I have to go away,' he told her, flatly. 'I have no choice. Things have become too complicated for me to stay. I have to think things through. Sort out my mind.'

Drawn again by his air of helplessness, Janice said, 'Can't I help you? Isn't there something I can do?' she asked.

Jimmy narrowed his eyes, suspicion and doubt battling with what could have been relief, though Janice was not sure. 'You'd like to help, wouldn't you? I can't imagine why. I'm not the easiest person in the world to get along with. I don't even get along with myself most of the time.'

Unsure if she was heading the right way or not, but certain that if she failed things could turn ugly, that whatever self control Jimmy had might crack, Janice said, 'I'll help you any way I can. I really will.'

Jimmy strode back to her and once more clasped her arms, though gently now. 'You don't want to know why I need help?'

'When the time is right, of course I do. Till then it's all right. I can wait.' For some inexplicable reason Janice felt an over-whelming sense of well-being, as if, absurdly, this very moment was what she had been born for, as if all of Jimmy's inner torments were somehow, for some inexplicable reason, hers to put right. If love there was, it was a love for someone she knew instinctively was weaker than her, who needed her much like child needed its mother. Fear may have played a part in it. The intensity of her fear only moments ago seemed to have left a vacuum in which she felt a desperate need to build something new. Just what that was, she had neither the intuition nor self-awareness to be sure, though she was certain the powder keg that was Jimmy Legg's troubled mind could only be kept safe if she showed him how much she genuinely wanted to help. His relief at her offer, as if the alternative was something he did not wish to happen, confirmed her feelings.

'I'm going in a few minutes,' he told her. 'I've packed my things. If you'd really like to help, come with me. Put what you'll need for a week or so in a bag and we'll load the car. Ten minutes from now we could be on our way.'

Janice stared back at him, startled. The speed with which he had accepted her offer surprised and alarmed her. She started to say that she perhaps wasn't sure she could go away as suddenly as this, but she stopped when she saw the anger in his eyes as he stared back at her. 'You offered to help,' Jimmy said. 'You trust me, don't you?'

Janice felt her fears re-emerge once more, realising the stupidity of her self-conceit, that Jimmy was not some helpless child in need of a mother, but a man whose violent anger she should shy away from. But what choice did she have? If he was who she thought he might be, he had a gun. Could she risk him using it on her? Or, worse, risk being attacked with his hands? Somehow she knew these were the choices left if she said no.

'Of course I'll help,' she said to him. 'It was the suddenness of it all. That's all. Give me a couple of minutes and I can be packed. I'll have to ring work.'

'You can do that tomorrow,' Jimmy said. 'There'll be no one there today. It's Sunday. You can ring in the morning and say you're sick. You can take a week off, can't you?'

Even while she said yes, of course she could, Janice felt as if her world had shrunk around her.

'I'll meet you by the car in ten minutes,' she said, but Jimmy shook his head. 'I'll help you pack. We'll go down together.'

25

Although he'd had a driving license for over a year, Toby Cartmel had never owned a car. Battered and ugly though the vehicle was, the prospect of having Jimmy Legg's van for a week or more had all the attraction of an extra Christmas so far as Toby was concerned. Even though tomorrow he would have to concentrate on buying all the materials Jimmy had listed and make a start on the job at Gladstone Road, there was enough money to pay for a full tank of diesel, and at least he could drive wherever he wanted in his own free time and have some fun. Sitting at the steering wheel with all the aplomb of a sports car driver, Toby grinned broadly, feeling like the King of the Road. On top of all this, he wouldn't have Legg on his back, nagging and snapping and shouting at him for over a week, perhaps even longer with any luck. Which was almost as good as a holiday itself.

By midday Toby had passed the first exhilaration of this unexpected bonus, especially since he had only himself to impress. Pulling up outside the Beggar's Tin on Balmoral Road, he jumped out and locked the van behind him. It might not look much parked next to all the other vehicles, but it was better than nothing.

Feeling as if things were beginning to look up for the first time for him, Toby sauntered jauntily into the pub.

He tossed his keys onto the bar and ordered a lager.

'Hey, look who's got himself wheels!'

Toby gloated as his ex-school mate, Petey Green, clapped him on the back, after sidling towards him with another classmate, Kevin Brite. Dressed in a suit that had seen better days, Petey was already the worse for wear. Hanging in unkempt locks across his forehead, his hair looked as if it hadn't been washed in months.

'Showing off, are you?' Petey picked up Toby's keys. He studied them in the palm of his hand as if he doubted they were real. 'What have you got, Toby? A Porsche?'

'Nah,' Toby laughed self-consciously. 'Jimmy Legg's van. That's all.' Toby's grin broadened as he shared the joke with his friends.

'So what's your bad-ass boss doing letting you drive his precious van? Doesn't he know you better?' Kevin asked.

'Doesn't he realise what a reckless tearaway Toby can be when he's in bad company.' Petey winked at his friend. The two leaned against each other like mismatched bookends, how much they'd drunk already obvious even to Toby.

'D'you fancy driving us somewhere later?' Kevin asked. 'We'd make it worth your while.'

His grin fading, Toby shook his head as he paid for his lager. 'I know you two, you'd have me ferrying you from one friggin' party to another. D'you think I'm stupid?'

'You work for Jimmy Legg, don't you? Anyone who can put up with that puffed-up pilluck must be stupid. Goes with the job.' Petey laughed at his own joke. He laughed even louder when Toby glared at him over his drink. Wishing he'd never shown the keys to them, Toby fell into a stony silence.

'Come on, Toby,' Kevin urged a few seconds later. 'It was only a joke, for fuck's sake.'

Toby shrugged. 'Some jokes aren't funny.'

'Bollocks!'

Toby turned away from them and glanced at a notice fixed to one of the wooden pillars spaced around the bar. As he read it the expression on his face made Kevin burst into a fresh bout of laughter.

'What's up, Toby? Seen a ghost, you sad bastard?'

Toby turned to them, his face white. 'What's this about?' He pointed at the notice with his thumb.

'Can't you read, you fuckin' moron?'

'Course I can fuckin' read. Is it a joke? Is someone trying to wind me up?'

'What the fuck are you talkin' about?' Kevin frowned at him, as if Toby was trying to get out of doing them a favour. 'Why should someone be bothered to wind you up?'

Toby looked at the notice again. It seemed official enough, with a police crest printed at the top. But he'd been the butt of enough japes in the past to be cautious now.

If it wasn't a trick, though, it did give him an idea for a trick of his own. Maybe...

'I know someone I could get a laugh out of with it.' Enjoying the curiosity of his friends, Toby grinned once more. Whether they went along with it or not, it would be good to get their jibes off his back, for a while at least. 'What do you think?' he asked.

'What do we think about what, for Christ's sake?' Petey sounded exasperated. 'You tryin' to wind us up or what, you twat?'

Toby nodded at the notice. 'I know someone who'd fit that description. I could ring the police and get them onto him.'

'Who's that, Toby? Your dad?'

'Yeah, battered by your mum.'

Toby scowled. 'I told you, you thick bastards, I know someone who fits that description.'

'So what?' Kevin asked. 'Half the fuckers I know fit it. Most of our friggin' friends ended up getting battered Saturday night. And if you don't start to make fucking sense, I think I know who'll be joining 'em.'

'Okay, you prats,' Toby said, rattled. 'What if I said I saw Jimmy Legg this morning when he loaned me the van? What if I said he told me he'd been in a fight? What if I said he looked like his face had been used as a bleedin' football?'

'Then get him,' Petey urged with a grin. 'Go get the fucking, stuck up bastard. Why not? Teach the bugger to be the bad tempered twat he is. He told me once he'd do me over, the fucking nonce.'

'I don't know.' Having blurted it out, Toby just as quickly started to regret having said anything. It was all right for them to say 'go get the bastard'. They didn't have to work for him. What if Jimmy found out who'd grassed him up? Toby would be lucky if he didn't end up in hospital. That'd be the least he'd expect from a hard-case like Jimmy.

'What d'you mean, you don't know?' Kevin snorted in disgust. 'Chickening out, are you? You're so fucking frightened of the bugger you won't even try something like this?' He nudged Petey in the ribs. 'I think Toby's frightened Jimmy Legg'll spank him if he finds out what he's been saying about him.'

Petey leered. 'One of us could always ring instead if Toby's too fuckin' scared to do it himself.'

Toby looked at his friends. 'What do you mean? You'd ring up if I didn't?'

'Why the fuck not? We're not frightened of Jimmy *fuckin'-*

shit-face Legg.'

Desperately, Toby looked at his change for a couple of ten pence coins. No one was stood at the pay phone at the far end of the bar. 'I'll be back in a minute,' Toby muttered.

'Hey, not without us,' Petey cried in protest. He hurried after him as Toby pushed through the drinkers crushed around the bar, ignoring the doubts that pounded his head as his friends called to him. Trying to disregard his qualms, Toby tapped the buttons on the phone, then waited till a voice came on the other end of the line.

'Hello,' Toby said, trying to keep control of his nerves as Petey and Kevin pulled faces at him, honking like pigs. 'Is this the number for information about the murder? No, I don't want to give my name. That's right. I think I know who you're after. I saw him this morning. Yeah, that's right. He'd really bad bruises all over his face. A fucking mess he was. But you'll have to be quick. He told me he's going away for the week. Probably till the bruises have healed, I s'ppose. His name's Jimmy Legg. He lives at flat 7b, Charlotte House, 63, Oakmere Road, Emlyn, South London. He drives a BMW. It's an old one. Red. That's right.' Putting the phone down, Toby felt hot sweat cover his face and his heart pounded loudly in his chest. He'd never rung the police before and the experience had frightened him. Now he'd finished, he was worried he might have gone too far. Besides showing off in front of his friends, spite had been the main reason for ringing up, even if he did wonder if his boss could really be the man they were after. Not that he believed it. Jimmy Legg might be a bad tempered bastard – he couldn't see him as the strangler. Still, it would give Legg a right royal pain in the arse having the police chase after him. Toby grinned to himself as he glanced at his friends. This had given them something else to laugh at besides him for a change.

'Toby, you bastard, that was fuckin' brill.' Petey's grin made him forget his doubts suddenly. Yeah, brilliant, he thought, imagining Jimmy's anger when the police turned up to ask him where he'd got his bruises. That would sour his holiday spirit, the pratt!

26

With clinical efficiency Jimmy helped Janice put what she'd need in a bag. Self-absorbed, he hardly spoke except to rap out instructions which Janice just as quickly obeyed. The change in their relationship came about so swiftly that Janice could hardly analyse how it happened. All she knew was that she had to do what Jimmy said, that she had no choice. It wasn't so much she was his prisoner. More, it was as if she had become a co-conspirator, that her future depended as much as his on getting away as quickly as they could.

Within little more than an hour they had driven out of London and were heading north up the motorway, the fuel gauge of Jimmy's BMW showing half a tank. Whenever she asked where they were going, Jimmy smiled in reply. He'd hardly spoken a word to her since they hurried out of the house, and Janice knew she had little choice left in what she did. There was an abrupt tautness about Jimmy's actions that showed the tension he was under. There was fear there, too. It was obvious in his every action, in the caution with which he drove, and the speed with which he headed up the road, never exceeding the speed limit, but never veering very far from it, as if he had to put as much distance as he could between himself and London as quickly as possible.

By midday they had passed Birmingham. At the first service station they reached once the city was behind them, Jimmy filled the tank, making Janice walk with him to the kiosk while he paid. His tact was far less prominent now and he made little secret to her that he had a gun in the inside pocket of his jacket. Nor was she under any illusions that she had any choices left except to do as he said. He never spoke of the alternative, but she could tell by the veiled desperation in his eyes she had to do everything she could to avoid it.

'I have to use the loo,' she said some time later as they passed a sign for the next motorway service station several miles south of Preston on the M6. Jimmy grunted in reply. He swung off at the first slip road they came to, leaving the motorway to make a tour of the town they reached a few minutes later till he saw the sign for public toilets at a tree-filled park by the roadside. No one else in sight, apart from a few passing cars, Jimmy drew up outside the Ladies. He went in with her, nodding when he saw the other exit leading to the park. 'Be quick,' he told her after he was satisfied the place was empty, and Janice hurried into one of the cubicles.

Later, as they drove past Lancaster, Janice was too tired to protest when he again came off the motorway and pulled up outside an off-licence. Reaching across, he pulled her hands to the steering wheel. A roll of heavy-duty gaffer tape lay under the dashboard. Tearing a strip off, he secured it round her wrists, binding them as tightly as he could to the steering wheel. Janice tried to protest, but his glance was enough to silence her.

'You wanted to help,' he said as he climbed out of the car and hurried to the shop. A couple of minutes later he emerged with a bag of crisps, some chocolate bars and a couple of cans of cola. 'These will have to do for tonight.' Stowing the food and drink on the back seat, he slashed the tape off Janice's hands with a Stanley knife. 'You can eat what you want when we arrive at our destination.'

'Is it far?' Janice asked.

A sign for Morecambe loomed out of the foggy gloom as they skirted the edge of Lancaster. Accelerating past the traffic over the wide bridge that spanned a dimly-seen expanse of river, Jimmy told her tersely, 'My mother left me a place near here in her will.'

Janice glanced at him, relieved that his forbidding silence had ended at last. 'What kind of place?'

'A boarding house. It's shut down now. It shut down a few years before she died. She was so far gone on drink she couldn't even keep this fleapit open any longer. The council closed her down in the end, even though most of her guests – if you could call them that – were on the dole.' He narrowed his eyes as he overtook a car that was turning left for Heysham, and took the road for the centre of Morecambe. Janice stared at the dark streets. Few people braved the cold winds that blustered around them. Just gone five thirty, it was too early in the year for holidaymakers to be out on the streets and the seaside town had a woebegone look. This impression grew stronger when they drove along the seafront, with its boarded up amusement arcades on one side and the utter blackness of Morecambe Bay on the other.

After driving several minutes down the Promenade, Jimmy turned off into a narrow side street. A short way along it, he turned left, drawing up by the kerb. He nodded towards a large, four storey building. Once painted white, its Edwardian facade was scabrous where the salt-laden atmosphere had eaten it away. Above the tall, colonnaded door hung an unlit neon sign, 'Arcadia' spelt in red italics.

Jimmy opened his door.

'Come on,' he said, adding unnecessarily, 'We're here.'

27

Janice could scarcely believe the squalor that confronted them when they stepped inside the building.

Her misgivings began as soon as they stood outside the door and Jimmy unlocked it. The smell from inside hit both of them at once - a vile mixture of stale urine, damp and decay.

By the time Jimmy realised the gas and electricity must have been cut off it was too late for them to go and buy alternative sources of light and heating. Their only light was a torch from the boot of his car, which they used to explore what was left in the boarding house, though it was soon obvious to Janice, after years of neglect, there was little to make their stay here pleasant or comfortable. Damp had reduced the few beds there were to mildewed heaps of sodden sheets, many of them rife with woodlice. Topping it all, it looked as if vandals had broken in and ruined what few sticks of furniture there were. The two largest ground floor rooms were what Janice supposed had been the lounge and dining room. Graffiti disfigured both of them. On what remained of the carpet lay scraps of mouldering food, empty bottles and used syringes. Jimmy turned away from them, his face filled with disgust as they headed for the stairs to the three floors above. He said they should at least find somewhere they could rest for the night. So thorough had the vandalism been, though, it was only when they reached the very top floor they finally found somewhere that hadn't been used as a public toilet, perhaps because the garbage hoarded on the bare floorboards looked bad enough already, hidden beneath mounds of dust and a haze of cobwebs.

'We can't stay here,' Janice said as she stared in the torchlight at the bare beds and dust.

'Just for tonight,' Jimmy told her. 'Tomorrow we'll find somewhere else. A hotel further north, perhaps.'

Janice glanced at his face, too dim in the afterglow from the torch to be clearly seen. The tone of his voice was enough to send a shudder through her. It was too cold and distant to reassure her of his sincerity. And she wondered if he meant what he said they would do, that he would risk taking her to a hotel.

'I'm sorry,' Jimmy said. 'I know how you fear the dark but

there's nothing I can do till tomorrow morning. You must see this,' he said with what sounded a close approximation to sincerity. But she wasn't sure. She wasn't sure about anything any more except her fear of this place.

'I don't want to die here,' she said. 'Not here – in the dark.' She could visualise her body lying cold and stiff on the bare floorboards of the rooms up here, with their spiders and dust and rat droppings and the cold drafts whistling through gaps in the windows. It was all too nightmarish to be true, as if she'd stumbled into one of her worst childhood dreams and couldn't escape.

'No one's going to die here,' Jimmy said. 'I told you. Tomorrow we'll drive up north and find a hotel, somewhere we can stay for a while till things quieten down and we can return to London.'

But she knew he was lying.

Janice slumped onto her knees, resigned, unable to see what else she could do. He was too strong for her to fight and too suspicious to let her out of his sight for more than a few seconds. What hope could she have of getting away from him here with so many unlit stairs beneath her to the street? She was trapped with him – trapped to whatever fate he decided to inflict on her.

'Here, have this,' Jimmy said. He passed her one of the bags of crisps he'd bought earlier, before opening a can of coke. 'You can wash them down with this. Not exactly haut cuisine,' he joked in what sounded to her like a cold, humourless voice.

She could have tried pleading with him, she supposed, as she ate the crisps, whatever flavour they were lost to her, but she knew she would be wasting her time. They hadn't known each other long enough for him to trust her, if men like him were capable of trusting other people. He was probably beyond that now. Perhaps because he knew no one could trust him either, she thought. She washed down the crisps with a mouthful of coke. It was lukewarm and fizzy and did little to quench her thirst.

'We'd be better off sleeping in the car,' Janice said. 'We could drive somewhere quiet, out of the way, somewhere no one would see us. Anywhere would be better than here.'

Jimmy swallowed his crisps and she could see him nod his head in the gloom. 'Perhaps,' he conceded thoughtfully, though without commitment.

'At least you could run the engine for a while with the heater on when we got cold,' Janice said. 'And we'd be able to set off at first light without anyone wondering what we were doing here in this abandoned place. If we left at night, we could get away without being seen. It would be harder to do that in the morning when it's busy outside.'

There was silence for a few minutes while Jimmy appeared to think about it as he finished his crisps. Finally, he opened a can of coke and drank its contents in several gulps.

Crushing the can in his fist, he turned his face towards her, a grey oval in the darker greyness.

'*Perhaps*, I said,' he reminded her. He glanced at the luminous dial on his watch, his eyes glimmering green for an instant. 'Now will you let it drop while I think.'

28

Despite her growing certainty that Jimmy had no intention of letting her leave this place alive, Janice had begun to doze when she heard voices on the lower floors of the hotel. Her first thought that this might be the police was abruptly crushed when she heard someone laugh. It was a nasty, nasal, baying laugh. The kind of laugh she could never have imagined a policeman making.

She saw Jimmy straighten in the gloom beside her, crouched tensely as he cocked his head to one side, at the same time holding up one hand for her to stay silent.

Despite this, she whispered: 'What is it?' though she knew he could have no more idea than her at the moment.

An irritable shake of his head was his reply as he slowly, carefully made his way to the stairs.

The noises from below were louder now as a group of people made their way up the stairs to the second floor. Janice wondered if they were the same people who had vandalised it. And felt torn between fear of what they might do if they found them here and the realisation that their numbers would probably be enough to overwhelm Jimmy and give her a chance to get away from him, *if only they knew they were here*. Which was the problem, she thought, knowing that she didn't dare try to catch their attention herself. Jimmy would probably kill her long before any of them could intervene if she did anything like that. His outrage at what he would see as her betrayal would be enough to unleash his violence. All she could hope for was that something would make them aware of their presence, something that Jimmy couldn't blame on her.

He shone the torch along the landing. Not far from them a metal ladder led up into the attic. Grasping hold of one of Janice's wrists Jimmy tugged her behind him. 'Up there,' he whispered.

'The attic?' Janice could barely restrain her horror at the idea of climbing up into the darkness that loomed above them.

'Don't argue,' Jimmy said. 'It's unlikely they'll come any further than here.'

Which she knew made some kind of sense. Why would

anyone want to go up there in a house with no lights? It was bizarre enough that a group of what sounded like men – she had heard no female voices amongst them – should be here at this time of night anyway.

Reluctantly, Janice climbed up the steps, finding herself in a long attic, its sloping roof sealed behind sheets of plasterboard, as if someone had planned to create more rooms up here. Even in her panic-stricken state, Janice wondered that Jimmy's alcoholic mother should have had the work done. The boards looked so clean in the torchlight, it was obvious they had not been here long.

Moments later, Jimmy stood beside her. He pulled the stairs up behind them, though Janice knew that if anyone wanted to use them they would only have to tug them down again from below.

Jimmy shone his torch the full length of the attic. A short distance further on a plasterboard wall sealed off the rest of the roof space. A solid-looking door stood in the centre, its unpainted, unvarnished panels and the bare surface of the plasterboards testimony that whatever work had been started here to extend the living area of the hotel had come to an abrupt end.

'Let's see where that leads,' Jimmy whispered. He pushed Janice towards the door, though it looked to her that all they would succeed in doing was trap themselves in an even more secluded part of the building with even less chance of escape. But she knew better than to argue with Jimmy. He reached ahead of her for the door handle and gave it a twist. It opened easily and a moment later Jimmy shone the torch into the room. It was so large that Janice realised the area they had been in was only a small part of the hotel roof space. At least eighteen feet square, it wasn't the size of the room that struck Janice as they looked through the doorway, but the skeletal body strapped to what looked like an operating table, high lit by spot lights trained onto it from either side of a professional-looking camcorder perched on a tripod. The light was dazzlingly bright, reflected back from stark white-painted walls.

'What the fuck?' Jimmy whispered as he stepped inside the room, a look of fascination on his face.

Janice felt bile in her throat as she stared at the body

manacled to the table. It was a teenage boy, perhaps fifteen, sixteen years old, emaciated to such a grotesque degree every bone seemed ready to cut through his thin translucent skin. The sight horrified Janice beyond belief. There were freshly healed cuts on every inch of the youth's body. Blood had leaked from the table onto the floor. Some of it looked as if it had clotted so long ago that many of the dark brown lumps were furred with mould.

'Is he dead?' Janice whispered, horrified at the state of the pathetic body.

Jimmy shook his head. 'He's breathing. Just.' He stepped around the table. On the far wall stood a glass-fronted cabinet. Stainless steel surgical instruments, knives, saws, scalpels, and drills, were neatly spread across its shelves.

'Do you think those people downstairs did this?'

Jimmy shrugged. 'Maybe.' He opened the cabinet and took out a couple of the largest knives, which he slipped inside his jacket pockets. 'What interests me is why the lights should work in this room when they don't elsewhere. Perhaps the power's not been cut after all. Perhaps it's just the fuses that have been removed for the rest of the house to give that impression.'

'Why?' Janice asked.

'So the place will look derelict and put anyone off from disturbing whatever they've been doing here.'

Jimmy returned to the doorway, where he listened intently for several seconds. 'If this is their work, they'll be up here soon.'

'What will they do when they find us?' Even as she asked it Janice realised how naïve that sounded.

Jimmy's lips moved into a cynical smirk.

'Probably invite us for a cup of tea,' he said, flatly.

Janice saw him reach into his jacket. He took out a gun. Even to her it looked old and rusty. Was this what he used to kill that woman's husband with?

His eyes met hers.

'It works,' he told her. 'But I only intend using it if those bastards make me. One way or another neither of us is going to end up like this,' he said, nodding towards the youth.

'Can't we help him?'

'How? Do you think he looks fit enough to get up and walk out of here? Do you feel strong enough to carry him if he can't?

That's assuming, of course, we could figure out how to get those manacles off. Besides, the way he looks, the shock of trying to get out of here would probably kill him.'

'They're going to kill him if we don't,' Janice said, though the irony of trying to plead with a potential serial killer to help save someone from being murdered made her feel sick. Jimmy had probably decided already how he was going to murder her in the next few days.

'I'm no knight errant,' Jimmy said. 'My priority is looking out for us. If we're lucky that'll be enough to get us out of this place.'

'Thanks.'

Jimmy's grin broadened.

'We've got to be practical,' he said. 'We don't know how many are down there, who they are or if any of them are armed.'

He looked around the room again, opening cabinets and pulling out drawers. He whistled appreciatively, stepping aside so that Janice could see inside the fridge he had opened. There were litre-sized bottles of what looked like blood stacked on shelves inside it.

'I suppose we can guess where this came from,' he said.

'But why?'

Jimmy shrugged. 'Who can guess what sick reasons lie behind any of this? Someone obviously likes prolonged torture. And is making some money out of filming it, too. Who knows why they want the blood?'

Despite the calmness of his voice, Janice could see his tension in the overly tight grip he held on the gun and the slight tremor in his voice. He might not be as scared as she was, but Janice could tell he was far from unaffected by their situation.

Before Janice could say any more there were sounds of movement at the entrance to the attic. The ladder rattled as it was lowered to the landing below, before footsteps could be heard ascending it. Moments later the footsteps approached the door into the room. Jimmy cocked the revolver and aimed it squarely at the door as it opened and a man stepped in, his surprise obvious. And for a moment he stared in disbelief at the gun pointing at him.

'Don't say anything and don't fuckin' move,' Jimmy said, his knuckles white as he aimed the gun at the stranger's head.

'Of course,' the man said, softly, recovering quickly. Of

medium height, he wore a plain suit and coat. Middle aged, he could have been any of a thousand office workers on his way home. His face looked mild, though there was a hint of something not quite right in the line of his mouth. His hair, which was light blonde and wispy, was beginning to recede. He was pale, though his lips, by contrast, were red, as if he was wearing women's makeup.

'Is something wrong?' A face, darker, with designer stubble and thick, untidily spiky hair appeared behind his shoulder.

'Both of you – in,' Jimmy said, his voice hardening. 'But slowly. And stop just inside the doorway.'

The first man shuffled forwards, stepping slightly to the left to let his companion follow him in. The other man was broader, with lively, dark, suspicious eyes. He too wore a nondescript suit and coat.

'Is that the lot of you?' Jimmy asked.

A sound of laughter from downstairs answered his question before either man had the opportunity either to lie or tell the truth.

'In the attic, yes,' the first man said a moment later, appraising Jimmy. His eyes settled on Janice with a look of curiosity.

'You're responsible for this?' Jimmy asked. He nodded towards the boy on the table.

'I'm afraid so,' the man said matter-of-factly.

'Who are you?' the darker man asked. His attitude was hostile and he regarded the gun pointed towards him with a look of contempt, almost as if he derided it as a threat.

Jimmy licked his lips, and Janice had the impression he was beginning to feel out of his depth. Next, she knew, he would start to feel angry. When that happened he was as likely as not to start firing.

'We're on the run,' Janice said. 'My companion's mother owned this place. That's why we came here.'

'On the run from whom?' the darker man asked.

Jimmy pointed the gun towards his face. 'I think this means I'm the one asking the questions. So shut the fuck up.'

'And we're the ones with numerical superiority,' the first man said. 'I don't know how many bullets you have in that gun, but I doubt very much it will have enough to deal with all of us.

There are more of us downstairs. One shot and they'll be here in seconds.'

'It's more than enough to deal with the two of you,' Jimmy grated meaningfully. 'That's all you need to know. I doubt the rest of your mob overpowering me would be much consolation if your brains were splashed across the wall.'

'He means it,' Janice added.

'I'm sure he does,' the man said with an impressive act of nonchalance, only betrayed by a sheen of perspiration on his forehead, though his companion looked as if he itched to act. And Janice knew the darker man posed the greater threat. That Jimmy shared this belief she could tell by the way in which the gun moved in his direction.

'What are you up to?' Jimmy asked.

'I thought that was obvious. We make a little money out of what the press call snuff movies. We make a bit more from allowing a few people to participate in them.' He smiled, amused. 'Not at *his* end of the business, of course,' he said with a meaningful nod at the boy. 'We'd find few takers for that. Even chronic masochists would baulk at that.'

Janice felt like gagging as the import of his words sank in. For all she knew that Jimmy was almost certainly a killer, at least that was because he had no choice in what he did, he was mentally ill. These men were different. She knew they were evil, with nothing to mitigate what they did. For the first time in her life Janice felt as if she was looking at men she would gladly, willingly kill if she could, who deserved to die – and for one moment she wished Jimmy would pull the trigger, whatever the consequences.

'Interesting,' Jimmy said finally, and Janice could tell he was having difficulty taking it in. Being a loner, reacting to his own compulsions was one thing, to see men go about something as calculatingly sick as this was something else altogether.

'Does this horrify you?' the man asked.

Jimmy twitched the gun towards him. 'Don't get clever with me,' he said. 'I'm still wondering whether to decorate the fucking walls with what passes as brains inside your head.'

'Tosser! You talk big behind that gun. I'd like to see what you'd say if we had you strapped to that table.'

'I'd like to see what you'd say if I had *you* strapped to it,' Jimmy responded aggressively.

Janice could all but smell the testosterone boiling between the two men as they stared at each other. Jimmy's face was already hardening as he ground his teeth, the knuckles of the finger hooked around the trigger of the gun white with tension.

The first man spoke to ease the situation.

'There's no need for any of this,' he said, calmly. 'You have the gun. We have the numbers. You're trapped. And your only way out is past us. I'm sure we could make a suitable arrangement. Depending on what can be agreed. After all, we don't want what's going on in this house being blabbed to the police.'

'Jimmy wouldn't go to them,' Janice said. 'He's on the run.'

'So you said,' the man answered. 'The big question is why? What's he done?'

The darker man narrowed his eyes. 'See those bruises on his face? I've been wondering about them. There was a news bulletin on the radio this morning. The police are looking for a man with heavy bruising to his face to do with a shooting in London. A serial killer, they said.' He smiled, his aggression seeming to dissipate. 'Some strangler they've been after for months.' He laughed. 'You wouldn't happen to have a red BMW, would you?'

'BMW?' Jimmy's face paled, and Janice could tell he was shocked another detail had been added to the rest, that he was beginning to realise how tight the noose was starting to close in around him.

'There was a BMW out on the street,' the other man said. 'I remember seeing it when we arrived. A bit of an old banger. Not dated enough to be a vet. Too old to be worth more than a few quid.'

'So you see,' Janice said, 'we could hardly go to the police. There's nothing we could tell them about this place that would stop them sending Jimmy down for life.'

'With no chance of parole,' the man added. 'Or time off for good behaviour.'

'Exactly,' Janice said, eagerly. 'So you see – you could let us go without having to worry about anyone blabbing to the police.'

'We'd have no reasons to worry about *him*,' the darker man said significantly. Janice felt Jimmy's eyes glance at her. 'What about it?' the man said. 'We might be able to trust you. How far

132

could we trust your companion if she got caught? Would she blab to save herself prison? How red are her hands? Or are they as lily white as I suspect?'

Worryingly, Janice felt some of the tension between the men relax.

'Perhaps you could do me a favour,' Jimmy said finally. 'Save me from having to do something which, to be honest, I wasn't all that happy about doing.'

'Jimmy!' Janice turned to him, suddenly frightened. 'I told you. I'd never betray you.'

'Be quiet,' the darker man said.

'The police can't possibly know much more about me than the car – and this,' Jimmy said, touching his bruises. 'Once these have gone in a few days' time, there's only the car. And how many clapped out BMWs do you think there are being driven about London? It would take more than that to connect me with anything.'

'And poor Craig here is, after all, beginning to get to the end of his tether,' the pale man said, with a glance at the boy manacled to the table.

'Jimmy, you can't do this,' Janice said, feelingly. 'You can't. I wouldn't betray you.'

He looked at her, an expression of regret on his face. 'Beggars can't be choosers, Jan. I didn't ask you to get involved. That was your choice. If you hadn't started poking around in things you should have left alone, you wouldn't be here now.'

'It looks like we see eye to eye,' the pale man said. He extended a hand, but Jimmy ignored it.

'I'd rather keep my distance if you don't mind. No offence, but I think we're a long way yet from being bosom buddies.' Jimmy nodded towards Janice. 'She can stay. You don't trust her. Neither, frankly, do I. All I need is for you and your pals to stay out of my way while I get out of here. Any funny business – any funny business at all – and I wouldn't hesitate in shooting anyone who got in my way. Understand?'

29

As he drove up north through the lowlands of Scotland Jimmy felt a greater sense of freedom than he had in years.

Despite the cold weather, he lowered the side window in the BMW as far as it would go so he could feel the fresh air blow in his face. Almost an hour had passed since Jimmy worked his way downstairs in the hotel in Morecambe past a motley assortment of men. Most of them had stared at him with so much hostile suspicion it bordered on paranoia.

Thankfully, the sound of Janice's pleadings as he walked away from her had been silenced with a couple of lengths of gaffer tape by the men holding her, who had just as quickly and just as efficiently bound and trundled her to one side. Proof, he supposed, they were well practised at this type of thing. It had, he supposed, been a small price to pay, though he knew he would miss her. It worried him, too, that Janice's disappearance might lead to some embarrassing questions from the police when he returned to London. How long it would be before she'd be missed, he did not know. A week, perhaps two. The first serious questions would come from her employers when she failed to turn up for work. Luckily, he knew she was not in regular contact with anyone from her family. She'd already admitted she rarely, if ever, returned phone calls from her mother. Even so, alarm bells were certain to start going off eventually. By which time he hoped to have settled back in London again, almost as if he had never been away. He doubted if anyone at the flats would have even missed him being there. Just like he was sure hardly anyone knew of his recent relationship with Janice. She'd never talked about any of her friends other than a couple of colleagues at the office. She was very much a loner. Like him, he supposed.

He eased off the accelerator as the traffic built up ahead of him, and wondered idly what was happening to Janice now.

Whatever it was it had nothing to do with him anymore. He had washed his hands of her. If the men hadn't taken her, he knew he might well have killed her by now. He would have had no choice. Though he would have made it quick and painless. Humane. Not the way it would happen now, he supposed. An unwanted image of the emaciated boy manacled to the table came to mind, disturbing his peace as he thought of the cuts and welts that covered the youngster's pale, transparent skin.

And why were those bottles of blood stored inside the fridge?

There was more going on than a few snuff movies, he was sure.

As he drew into a motorway service station for something to eat, he told himself it was none of his business. He had done well to get out of that place in one piece. Without the gun he knew he wouldn't have made it alive.

Jimmy bought some sandwiches and a coffee from the shop, then sat in the car park to eat his food in privacy and get some rest. It was barely dawn and he was tired. He hardly slept last night and it was still pitch black when he left the hotel. *His* hotel, he amended, resentful that the place had been taken over. The men claimed to have leased it from the solicitor who'd handled his mother's will. And well they might. He'd handed over control of the place to that bastard after his mother's death, hoping the building could be sold off quick, though no offers had been passed on to him. He wondered whether the solicitor was craftily pocketing the rent from the place while he was out of the way in London.

One thing was sure: the men wouldn't have leased it under their real names. Nor did he suppose the solicitor had bothered to check on them. He remembered him now. A weasel of a man with a pencil moustache and bad breath. Just the sort of solicitor his mother would have to sort out her will. Seedy and crooked. Like most of the men she'd ever got herself involved with – apart from his father, who'd been the only decent one amongst the all sorry lot. And the worst treated.

Jimmy screwed up the empty cartons of food and drink and flung them outside his car.

He'd had enough introspection. Time to be on the move again.

Though he could not help picturing Janice's face when he last saw her. Looking even larger than normal above the silvery grey tape stretched across her mouth, her eyes stared at him as he walked across the attic floor away from her, the gun held tight against his chest, cocked and ready. It was not a moment he relished. It soured the aftertaste of the coke as he reached for the ignition keys to start the car. For one insanely Quixotic moment he had even contemplated playing John Wayne and shooting the men he was leaving her with, though there were more of them than he had bullets in the gun.

Perhaps if he had got to know Janice better things might have been different.

He might have been different.

Then again, he thought, things could always have been different.

He remembered the first woman he killed.

He had hardly slept for weeks. His divorce came through at the same time as his bankruptcy. His car was repossessed and he had barely enough money to pay the rent. Rage, resentment, self-pity, bitterness, all plagued him, his head so full of vengeful thoughts he felt it would burst. The worst were the nightmares he had each night about his mother. Sometimes her face was mixed with that of his ex-wife. Those dreams had been the worst.

If his ex-wife had not run off to Spain she might have been the first, he knew. Maybe the last, too.

Even now he was unsure why he did it. Looking back on the killings they now seemed dreamlike, as if he had only been partially there and had sleep-walked through them, as if someone else had been in control even when he was getting himself ready: the dark clothes, the balaclava, the heavy duty rubber gloves – the grease paint he had taken from his mother's belongings when he went through them to see if there was anything of value after the funeral – the same grease paint she'd daubed him with all those years ago.

And the knife.

That had been bought weeks before.

Which was why he knew he must have had what he did on his mind all the time. So long ago now, looking back on what happened it all seemed so blurred.

The knife...

He'd not even known if he could do it at first, though he had fantasized doing it often enough when the rage came on him.

That cold, insidious, burning rage.

That rage that had left him outwardly calm.

And inwardly, *inwardly* so mesmerically strong.

He knew he had imagined doing things like that since he was a child. It had always been there. Small and furtive, a nasty secret tucked away at the back of his mind – though sometimes, when the mood took him, it would creep out of the shadows. Especially in his dreams. In his deepest, darkest, dirtiest dreams.

When young he had sometimes used a knife on animals. Secretly, of course. How his mother would have rejoiced if she could have discovered a weakness like this in him. It would have made her day. He could imagine how she would have humiliated him for it, just as she delighted in humiliating him about everything else, from wetting his bed to his first erection. His face still burned when he recalled the time she had caught him masturbating. That was something he had not been allowed to live down for months – if ever. She rejoiced in bringing it up in front of whatever man she was living with. None of them had failed to play along with her in ridiculing him.

As if none of them had ever done it, he thought heatedly, his hands unconsciously clenching so tight on the steering wheel it hurt his fingers.

As if none of those dirty filthy bastards hadn't done much worse in his mother's bedroom.

Calm down, *calm down*, he thought to himself, easing back on the accelerator.

He wiped his forehead, feeling the sweat that seeped into his eyes.

The last thing he needed was to be caught speeding.

There was no point in calling attention to himself, not when he had so much to hide.

Still, it was difficult not to keep remembering things, especially when he felt twinges of guilt come over him how he abandoned the girl. As if he could afford the luxury of guilt – as if he had not been thinking of killing her himself.

Though he knew he had still not decided when events over-took him.

Would he, he wondered, have killed her if she had stayed with him?

Would he *definitely* have killed her?

He was still not sure. Even though she posed a threat, he had not convinced himself she couldn't be trusted, that she would have betrayed him. Ironically, he was the one who had betrayed her in the end, not Janice, he thought as he stared through the windscreen.

30

DS McKenna read the report with cautious optimism. Ever since the investigation began they had been inundated with hundreds of names of suspected murderers, all of which had eventually been eliminated, and he sometimes wondered what motivated people to send in tip-offs that were blatantly ridiculous. Vindictiveness? Grudges and malice? Or plain, old-fashioned stupidity?

This, though, was different.

He recognised Jimmy Legg's name as soon as he saw it. And even though the recorded message hardly inspired much confidence, with its background noises inside a pub and the nearby sounds of someone sniggering, nevertheless it gave him pause for thought.

'What do you think, sarge?' Perched on the chair next to his, DC Barnes was eager to act. 'Sound like a positive lead to you?'

'He has a BMW,' McKenna said. 'And a record of violence. They're a start.'

'A bloody good start,' Barnes said.

'Anyway, we have Legg's address, so we might as well call and see him, hear what he has to say for himself.'

Half an hour later the two policemen drew up outside the Victorian villa in which records showed Jimmy Legg rented a top floor flat. The parking space outside was empty.

The doorbell listed three people: Mr and Mrs Fry on the ground floor, Miss J. Burroughs on the first, and Mr J. Legg on the second. Barnes pressed the bell for Legg, then stood back and waited. A couple of minutes later he rang again, longer this time.

'Looks like he's not in,' McKenna muttered. 'Let's try the ground floor. There are two people listed. There's a chance one of them might be in.'

A tinny voice answered over the intercom a few seconds later.

McKenna introduced himself and asked if he could ask a few questions.

Mrs Fry was an elderly woman with heavy-looking glasses and a querulous expression on her large, pinched face. She ushered the policemen into the hallway where she studied their warrant cards for several seconds, then said: 'How can I help you, Sergeant McKenna?'

'We're looking for your neighbour on the top floor. Mr Legg. We need to ask him a few questions. Do you know where we might find him or when he'll be back?'

'I've no idea where he works. All over the place, I think. He's self-employed, you know, though I don't think he has any premises – other than this place. I haven't seen him today. His car wasn't parked outside this morning. Funnily enough, his van's gone too, which is unusual. There's always one of them there, hogging the space.'

'You don't know if anyone else might know where he could be? Your husband perhaps?'

The old lady shook her head. 'Hubert's been confined to his bed for months. His legs. Never sees anyone these days other than the district nurse, who pops in every morning. The only other person here is Janice Burroughs. She has rooms on the next floor. I think she sees a lot of Mr Legg. I've seen him giving her lifts in his van. There's definitely something going on between them. Though it's not from want of trying, I'm sure. He's been after going out with her ever since she moved here.'

'Barnes, nip up and see if Miss Burroughs is in?' McKenna did not relish the steep flight of steps to the next floor.

A few minutes later Barnes was back.

'No one in. I tried the top floor too, just in case Legg's not answering the doorbell, but nothing.'

'That's strange,' Mrs Fry interrupted. 'I've not heard Janice go out today. The front door shuts with such a bang you can't miss it.'

'Perhaps she's gone to work,' McKenna suggested.

'I suppose,' Mrs Fry said, doubtfully. 'Normally she would have. Though I didn't hear her. And I always do, you know. I haven't any choice. I get up at six to make Hubert a cup of tea. I can't sleep after that. Not for years. I always hear Janice when she sets out, usually at eight.'

'Are you sure she didn't leave today? Could you have missed hearing her?'

'I'm definitely sure, Sergeant McKenna. I might be getting on but I'm not forgetful. In fact, I remarked on it to Hubert. I wondered if she'd taken the day off.'

'And Mr Legg?'

'I haven't seen sight nor sound of him since yesterday.'

'And his car?'

'Either that horrible old car or his van are always there. It's odd they're gone. I didn't think he let anyone else drive them.'

'Have you heard anything strange? Loud noises, perhaps? Arguments? Shouting? Bumps and crashes?'

'Nothing, Sergeant McKenna. Though…' She frowned slightly, as if she was trying to remember something in detail. 'There did seem an awful lot of hurrying about yesterday morning. Doors being slammed. Footsteps up and down the stairs. I think Mr Legg was loading something into his car. In fact, now I come to think about it, that's the last time I heard him, I'm sure.'

'When was this?'

'Yesterday morning, sergeant. I remember *The Archers* had just finished on radio four and I was waiting for *Desert Island Discs* to start. I love listening to that on Sunday mornings. Which would make it quarter past eleven, wouldn't it?' She grinned triumphantly.

'And Miss Burroughs? Do you have any idea when you last heard her?'

'I think she may have been with Mr Legg, sergeant. In fact, I'm sure I heard her voice.'

31

There were still fifty miles to go before Glasgow when Jimmy was forced to drive off the road and pull up. His stomach had been spasming for the past few miles, getting steadily worse. He groaned as the pain intensified till he pushed the car door open and rolled onto the grass verge, where he was suddenly, violently sick.

He gazed down the road through the glowering twilight. Clouds hung low overhead and, even though it was early morning, most cars had their headlights on.

Again, he felt spasms sweep through his abdomen and what was left of his sandwich was heaved on the grass.

When he felt as if he had begun to recover Jimmy wiped his mouth with the back of his hand and stood up. The cold air felt good on his face and he breathed in gulps of it, though he could feel the tension harden again into a knot inside his stomach. What the hell was wrong with him? For the past hour he had done nothing but think about Janice, however hard he tried to dismiss her from his mind. He had begun to think, too, about the men in the hotel, especially the darker of the two he'd spoken to. The man had started to get so far under his skin he'd had to fight the urge to fire the gun at him. He wondered what the hard-faced bastard was doing now. Had they got rid of the youth, who surely could have only been days away from death, and fastened the girl to the table in his place?

Jimmy swore beneath his breath.

He had enough problems ahead of him without worrying about Janice, for God's sake. Whatever trouble she was in was her own damn fault. If she hadn't poked her nose into things she should have kept out of, she could have been nice and safe in her flat in London, not locked away with a bunch of perverts in Morecambe.

It was nothing to do with him.

But the assertion irked him. And he could feel the spasms again in his stomach.

For reasons he could not even analyse he knew he could not stop worrying about her. He tried not to do. Desperately, he tried. He told himself she wasn't his responsibility. She never had been. She meant nothing to him. *Nothing at all.*

Climbing back into his car, Jimmy checked the revolver, counting the shells in its chambers, then tucked it deep in the pocket of his coat. Restarting the car, he swerved onto the road, his face expressionless. At the first opportunity, he swore to himself and turned back south.

Armed with a search warrant, McKenna stood back while a uniformed constable forced the door into Jimmy Legg's flat open.

'This feels like it, doesn't it, sarge?' Barnes said, his voice shaking with an adrenalin rush as the door gave way and four armed officers from the Tactical Aid Squad in Kevlar vests rushed in.

McKenna did not know whether to feel surprised or worried by the Spartan tidiness of the rooms as they began to search them. There was a utilitarian look to everything which somehow went far beyond the bounds of plain economy. It was almost obsessive. There were no books or photographs or anything else of a personal or recreational nature. The only TV was a twelve-inch monochrome, and far from new.

'Doesn't seem to be much of a fun guy,' Barnes said.

McKenna nodded. The same thought struck him too.

He glanced through some of the items in the wardrobe.

'I don't know what this metal box is for. There's nothing in it, sir,' one of the uniformed constables said. He placed it on the neatly made bed. 'Bit of a strange smell in it.'

'Like gun oil,' Barnes said. He held a piece of cloth he'd pulled from inside it close to his nose. 'What do you think, Craig? You're experienced in handguns.'

The PC took one sniff, then nodded. 'Definitely gun oil, sir. There's no mistaking it.'

Barnes glanced at McKenna. 'Could have been where the gun used to kill Barry Greenwood was kept.'

'If Jimmy Legg did it,' McKenna added.

Barnes shrugged. 'Looks as if the evidence is starting to build up.'

'Which is why we must find out where he's gone. And Janice Burroughs.'

'Who's probably with him?' Barnes said.

'Probably. Whether willingly or not remains to be seen.'

Jimmy pulled off the motorway and followed the signs for Lancaster, then Morecambe. It was mid afternoon by the time he reached the outskirts of the seaside town, by which time he felt hungry and tired, his nerves stretched raw as thoughts ran out of control through his head, returning again and again to Janice and his betrayal of her, of the pleas he had done his best to ignore when he walked out of the hotel. The experience left him feeling emotionally drained. It seemed impossible to remember how he had been able to abandon her so easily. It was almost as if he had been another Jimmy Legg. A Jimmy Legg he barely recognized now.

He drove off the almost deserted seafront towards the hotel, when he was suddenly forced to brake. Two fire engines and a number of police cars, warning lights flashing on their roofs, filled what space there was along the street. Already it had been sealed off. Clouds of smoke were drifting along it, though Jimmy could tell the fire itself had died – or burnt itself out. The hotel – *his* hotel, he thought, appalled at the sight – had been gutted. Its roof had collapsed and what little still stood above the second floor, other than blackened rafter beams, looked ready to keel over. Shocked, Jimmy stared at the charred shell of his legacy till someone jabbed their car horn behind him. A policeman looked across at him from behind the tape stretched across the street and waved him on impatiently. Changing gears, Jimmy bowed his head to hide as much of his face as he could and shot forwards, even though he could barely concentrate on where he was going. This was brought home a few seconds later when had to brake to let a group of teenagers dash across the front of his car to the opposite pavement.

'Bloody fools,' someone shouted, but for once his own anger felt muffled, unfocussed, as he slowly drove forwards through the maze of narrow, one way streets with obsessive caution, till he spotted somewhere to park near a row of shops. Handbrake on, Jimmy turned off the engine and stared through the windscreen. Which was when he found his hands had started to shake as the knot of tension inside his stomach tightened once more.

What have they done?

What have the fucking bastards done?

Feeling nauseous, Jimmy wound down his window. Outside, even here, several blocks from the fire, he could smell it, a harsh sooty stench which even the non-stop drizzle and overlying tang of the sea couldn't dampen. Jimmy craned his neck and looked towards the hotel, hidden beyond the shops and cafes on the opposite side of the street.

Their dirty little secret exposed to him, the men must have decided there was too much risk that Jimmy would say something about them if he was caught. And what better way to destroy any evidence than reduce it to ashes?

But what of Janice? What had they done with her? He clenched his fists about the steering wheel. He had to think logically. Ignore his anger and whatever bullshit emotions he felt.

Think.

Think Coldly.

Logically.

Carefully.

He stared ahead of him, though he barely saw the few pedestrians or cars that made their way along the rain-washed street. Whoever the men were he knew they would not have left any bodies in the place when it was torched. A fire was bad enough. But deaths inside the hotel would attract attention, especially if it looked as if they had been murdered. Besides, he was sure the men had other things planned for Janice.

What, though, would they have done to her?

Somehow he was sure she would have been bundled out of the hotel, almost certainly long before dawn when they were less likely to be seen.

But where would they have taken her?

And how could he find out where this was when he didn't know who any of them were?

A thin smile suddenly parted his lips.

What an idiot he had been. What an absolutely stupid, cretinous idiot. There *was* a link. That slimy git of a solicitor who leased the hotel to them was all the link he needed.

His smile touched the corners of his mouth as Jimmy remembered the solicitor's name: Christopher Maitland. It was

145

time he had words with Mr Maitland anyway after the way he rented the hotel out to them without his knowledge – and without him being paid his share. In any case, Jimmy had already disliked to the man. That had come on first sight. Perhaps because he was sure that Maitland had been another of his mother's 'boyfriends'.

Jimmy remembered visiting the man's office after his mother died. It was a crummy little place, hidden between a dry cleaner's shop and a cut-price off-license on the main road to Heysham. Only a one-man band, Maitland employed a couple of girls as secretaries and seemed to scrape most of his living off conveyancing. Perhaps Maitland's personal appearance had a lot to do with it. There was definitely something wrong with the man. For all he had intelligence enough to have qualified as a solicitor, he looked more like a low class pimp than anything else. In a way, Jimmy relished the idea of dealing with him.

But he knew there were other things first.

The most immediate he resolved when he hurried across the street and bought a duffel coat from a charity shop. Its large hood hid most of his face. Feeling secure inside it, he went on to buy some fish and chips and a carton of coffee from a take-away, taking them back to his car. This time he hoped he would be able to keep the food down. At least the knot of tension inside his stomach had eased since he'd decided to do something about Janice. His only remaining worry was the BMW. It was too conspicuous, and he knew he would have to ditch it somewhere for something mundane.

He called into a newsagent and bought a copy of *The Lancaster Guardian*. A quick scan of its classified pages soon found what he wanted:

Ford Fiesta
M reg. 10 months MoT
5 months tax.
Good runner.
£350 ono

This was followed by a mobile number.

Jimmy fished out his phone and rang the number in the advert. Luckily, the man was at home and a few minutes later Jimmy was on his way to a council estate on the outskirts of Morecambe. Not worried about any of the car's defects, like the

146

filthy state of its upholstery or the patches of rust that were flaking off the edge of its doors, it took less than ten minutes. By which time Jimmy had handed over two hundred pounds and left the BMW in part exchange. And, although he'd promised to send the BMW's documents in the next few days, he could tell the man was convinced it was stolen – though that didn't seem to bother him.

In a way, Jimmy was glad to see the back of it. The car had always been too conspicuous. And he had been stupid to keep it as long as he had. His new car was certainly mundane enough, if less fun to drive.

When he checked his watch, he was surprised to see it was half past four. Time to be heading for Maitland's office. He didn't think the solicitor would hang around late.

It was ten to five by the time Jimmy parked a few yards from the solicitor's premises. He rang directory enquiries for Maitland's number, then telephoned to make sure he was still on the premises. A young girl answered.

'Do yuh want to talk to 'im?' she asked in a blunt Lancashire accent.

Jimmy hung up. He'd found out all he needed to know. There was a metallic blue Alpha Romeo parked outside, which he suspected was probably Maitland's. It looked his style.

Sure enough, a short while later a dumpy girl in padded sports pants and a woollen hat left the building. She was followed by an older woman, short, stocky, with cropped hair and the mannerisms of a man. Jimmy remembered them both from his visit last year. He watched them call good-bye to each other, by which time Maitland had also emerged. Of medium height, he had an odd, ingratiating stoop which made him look shorter than he was, though it was his face that Jimmy remembered clearly. There was something so startlingly unhealthy, not only about his greasy, pock-marked skin, but the shifty look in his eyes. Maitland paused for a moment after locking the door to glance up and down the pavement, scanning it carefully as if he half expected someone to be spying on him. Despite this, his eyes failed to settle on Jimmy's car. Then Maitland pointed one of his keys at the Romeo; its indicator lights flashed on and off and there was a loud click as its doors unlocked.

Jimmy smiled, satisfied that his assumption had been correct.

Now all he had to do was follow him discretely. Which was something the Fiesta was suited for. He doubted if Maitland would give such a car a second glance.

Maitland did not drive home straight away. Instead, within half a mile, he pulled in at a Mock-Tudor pub. Once the solicitor had disappeared inside the pub, Jimmy followed him onto the car park, reversed into a spot several spaces away from the Romeo, where he could drive straight out onto the road when Maitland left, then settled back to wait for the him to come out. After an hour had gone by, Jimmy was glad he had decided to have a snack earlier. As it was he felt thirsty by the time Maitland returned to his car.

'I hope you fucking well enjoyed your meal,' Jimmy muttered to himself as Maitland set off with a squeal of over-accelerated tyres on the wet tarmac. Jimmy drove as fast as he could behind him, but the Fiesta struggled and he was soon more than a hundred yards behind the Romeo. Luckily, traffic ahead was heavy and slow and he soon began to catch up again.

A short distance further Maitland headed off the main road. The tree-lined avenue into which he drove hid detached villas hidden behind hedgerows. Jimmy reckoned they had once looked better than now. The bushes and shrubs looked overgrown and dismal in the growing gloom as night settled in, while the road was rough, with enough potholes to make the clapped out springs on the old Fiesta creak, even though he slowed to a crawl.

Maitland's Romeo stopped at an open gateway, before slowly turning down the drive of the last house on the cul-de-sac. Like most of the others, it was a two-story villa with a red-tiled roof, barely visible above the hedgerow. Jimmy followed him to the end of the avenue, did a three-point turn, before parking his car next to the gate to Maitland's house. He checked the pockets of his duffel coat. Inside the right hand pocket was the gun. Its metal felt warm to his touch. His skinning knife and a couple of the knives he'd helped himself to in the attic were in the other. These would be more than enough for his purposes. A good six inches taller than the solicitor and at least a couple of stones heavier, he did not anticipate any problems dealing with him. In fact, he looked forward to meeting him again, when a few grudges could be resolved.

Shutting the driver's door as quietly as he could, Jimmy stole towards the gate. The driveway was impenetrably black apart from a glow from one of the downstairs windows. Its bay jutted out into the garden, surrounded by a concrete path, which he skirted as he headed towards the back of the house. For a moment he paused and listened at the window. The heavy drapes drawn inside prevented him from seeing into the room. All he could make out were the murmurs of a television set, which sounded as if Maitland had settled down to watch the news.

A latched door led to the rear of the house. It was even darker here, and Jimmy wished he had brought a torch, though if any of the neighbours caught sight of one they would straight away think of burglars. No doubt they had their own Neighbourhood Watch in an area like this and it wouldn't take much to get one of their curtain twitchers to ring the police. Working mainly by touch, till his eyes had begun to adjust to the gloom and he could make out vague shapes in it, Jimmy crept to the kitchen door. It was locked, but it was an easy task, using one of the knives he had taken from the hotel, to force it open. The wood was soft where the paint had weathered and rain had managed to soak into it. It parted with no more than a faint crack.

Jimmy put the knife back in his pocket. He did not know whether Maitland was married or not – or even if he had a family. For some reason, though, he had a feeling the man lived alone. Perhaps from something he said when they met. Or an impression he'd been given about him. Even so, the gun was the most effective way of making sure, if there was anyone else in the house besides Maitland, he could keep them under control.

Besides, he had begun to like the feel of it.

Quietly, Jimmy worked his way through the kitchen, his fingertips touching the edge of the worktops. The door into the rest of the house opened silently for him. The first door he looked through led into the dining room. Its air was damp and smelt of neglect. Maitland obviously preferred to eat out – and could afford to, Jimmy thought. A corridor headed towards the entrance hall. Halfway along a partially open door spilled light across it. He could hear the television clearly now. There was a voice, speaking low, which Jimmy realised was Maitland talking on the phone.

'What do you mean, there wasn't any choice? The police have been on to me all fucking afternoon. Someone's suggested arson, damn it. Do you know what that means? It means a fucking investigation. I just hope for your sakes it was the owner you saw. If he's on the run for murder, he'll have more on his mind than me letting you have use of that place. I know. I know. You made sure there's nothing to incriminate us. There'd better not be. What? Of course I'm not threatening you. You know me better than that. We just have to take care, that's all. There's too much at stake.'

For a few more minutes he rambled on, though now it was mostly the occasionally mumbled 'Yes' or 'No', till he finally finished, sighed as if all the worries of the world were on his shoulders and dropped the telephone on its cradle.

Jimmy heard a tinkle of glass as the solicitor poured a drink.

Which was when Jimmy stepped through the open doorway.

Maitland's face looked grey when he glanced up, a heavy decanter almost slipping from his fingers.

'What the fucking hell are you doing here?'

Jimmy pulled out the revolver and pointed it towards him from waist height.

His hand shaking as he stared at the gun, the solicitor slowly, ever so carefully placed the decanter back on the table

'I think I'll be asking the questions,' Jimmy said. He cocked the revolver.

'What do you want?' Maitland's voice stuttered when he spoke.

'Information about certain people you're involved with,' Jimmy said. 'You know who I'm talking about. You've just been chatting to one of them on the phone.'

Maitland squinted at his face. 'You're Legg, aren't you? I handled your mother's will.'

'That's right. The idiot whose hotel you've been renting out and keeping the cash – whose hotel I was under the impression you were trying to sell for me. Which is no bloody wonder the place has had no offers. I don't suppose you ever even put it on the market.'

'It's not fit to sell. The place was condemned even while your mother had it. Any buyer would have to spend more restoring it than the place is worth. Do you know what prices are for derelict properties like that in Morecambe these days?'

'It was fit enough to rent out,' Jimmy said.

'I don't know what you mean. Rent out? To whom?'

'You know very well who rented it. I heard you talking to one of them when I came in.'

'That was about something else. It had nothing to do with your hotel. In fact, I was going to write to you this week about it. I had a structural engineer in recently. He warned me it was unsafe inside. Dry rot throughout.'

'Liar. There might be dry rot. I wouldn't know. But no one's inspected it recently. If they had, how would you have explained your torture chamber in the attic? Or did this structural engineer not bother checking there?'

'Torture chamber?' Maitland laughed. There was a brittle ring to it.

Jimmy raised the gun, pointing it towards the solicitor's face. 'Don't treat me like a fool. I've been there. I saw it. Before your associates decided to burn it down.'

Maitland made to shake his head, when Jimmy suddenly lunged forward, angrily hitting him across the face with the end of the revolver. It impacted with his cheekbone and threw the solicitor back across the room. Maitland clutched at his face, groaning as blood seeped between his fingers where the skin had been opened to the bone.

'You fucking bastard,' Maitland muttered, backing away. He was hunched up double and gritted his teeth against the pain.

'That's my middle name,' Jimmy said. He raised the gun once more. 'I don't care how many times I have to hit you. That doesn't bother me. Because I'll keep on doing it till you tell me what I want to know. Curse me, swear at me, call me every fucking name under the sun, I – don't – *fucking* – care. That won't stop me from hurting you. Nothing you can say, apart from answering my questions, will stop me from hurting you. I'll enjoy it, in fact. It would give me a kick. Do you understand?'

'You're a sick bastard, Legg. Did you know that?'

'Sicker than someone who associates with torturers, with people who film snuff movies for money? Who drain the blood from their victims? Did you know that, Maitland? I saw the bottles they stored it in. Pints of it were stashed away. I saw the lad who was strapped to the operating table they'd installed up there. I saw what he was like. How they'd cut him. And starved him. Did you ever see that?' Jimmy asked. 'Or was it a case of turning a blind eye so long as you got paid?' He stepped towards Maitland, who backed away as far as the wall and could go no further. 'What do they pay you, Maitland? I'll bet it's a lot. I'll bet it's a hell of a lot. For an operation like that, with total secrecy, no questions asked?' Jimmy raised the gun as if he intended to hit him again. 'How much, Maitland? A thousand? Two thousand? More?'

'What do you want?' Maitland cringed as Jimmy stepped closer, the gun still raised above his head.

'Where have they moved to?'

'*Where?*'

Jimmy held himself back, though the urge to bring the gun down on the man's head was almost overwhelming. As if sensing this, Maitland bleated: 'No!'

'Then stop fucking well pissing me about,' Jimmy said. 'Where the hell are they?'

'Why do you want to know?'

Jimmy took a deep breath. 'Do they scare you more than me?' Jimmy asked. 'Is that why you're trying to squirm out of telling me?'

'You don't know them.'

'I don't fucking well *want* to know them,' Jimmy said. 'I only want to know where they are.'

'But why?' Maitland shook his head as Jimmy stepped towards him again. 'You don't understand. If you did, you wouldn't be asking questions about them. You'd be glad just to have got away from them in one piece.'

'How much do you know about what happened?'

'I know you were hiding there with some girl. I know you managed to persuade them to let you go, though you left your companion. Abandoned her.' Maitland was unable to suppress a knowing smile that almost earned him another blow from the gun, but Jimmy decided to let him continue now that he was talking at last. Retribution could wait. For a while.

'Go on,' Jimmy urged.

'They didn't trust you. There was an argument after you'd

gone. If not for the gun, there's no way you would have walked out of there.'

'I can imagine,' Jimmy said. 'What did they do next?'

'They always have contingency plans. They're organized. They've been doing this for years.'

'How many years?'

Maitland shook his head. 'Who knows? Lots. A lot more than you think, probably. They know what they're doing.'

'I'm sure they do.'

'Afterwards, when they'd finished discussing you, it was decided to move out of the hotel and take everything with them.'

'Including the girl?'

'Everything. They wouldn't leave anything behind. To make sure there wasn't the slightest chance of anything being found that could link them to what had been going on there they set fire to the building.'

'In case of forensics?'

'Fingerprints, DNA, anything. They know what they're doing.'

'So you keep telling me.' Jimmy let the revolver roll from side to side in the palm of his hand. 'Where did they take the girl afterwards?' he asked as Maitland's eyes followed the movements of the gun, his pupils dilated with fear.

'I don't know. They didn't tell me.'

Jimmy smiled. 'I think you're a lot more closely involved with these people than you let on. You wouldn't know as much about them as you do if you were just their landlord. I'm sure you're much more than that. Otherwise you'd be worried about your skin. And one of them would probably be here right now making sure you didn't talk. Don't think you can fob me off. You're one of them, Maitland. I know it.'

'It wouldn't do you any good. Do you think you could just walk in and take her with you? That's what this is all about, isn't it? You've had second thoughts about abandoning the girl. Now you're thinking you're some kind of knight errant, riding to the rescue.' Maitland's eyes twinkled with cynicism behind their fear.

If Maitland had expected a violent reaction, Jimmy astonished him by carefully easing the cocked hammer of the revolver down, before tucking the weapon inside his coat. For a

153

moment, Jimmy saw a sense of relief pass over the solicitor's face, which was when Jimmy reached into another pocket and brought out a knife.

'You wouldn't...' Maitland's face went even paler than before.

It was long and shiny, made of stainless steel, with an edge that looked incredibly sharp. Perhaps Maitland recognized it from the operating room. Perhaps he'd watched it being used on the youth. Jimmy weighed the knife in his hand. It felt good. Useful. Practical. And would probably slice deep without too much effort.

Their eyes met.

'I've used a knife before,' Jimmy said.

'I've been going through all the papers we found in Legg's apartment,' DC Barnes said, his face flushed with success. 'I think I might know where he's gone.'

He placed a solicitor's letter on McKenna's desk. 'It turns out his mother died a couple of years ago. She left him a private hotel. Probably a boarding house. You know the kind of thing.'

'Don't I just. When I was a kid it wasn't holidays abroad with the parents. It would be the Buena Vista Hotel or some such dump on the promenade of some crummy seaside resort. Though we never quite made it to the heights of Morecambe.' McKenna whistled, lightly. 'That's far enough away to take some of the heat off him. Is it still up and running?'

Barnes smiled, tightly. 'That's the thing. I rang our colleagues in Lancaster to see if they could find out anything about it. Which surprised them, since an investigation has already been launched by the fire brigade. The place burned down last night.'

'Burned down?' McKenna narrowed his eyes. 'Arson?'

'They're ninety percent sure.'

'Was anybody hurt?'

'Apparently not. The place has been shut for years. By all accounts it was a dive. Overdue for demolition. Except that costs money. So far no bodies have been found, so it looks as if it was empty at the time.'

'Though somebody must have been there if there was arson. A bit of a coincidence our friend Legg should have disappeared at the same time. If he doesn't know he's under suspicion for murder you'd be tempted to suspect he might be trying for an insurance claim.'

'About the only way the place would raise cash from what my contact in Lancashire said.'

'Which could mean his disappearance hasn't anything to do with the murders at all. That he's other things on his mind.'

'We can't be sure of that, sarge. And he does drive a red BMW.'

'Very true,' McKenna said. He stood up. 'I'll have a word with the guv'nor. It might be worth our while taking a trip up north. I could do with a touch of sea air.'

Janice could neither move nor see. Her world was confined to a narrow box that might as well have been a coffin for all the space she had. And though she knew this was only temporary, that soon she would be released from it – or so she had been told – this was still like her worst nightmare as she stared into the darkness all around her. Even so, in a paradox that would have earlier confounded her, it was her release from the box she dreaded most. Inside she was safe. At least temporarily, she thought. When they removed her from it her real torments would begin, probably manacled to the same table she had seen the boy fastened to before.

Would they move her to it after he died? From what she had seen the youth hadn't looked as if he could last another day. *If* he even had stamina enough left to survive his removal from the hotel, she thought. That had been traumatic enough for her, her wrists and ankles bound together so tight they hurt, while a couple of the men ignominiously hauled her down the flights of stairs to the ground floor, where she was roughly bundled into the back of a van, her body covered in more bruises than she'd had in her life, then sealed in this box. Though the youth's emaciation meant he would be considerably lighter, she doubted if he would have been treated with any more consideration. There was a callous indifference about the men that chilled her, as if she was no more than an animal being dragged to slaughter.

Outside it was silent at last. For hours she had heard them moving things. They did not speak much, perhaps because there was so much work to do, but when they did it was in low, furtive voices as if they were bothered about being overheard by someone in authority – someone with little time for complaints or grumbles, someone with a short and frightening temper.

Tears of frustration welled in her eyes. She still found it impossible to believe Jimmy had abandoned her with these men, walking out as if he felt nothing for her, as if she were no more than a stranger to him. She knew he had been involved with the murders – that he would have probably killed her later that night – yet still his betrayal had come as a shock. It had looked so easy for him to do, with such indifference, like swatting a fly. If he had killed her she knew that would have been as quick, as merciful, as painless a death as he could manage. It would not have been like the lingering, pain-filled death these men had been exacting on the youth – which she was certain they would start soon enough on her. How could Jimmy have left her to this? Or had he been so frightened, for all his bluster and pent-up violence, that he preferred to sacrifice her like he had than fight?

From his perspective it had been the logical thing to do, cold blooded though that seemed to her. What could she have expected from a man who was nothing more than a murderer? She felt salt from her tears form crusts about the edge of her lips. His skin was all that mattered to Jimmy. What happened to her was irrelevant. All his words had been nothing but lies, and she had been a fool ever to have thought she meant anything to him other than someone with whom he would eventually have talked his way into bed.

Her only hope now was that somehow, in some way the police would find out what had happened, but even that chance looked remote. Maybe the youth had had hopes like that when he was manacled to the operating table. Much good they had done him, Janice thought, feeling sick with fear.

36

The deep pile carpet of Christopher Maitland's living room was soaked with blood. The area where it was drenched the most was immediately before the ornate Queen Anne fireplace where Maitland's body twitched with unconscious spasms. His shirt had been cut from him, though there was so much blood on his torso it hardly looked naked at all.

Jimmy sat on the sofa facing him, resting, his body almost as drenched as Maitland's. He felt exhausted, yet at the same time elated. It had done much to ease the knot of tension in his stomach. It was still there, of course, but quiescent now. In some way he felt satisfied.

It had taken him less than half an hour to find out everything he wanted to know. In reality, the solicitor had not needed all that much persuasion once he realized Jimmy had no qualms about using the knife, that, on the contrary, he actually derived a great deal of pleasure from using it. By the third severed finger Maitland would have sold his soul to the Devil if Jimmy had told him to, blabbering and pleading shamelessly, his wrists and ankles tied up tight, though not surprisingly, he still tried to fight when Jimmy began to work on him. Considering the amount of pain being inflicted, Jimmy had expected this. To help subdue him he'd punched Maitland a couple of times in the face, then held him down as he amputated the first of his fingers with a single downwards lunge of the knife, its point penetrating the carpet and sticking for a moment in the floorboard beneath. Maitland had all but bitten through the gag Jimmy had tied across his mouth, tears streaming from his eyes and down his face. Two more fingers left him weeping and screaming, the sounds barely muffled by the gag. It had taken the threat of the now bloodied blade being pointed at one of his eyes to shut him up. Leaning over his head, Jimmy whispered, 'One scream, just one fucking scream, you'll lose this eye. Understand?' With that he carefully eased the cloth from the solicitor's mouth. 'This is just so you can answer me when I ask a question. Otherwise say nothing. Nothing at all. Or say good-bye to Mr Eye. And, believe you me, Maitland, I'll do it. Do you understand?'

Too frightened to speak, Maitland nodded his head.

'First off all,' Jimmy said, 'who are these men?'

Even with the threat of the knife only inches from his face, Maitland hesitated. Just how frightening were these people? Jimmy lowered the knifepoint towards Maitland's eye. 'I'm waiting,' he said in a soft, determined voice.

'They'll kill you if you try to contact them. They'll kill me too if they ever find out I've told you anything about the Group.'

'Is that what they call themselves, the Group? Like they meet every Friday to strum their guitars?'

'You wouldn't joke about them if you knew more.'

'Maybe. And maybe they've more to worry about me. I don't like being kicked off my own property. I don't like being threatened either. Nor do I like having to ditch my girlfriend to them.'

'Your girlfriend? They said you were thinking about killing her.'

'Maybe I was. Maybe I wasn't. That was for me to decide in my own good time.' Jimmy waved the knife back and forth before Maitland's eyes for emphasis. 'Back to questions and answers. Enough chitchat. We can leave that till later.' He smiled coldly. 'If there is a later.' He smiled more broadly when he saw the fear in Maitland's eyes. 'Where have they set up their torture chamber now?'

Maitland gulped.

'If you have a death wish I'll tell you, but you would be stupid to go there.'

'That's my decision.'

Maitland nodded, cautiously. 'They've moved to a farm. It's not a working farm, mind. Most of the land was sold off years ago. There's just a farmhouse, a barn, some outbuildings, three or four acres of land.'

'Is it secluded?'

'The house and barn are set back from the nearest lane. There aren't any buildings nearer than a mile away. And there's plenty of land surrounding it to keep eavesdroppers back.'

'How secure is it?'

'There's fencing all around, much of it covered in barbed wire. There's a wall along the lane. And padlocked gates.'

'Any surveillance cameras? Anything electronic?'

'I don't know,' Maitland said.

Jimmy lowered the knife till its point almost touched the solicitor's lashes.

'Are there any surveillance cameras? Electronic sensors? Burglar alarms? Automatic lights? You'd better loosen up and start telling me these things. If I go there and find you've been lying to me, or missing out stuff I should know, I'll come back and cut you again. Properly this time. You'll be feeding through a tube for the rest of what's left of your short, miserable, pain-wracked life.'

'No cameras. There is a burglar alarm in the farmhouse, but not the barn, which is where they've moved everything. I told you, it's only temporary. They don't need anything more elaborate. There'll be someone there all the time anyway.'

'Why temporary? The place sounds perfect for what they're up to.'

'Too much activity would be noticed. People would start to ask why there are so many men coming and going. It's not a working farm, so questions would eventually be asked. It would stand out a mile. People would get suspicious there was something criminal going on. The police would get involved.'

'And that's something the Group wouldn't want, is it? Too much to hide.'

'Secrecy is everything.'

'I'll bet it is.' Jimmy stood up. His mouth, parched earlier, was so dry now he felt desperate for a drink. He glanced at the whisky, but it wasn't alcohol he wanted now. Water was what he needed with all he had ahead of him tonight. 'Don't even think of crying out for help while I'm gone. I'll only be in the kitchen. Before anyone could hear you I'll be back.'

With that, Jimmy padded out of the room. He downed a glass of water in one gulp. He hadn't realized how thirsty he was. But it had been a long day and, apart from a cola earlier, which he'd thrown up on his way to Scotland, and a carton of coffee in Morecambe, he'd had nothing to drink. Which was no wonder he felt dehydrated. He poured himself a second glass, then took it back to the living room.

Maitland was sat on the carpet. A quick glance showed he had managed to gnaw his way through the bonds on his wrists and was busily untying the rope around his ankles. Jimmy crossed the room in three strides, the glass of water cast to one side as he whipped up the knife from the seat of the sofa where he had left it. His foot took Maitland on his upturned chin as he tried to dodge away from him. His head shot back, then Jimmy grabbed him. Twice he cut him. Two shallow lines crossed his chest, each of them twelve inches long. Maitland screamed, till Jimmy slapped him across the face and, glowering at him, held the knife blade inches from his eyes.

When Maitland realized the seriousness of the threat and was silent again, Jimmy half turned from him, stabbed the knife into the floor where he could reach it easily, then pulled the gag across the solicitor's mouth, stifling his moans.

'This is to teach you what happens when you make a mistake,' Jimmy said between panting. With that he reached down and grabbed Maitland's hand. 'Time for one more digit to show you I mean business.' He reached for the knife. Its blade came down with a thump on the carpet, severing the index finger of the man's right hand with so much force it jumped two feet through the air.

Maitland fainted.

While he was out, Jimmy retied his wrists, making sure they were tight, then returned to the kitchen for another glass of water. The last dregs he used to splash the solicitor's face.

'Wakey wakey. Rise and shine.'

Jimmy grinned as the man regained consciousness. For a moment Maitland seemed unable to take in his surroundings. Then his memories cleared. And with that his eyes opened wide in fear.

'I'm glad to see you're with me again,' Jimmy said. 'I was beginning to get worried I'd lost you for good.' He reached down for one edge of the gag. 'Remember what I told you. When I release you from this I want no shouts. No pleas. No cries for help. Not if you want to have anything left to scratch yourself with.'

Maitland's tongue licked across blood-caked lips.

'What else do you want to know?' he asked in a desperate croak.

'The exact location of the farm. Do you have maps? If you have, tell me where they are.'

There was no evasion now. Pain-wracked and frightened, he had no resistance left. A briefcase, left by the door, contained an

Ordnance Survey map, he said. This not only had the farm on it, but had it highlighted in an orange Day-Glo circle.

'Is the girl there?' Jimmy asked. 'Will they have harmed her?'

'She's there. I doubt anything will have happened to her yet. They prefer to wait till later at night.'

'Why?'

Maitland shook his head. 'I don't know.'

Somehow Jimmy suspected he did. And was tempted to use the knife again when Maitland passed out.

Cursing quietly, Jimmy got up and sat on the sofa. Which was when he realized just how tired he was. He may have quenched his thirst for the time being, but his body felt drained.

He gazed at Maitland. The man was a mess. And for a moment Jimmy wondered whether he should finish him off, even though he knew that Maitland would not go to the police. Killing him would be the simplest solution. No comebacks. No complications. All it would need was one quick slice across the throat.

But there could be more to be found out yet about this Group. And Jimmy was far from sure everything he had been told had been the truth. What if there was nothing at this farm? What if it was no more than a red herring, which Maitland hoped would give him time to escape from here? He couldn't risk it. Maitland was his only link to the Group. And Janice.

37

Janice had already peed herself twice while locked in the box. She felt cold and miserable and grubby. Her throat burned and she knew she was beginning to hallucinate from a combination of hunger, thirst, fear and despair. It was so long since she had been imprisoned she'd lost track of time. It could have been hours or days since they threw her inside the box and screwed down the lid. In reality, she knew it could hardly have been more than a day. Bad though that was, her thirst would have been even worse by now if she had been imprisoned any longer. Worryingly, though, she hadn't heard any sounds of movement for far too long, and she was beginning to worry the men had abandoned her. This led to her feelings of claustrophobia becoming so intense she would have been pounding and scratching with all the mindless hysteria of blind panic on the wooden lid only inches from her face if not for the bonds that restrained her wrists so tightly she could barely move.

Worse still, she was aware that the silence outside was far from absolute. There *were* sounds. Light and furtive. And sometimes she could hear scurrying. In her heightened imagination she could clearly see scaly tails and the dark, flea-ridden bodies of scavenging rats as they rustled inquisitively around the box, sniffing at it. She could hear the wind, too, as if through a tree or rafter beams. And all the time she could hear the sound of dripping water. Not just from one place, it seemed to echo all around her, some far away.

Though she knew it was pointless, she tried to picture where she had been left. At times she saw the box laid in a pitch-black cellar deep underground, full of stone archways, cobwebs and mould. Sometimes this terrified her the most, intensifying her feelings of claustrophobia, of being alone in perpetual darkness, of dying of thirst, forgotten and alone. Then she would imagine it had been stored in a large warehouse, perhaps one amongst hundreds of similar boxes, stacked beneath windows high in its walls, light beams shining down on it. In truth, she had no idea where she was – which perhaps disturbed her most of all. She knew none of her speculations might be correct. For all she knew she could have been left somewhere even worse than anything she could imagine.

She remembered the white-painted room she and Jimmy found in the attic, its bleak, antiseptic appearance like that of an operating theatre, though its purpose was all too clearly that of torture and death. And she knew, deep down, this was probably out there too. That it was to something like that she was going to be taken when the lid was removed and they hoisted her out.

Why did you leave me, Jimmy Legg?

Why did you leave me?

She thought yet again of Jimmy's glance as he left the attic, his body stiff, alert to any threat from the men surrounding him as he pressed the gun tightly to his chest where they couldn't grab it. His eyes had barely looked at hers. And when they did they were cold. A dead man's eyes.

The eyes of a psychopath.

Which was why she knew she was fooling herself if she thought he had the slightest affection for her. He never had, she knew that now. Perhaps he wasn't even capable of grasping what the concept meant. To him were people just objects? Things to be used? Or killed? Or both?

No better than the bastards he had left her with.

The sound of footsteps heading towards her, echoing across the room outside, made Janice tense with apprehension. She stifled the urge to scream for help as her eyes strained against the darkness.

Someone touched the box. A moment later there was a bump, a whirring sound and she realised that someone was using an electric screwdriver to unseal the lid.

38

Jimmy made sure Maitland's hands and feet were securely fastened, then retied the gag. He did not want a repetition of the solicitor's attempt to free himself by chewing through his bonds, though he looked in too poor shape to be trying tricks like that for a while as Jimmy glanced over the man's badly cut-up body. Still, it was his fault. If he hadn't been evasive or tried to escape, Jimmy wouldn't have had to deal with him as severely as he had, though he knew, deep down, it would have taken little excuse to hurt the man. There was something about him that was begging for it.

Jimmy strode across the room. Upstairs, he took a long shower till every drop of Maitland's blood had been swilled from his body. Afterwards, he felt revitalised. And cleansed. He dried himself in Maitland's bedroom, where he regretted the solicitor was so much smaller than him. He could have done with a change of clothes. But the only things he could find that would fit were some pairs of socks. Jimmy's own extra clothes had all been left in a travel bag back at the hotel in Morecambe. With other things on his mind at the time, he had forgotten about them. Fortunately, his money and any documents he had brought with him were on his person. As for his clothes, he would replace them as soon as more pressing matters were out of the way.

Returning downstairs, Jimmy rummaged through the kitchen for something to eat. Finally, he decided on a three-egg omelette, some bacon and several slices of toast. He poured himself a mug of coffee and, although he didn't normally use it, added a couple of spoonfuls of sugar.

Afterwards he checked on Maitland again. The solicitor was still unconscious and breathing noisily. Jimmy wondered if he might have hurt him more than he thought, though he was not overly concerned. He would have preferred to keep him alive for a while in case he needed to question him, but it was not something he was bothered about.

In the meantime, he laid the Ordnance Survey map on a table, studying it till he was sure of his route to the farmhouse. Situated deep in the countryside to the south of Morecambe, he estimated it would take him half an hour to drive there from Maitland's house, perhaps less at this time of night.

In the hallway he found the solicitor's keys. Picking them up, he let himself out the front door and locked it behind him. For a moment he wondered whether to borrow Maitland's Alpha Romeo, but his own car was much less noticeable and certainly more than adequate for the short journey ahead. In the end he decided a low profile was better than an ego trip.

Checking to make sure he still had the gun in his pocket along with the knives, he returned to his car. A couple of minutes later he was on his way.

Heavy clouds hid what moon there was, which suited Jimmy; it would make it more difficult for anyone to see him when he arrived at the farmhouse. Though what he would do when he got there he was still uncertain. Even why he was going seemed blurred. Did he care that much for what happened to the girl? He hadn't cared that much about her when he left her at the hotel. He had gone with a clear conscience then. Or so he thought, he added to himself. He frowned, unwilling to go down that road. He had cared for someone once before and look what that cost him: an expensive divorce and a suspended sentence. But Janice seemed different. Like him she had been burdened with an oppressive mother. A mother who would have stifled and bullied her into being nothing more than an unpaid servant if she hadn't managed to get away and make a life of her own in London. Though he didn't think anyone's mother could match his own and, for all that Janice disliked hers, at least she wasn't a self-centred, alcoholic slut like his.

Rain swept in, making the night darker. He would be soaked within minutes of leaving the car. But even the most paranoid of people would hardly expect someone to be prowling about a place like the farmhouse in weather like this. Not that they would expect him in any case from the way he behaved when he left the hotel. Which was where his apparent callousness would give him an advantage. So far as the men were concerned (the Group, he added), he would be miles from here with other things on his mind than the fate of some girl he had already admitted to thinking about murdering.

The farmhouse was almost impossible to make out in the rain. As a result of which he drove past it before he realised where it was. Spotting a junction ahead of him, he pulled up, cursing angrily. The junction was well marked on the map and lay a mile and a half past the farmhouse. Carefully, he backed into the drive of a house further down the road, then headed back the way he had come. This time he kept a careful eye on his milometer and as soon as it started to reach a mile and a quarter he slowed to a crawl. Fortunately, there was no other traffic on the road. He could go as slow as he liked while he kept his eyes open. Sure enough, a few minutes later he saw it, a dim huddle of dark buildings in the distance. A tall, simple, wrought iron gate, set back several yards from the road, its outline blurred by coils of barbed wire, marked the entrance to its grounds.

Now that he knew where it was, Jimmy drove on till he reached the first turn off. Little more than a path for tractors, the narrow dirt track cut through the surrounding fields between an overgrown hedge and banks of trees. Deciding that this would do, he reversed the Fiesta onto the path and drove back far enough for the car to be hidden from the road. From here, invisible in the rain between the hawthorns that dominated the hedgerow on either side, he knew it would be safe from detection, especially when he switched off the lights.

Pulling a woollen hat on, Jimmy climbed out into the rain where he was instantly drenched. Though he slammed the car door shut behind him, he left it unlocked with the keys in the ignition, knowing that no one was likely to try and steal it here – if a banger like this was even worth stealing anyway. More importantly, he knew there was a chance he wouldn't have time to start fiddling with keys when he returned.

Head bowed beneath the downpour, he jogged down the path, turning left at the road. A few minutes later he was stood at the iron gate. Barely visible a hundred yards away across a rain-swept field, the dark bulks of the farmhouse and nearby barn were relieved only by a couple of lights near their doors. A concrete drive led from the gate towards them, where a broad yard separated the two buildings, on which he could make out several cars and a van.

A padlocked chain, too heavy to be forced open, secured the gate. The height of the gate itself and the barbed wire tangled round its outer frame made it impossible to climb, while the wall along the roadside was at least eight feet high. If he was to get in his only hope lay in finding a weakness somewhere around its boundaries.

Holding his hand above his eyes to shield them from the rain, Jimmy scanned the edge of the grounds. The nearest field was meadowland, with a drainage ditch along the hedgerow that divided it from the farmhouse and its acres of grounds. Getting into the meadow looked easy: the only barrier was a metal gate, wide enough for livestock to be herded through. As it was barely four feet high, he climbed it in seconds and was ankle deep in mud the next. What grass there was around the gate had been churned into a quagmire by the hooves of countless cattle that had passed through it. Cursing beneath his breath, Jimmy waded clumsily to firmer ground, then hobbled towards the hedgerow. Feeling along it, he found that a couple of lines of barbed wire had been threaded through the bushes to form a second barrier. Which was adequate enough where it was thick, but he suspected there would be sections where the hedgerow had been damaged, either by cows or because the soil underneath had given way.

Foot by foot, Jimmy felt his way along the bushes. Towards the end, the land dipped down towards a brook. It wasn't really much of a stream, little more than a few feet across, but it had eroded the land around the roots of the bushes closest to it, some of which had been exposed to the elements. A section there had begun to collapse. And, although there wasn't a gap as such, Jimmy could feel how weak the barrier was. Taking out one of the heavier knives he began to hack at the base of the hedgerow. Some of the roots were already dead and were so brittle he could snap them off with his fingers. The barbed wire strung through the branches above was looser here. Raising his foot, it did not take much effort to force the wires till they were crushed into the ground. Even though he had still not managed to clear more than a couple of feet for him to slide through, that would be enough. His clothes would take the brunt of the damage inflicted on him by the thorns.

Despite getting snagged again and again and hearing a long tear from his trousers, Jimmy finally managed to work his way through. Panting at the effort, he fell into a crouch on the far side to catch his breath while he kneaded his hands. Despite the thick leather of his gloves, thorns had managed to stab his flesh. In the meantime, he gazed around, trying to take in what he could of his surroundings. The ground was firmer underfoot on the other side of the hedge, though it was still very muddy. No animals had damaged the grass here, though, which was as tightly packed as a lawn. A short distance away loomed the unlit back of the farmhouse, impenetrably black in the darkness like a huge block of coal. To one side he could see the afterglow from the lights at the front.

Moving confidently, Jimmy sprinted to the building and began to feel his way along its granite and flint walls. Pausing, he listened for a moment at the kitchen door. There were no sounds inside, nor could he see a hint of light when he peered through the window. Carefully, he inched towards the corner of the building. Here he paused again, moving his head as gingerly as he could to peer around it, but there was no one in sight. The lamplight from outside the front door of the farmhouse and from the door into the barn shone across the vehicles parked in the space in between. There was a Land Rover, a Ford Mondeo and a couple of large estates, besides a dark blue transit van.

When he was satisfied there was no one here, Jimmy ran as quietly as he could to the vehicles, sheltering for a moment in the darkness between them, before moving to the barn. He shoved one hand into his coat pocket where he grasped the revolver.

Standing again, he sprinted towards the barn door, making as little sound as he could. He did not believe there would be no form of security here. There had to be something, if only a lookout. He was doubtful of Maitland's insistence they had no CCTV cameras or any other electronic devices hidden about the place. Maitland probably hoped he would blunder into one of these and get himself caught, which would null any fears he might have had about retribution. How the slimy solicitor would enjoy that, Jimmy thought, remembering some of the things he'd done to him. Tit for tat wouldn't come into it, he was sure.

Tensely, Jimmy circuited the barn, but the only entrances he saw had been bricked up or were far too heavily locked. Which left the door near the vehicles, which was sure to be guarded.

When he returned to the front of the barn, Jimmy wondered how many men were here. The five vehicles parked outside probably meant there were going to be at least that number, but undoubtedly there were more. Even though he still had a half dozen shells left in the gun, with another half dozen in his pocket, that was pushing things. After he used up what ammunition he had there would only be the knives to defend himself with. He wondered if any of the men would be armed. A shotgun or two wouldn't come as a surprise, especially in the countryside where they were common. In a struggle at night, where clear targets were hard to see, shotguns were probably more effective than a revolver.

His heart pounding, Jimmy gritted his teeth. He knew it was decision time. Either he went ahead now or backed off. If he carried on there would be no going back. But if he backed off, he knew there would still be consequences: what he had done to Maitland, what Janice would reveal about him – and the suspicious nature of the Group and their willingness to take violent action.

To have any chance against the odds stacked against him, Jimmy knew he would need a diversion, something that would give him an edge. Just forcing his way inside the barn, knowing nothing of what to expect once in, would be tantamount to suicide – and an agonising one at that if he was taken alive.

Jimmy glanced at the vehicles as an idea occurred to him. It was risky, and would bring more attention to this place than anyone wanted, but he knew he had nothing to lose. Even if he managed to keep a low profile till the bruises on his face had disappeared and avoided drawing attention to himself from the police over the murders in London, it would not take long for the men who had Janice to find out who he was from her. In a day or two they would be looking for him. He was certain of this. He knew too much. Especially when they discovered what he had done to Maitland. Even if Maitland died before he could reveal who had tortured him, it wouldn't take a genius to deduce it was just too much of a coincidence for it not to have been him.

If not just for Janice, he knew he had to do something. There was no way he could ignore these people and hope things would go on as before.

Prowling amongst the vehicles, Jimmy ignored the Land Rover. A glance showed it was diesel, so no use for his plan. Instead, he went to the Mondeo. Its fuel cap was locked. And, although for a moment he was sorely tempted to prise it off with one of the knives, he was far from sure it would work. And would probably risk making too much noise anyway. Instead, he went to the older of the estates. It was a Corsair, twenty years old at least. Luckily, its original petrol cap had been replaced with a plastic substitute, little more than a bung, which came off with no effort.

Jimmy unfastened his coat and cut away several lengths of material from his sweatshirt. Tying them together, he fed one end into the petrol tank. After leaving it long enough to soak up some of the petrol, he pulled it out and rolled the material into a ball so all of it was saturated with fuel.

By now his heart was pounding so heavily he felt as if he was on the verge of a heart attack as he carefully fed half of the material back into the fuel tank again, letting the remainder hang down the side of the car. He took out his cigarette lighter, cupped it in his hands against the wind and ignited it. Before the wind could blow it out again, he brushed the flame across the bottom of the material. Immediately it caught fire. So rapidly, in fact, it took him by surprise. White-faced, he leapt away as flames rushed like pale blue phantoms up the petrol-soaked fabric towards the fuel tank. Turning, Jimmy sprinted as fast as he could towards the edge of the barn, intent on using its solid wall as a shield from the blast, when he heard the explosion close behind him. A wave of intense heat thumped into his back, pushing him round the end of the barn and falling flat on his face on the grass.

Most of the force of the explosion soared skywards as the estate bucked, then split apart, and sheets of twisted metal, smouldering upholstery and burning plastic shot into the air. The heat intensified, and Jimmy kept his face back from the corner. There was a loud *crump* as the car close to it caught fire, adding to the heat.

The farmyard was engulfed with light. Shadows leapt across the grass, dancing like grotesque marionettes. Above the roar of the flames, Jimmy heard someone shout. Which was when he took the gun from his pocket. At that moment a man rushed round the corner. Perhaps he was looking for something with which to extinguish the fire. Maybe there were hosepipes on this side of the barn. Jimmy did not stop to think what the reason might be. Instead, instinctively, he struck, hitting the man across the temple with the barrel of his gun. The man fell without a sound. The next instant Jimmy leant over him, pummelling his head till his skull give way.

Immediately he was sure he was dead, Jimmy ran back to the barn. He was barely in time. Yelling: *'Hill! Hill! For damnation's sake, hurry up with that foam,'* a man rushed past the end of the barn. He was tall and stocky; a hospital coat hung open to reveal a dark tracksuit. He stopped in mid shout when he saw Jimmy in the shadows. A puzzled frown crossed his face, perhaps wondering if he was 'Hill', before Jimmy shot him. Which changed his frown to a look of bewilderment. Blood spread across his chest as he slumped to his knees, dead before his face hit the grass.

Three bullets left, Jimmy thought, the man forgotten as he turned the corner to the front of the barn. In one hand he had drawn the knife that had proved so effective against Maitland. It proved equally effective against the first of the men he encountered. With an easy underarm motion Jimmy jabbed it hard into the side of his neck.

In the confusion, even now no one had seen what was happening. As if invisible, Jimmy strode towards another of the men. Half blinded by the blazing cars, he didn't see Jimmy till the knife hit him in the throat.

Jimmy ran towards the barn and pushed open door into it.

Which was when he made an almost fatal mistake.

After the light of the fires, his eyes were unable to adjust quickly to the subdued light inside to see the man stood guard behind the doorway. The man, though, was only able to make Jimmy out as a silhouette. By the time he realised he wasn't looking at one of his comrades, the man's movements had already caught Jimmy's attention. Automatically, he sliced his knife in an arc before him. It struck the man's hands as he reached out to grab him. Screaming as the knife cut through his fingers he desperately tried to back away, but Jimmy pressed his attack, head butting him on the bridge of his nose, then stabbing the knife as hard as he could in his abdomen.

It was a lethal combination, followed by Jimmy, grinning fiercely, hitting the man again and again on the crown of the head with the barrel of the gun in a sudden, all consuming rage that almost obliterated everything else from his mind.

As he struggled to pull himself out of the frenzy, and almost reluctantly rose from the bloodied ruin of the man, Jimmy started to take in his surroundings. What he could see of the barn in the subdued light appeared to have been converted into an open-plan living area, with leather sofas and a scattering of tables. To the right of the entrance a flight of polished wooden stairs led to an upper floor. Perhaps a suite of bedrooms had originally been planned, but Jimmy suspected he'd find something totally different now as he headed towards the stairs, determined to see this through to the end.

Janice tensed as the lid slid open.

She had become so used to the utter darkness inside the box the light hurt her eyes.

Before she had time to take in what was happening, two pairs of hands grasped hold of her arms and shoulders and hauled her out. Her ankles were dragged across the rough edge of the box before someone grasped her feet and she was carried across the glaringly lit room.

Helpless, she could not stop herself from making what sounded even to her like pathetically inarticulate pleas for help.

Her mind was in a whirl as she was lowered onto a leather chair. Her soiled clothing clung to her lower body, cold and wet and rank with urine, and she could feel her teeth chatter. The next moment she was pulled to her feet again. Someone slid what felt like a knife through her clothing. It fell to her feet in a sodden heap, where it was just as quickly whisked away. Her arms were guided into the sleeves of a cotton-fibre dressing gown. Its belt was drawn about her waist, tied in a knot, before she was guided back to the chair. By now her eyes were beginning to adjust to the light, which was far from as bright as she first thought. She could see she was in a large, wood-panelled room. As she gazed about it, she realised it wasn't just large – it was huge, its far walls fading into the gloom more than thirty feet from her. In front of her a group of men stood watching. One was stuffing her soiled clothes into a bin bag. Three others stood in a line, their arms folded in contemplation. There was a dispassionate look in their eyes that chilled her despite the warmth of the dressing gown.

She recognised two of them as the fair-haired man and his darker companion who confronted Jimmy and her in the attic what seemed like ages ago now, though she knew it could not have been much more than twelve hours since it happened.

'Aren't you going to introduce yourselves?' Janice managed to croak, her throat parched. The effort used up all the bravado she could muster and she was unable to stop herself flinching like a whipped puppy when the dark haired man took a step towards her, even though he smiled.

'Conrad,' he said. 'Conrad Phillips. My colleague to the right,' he added, with an affectation of affability, indicating the fair-haired man, 'is Kingsley Wellington. And this,' to a taller, stockier man with short-cropped hair and a hard, brutal face, a hospital coat covering the dark tracksuit beneath, 'is our esteemed colleague, Doctor Montague Stephens.'

Janice wondered if any of these names were real. There was a grim look of suppressed merriment in Phillips' eyes that made her doubt it. It was the kind of cruel hoax she would have expected from them, coaxing her into a false sense of bonhomie.

'And your name?' Phillips asked. 'We never did get to formal introductions in your friend's hotel.'

So dry was her mouth it took Janice several attempts to blurt it out.

The man who called himself Kingsley Wellington walked away for a moment. He returned with a tumbler filled to the brim with iced-water and a slice of lemon.

'Sip it slowly,' he said in a mild voice, almost solicitous.

Though she despised what she was sure was sham concern, Janice needed the drink too much to care. At least for the moment she was not being hurt, which was all she was concerned about. And the longer she could prolong this state of affairs the better, she thought as she took a long, leisurely sip of the water, savouring the pleasure as it passed across the parched surface of her tongue.

'You must tell us more about yourself and how you came to fall in with your friend,' Phillips said with a hint of sarcasm. His dark eyes flashed interrogatively. 'It's not every day we bump into someone on the run from the police, suspected of murder. Nor who would so easily dump someone as lovely as you.'

Still mindful of the filthy clothes they had just cut from her, Janice resented the compliment. For a moment more she sipped the water, before lowering the glass from her lips.

'What do you want to know about him?' If it would buy her time or score some brownie points with her captors, she had no compunction about telling them everything they wanted to know about him. She didn't owe Jimmy anything now. Not after he deserted her. Janice felt tears burn the corners of her eyes when she thought about him, how his attitude had begun to change towards her and the air of menace she had started to feel towards the end, even before he left her to whatever fate she faced amongst these men.

Brushing a hand through his thinning hair, Kingsley Wellington – surely a name better fitted for a jazz musician, Janice thought, feeling its falsity grate her – drew up a chair and sat down, fastidiously crossing his legs. Phillips sat beside him, hunched forwards, his dark eyes attentive, while the taller man, Doctor Stephens, stood behind them, his face expressionless.

'Go ahead,' Wellington said. 'Start by telling us where he lives and what he does. Then how you became involved with him. And why you think he's on the run.'

For the next few minutes Janice talked, stopping only to freshen her throat with another drink of iced water, which Phillips immediately brought to her as if nothing mattered more to him than her well being. She had to keep reminding herself it was fake, that they did not care anything about her, only what she could tell them about Jimmy Legg, and that sooner or later she would be taken to replace the youth on the operating table, when any pretence of compassion or concern would disappear. She knew that part of why she was prepared to tell them what she knew about Jimmy was to repay him for his betrayal, especially since she would have never ended up in that wreck of a hotel if not for him. His abandonment hurt her emotionally more than she would have expected.

By the time she had finished she felt exhausted.

She looked up at the men, fully expecting that things would start to change now they had everything they wanted to know about Jimmy. To her surprise Wellington nodded his head as if in appreciation, and said:

'You must be starving, Miss Burroughs. When did you last eat?'

Flustered, Janice said:

'Last night sometime. Some crisps.'

Wellington shook his head.

'It's time we provided you with something. Don't you agree, Conrad?' He turned towards Phillips, who nodded his agreement.

Janice's eyes followed them, suspicious they were playing a spiteful trick.

But Phillips stood up.

'Would cold meat, bread and cheese be okay?' he asked.

Too uncertain about their motives to speak straight away, Janice nodded her head.

Phillips laughed.

'I don't think you trust us, do you?'

'Do you blame me?' Janice blurted. The question burst from her as an accusation.

'Not at all. Not at all. But you've only seen one side of us so far.'

'What other sides are there?'

Wellington interrupted. 'What was happening to the boy was part of it. An essential part, unfortunately. But a part, nevertheless. Sometimes necessity forces us to do things we would otherwise prefer not to do.'

Despite her fears and uncertainties, Janice felt compelled to say: 'What could force you to torture the boy like that?'

'I'll get you something to eat,' Phillips said, ignoring her question with a smile. 'You'll be able to take things in better on a full stomach. Would you like something to drink? Some tea, perhaps? Or coffee?'

Janice said: 'Coffee would be fine.' She settled back on her chair as Phillips wandered away. She watched the remaining men warily, certain they were only playing with her and any moment the reality of her situation would be revealed with devastating effect. Was this how they lulled the youth when he met them?

'When we found that room in the attic...' Janice said, her voice faltering.

Doctor Stephens frowned at her, but Wellington merely nodded his head in acknowledgement. 'Where you saw the boy,' he added, helpfully.

'We found bottles...' Somehow Janice found it impossible to go on.

'You found bottles that looked as if they were filled with blood?'

'It wasn't blood?'

Wellington laughed. 'Of course it was blood.'

Janice suddenly felt sick. 'But why?'

'Because we need it,' Phillips said as he returned with a tray. Janice saw a plate piled high with slices of ham, salami, a wedge of brie and some thickly buttered bread next to a mug of coffee. The coffee's aroma had already reached her, making her feel even more hungry than before. Phillips set the tray on a table close to her. 'Help yourself,' he said.

Janice needed no urging. Whatever they decided to do later, she would make the most of this opportunity. She had already passed through more fear while locked inside the box than she had experienced in her life. In a way she felt as if it had hardened her.

In less than ten minutes she had emptied the plate and drunk most of the coffee.

Phillips said: 'You were asking about the blood.'

Warily, Janice put down the mug and stared back at him. 'You said you needed it.'

'Sounds awful, doesn't it?' Phillips said.

'No more awful than what you were doing to the boy.'

The men exchanged glances. Janice was sure she could sense amusement pass between them, which only reinforced her certainty they were toying with her for perverse reasons of their own.

'You really think the boy was suffering?' Wellington asked.

'Is that a joke?' Janice heard her voice harden despite her fear, goaded by their arrogance. 'Of course he was suffering.'

'Perhaps you should see him.'

Janice felt her heart sink. This was it. No more pretence. No more poorly acted concern for her welfare. She was going to be taken to that operating table, certain the boy must have died and it was her turn to take his place.

'You have gone quite pale, Miss Burroughs,' Wellington said. 'Did my words surprise you?'

As if exasperated, Doctor Stephens broke in: 'Let's finish this charade. It's starting to get on my nerves.'

'You never have had much patience, Monty,' Wellington said reprovingly. 'On the other hand, perhaps you're right. We've teased our guest long enough.'

Janice felt herself tense as they approached her. Wellington took her by one arm.

'It would be better for you if you didn't resist or try to fight,' he warned. 'Either way you're going to go where we take you.'

Her muscles, though, were too weak suddenly for any

attempt at resistance. Janice felt as if she might faint as Wellington guided her to a staircase that led to the floor above. It was broad, with an air of luxury in stark contrast to the semi-derelict hotel of last night.

'This is just temporary,' Wellington said as if reading her thoughts. 'We would not normally work from here. But we couldn't risk staying where we were, not with your friend Legg on the loose, liable any minute to be picked up by the police. I don't suppose he would hesitate in telling them everything he'd seen of our activities, if only from spite.'

At the top of the stairs a corridor led to a series of finely-panelled doors. One of them was open, the room beyond brightly lit. Whatever furniture it might have contained before had been replaced by the hospital equipment Janice saw last night – including the operating table. Now empty, its opened manacles hung by its sides.

Of the emaciated boy there was no sign.

'He's dead, isn't he?' Janice said, wanting to resist the men as they guided her forwards, but feeling too weak to do anything. Her bowels felt as if they were going to release whatever they contained, however shameful that would be. She had thought she had become hardened, but the sight of the table filled her with such terror she could do nothing but stare at it.

'Dead?' Phillips chuckled.

Janice looked at him, shocked at his humour, when she caught sight of a slight figure in the corridor, stood between two men. The boy's face was so pale it was almost blue. Even from here she could see fine networks of veins across his forehead like the markings on a piece of high-quality marble. His deep sunk eyes were red around their edges as if they were bleeding; they looked desperately tired. Paradoxically, there was an unmistakable brightness to those eyes, as if a strange light lay behind them deep inside his skull.

Janice tensed at the sight, shocked more than if she had glimpsed the youth's corpse.

Phillips' chuckle deepened, though Doctor Stephens emitted a sigh of exasperation.

'Take the boy away,' he snapped at the men.

'Don't you think it fair our guest should have a chance to see the end product?' Phillips asked. 'It might help her endure what's ahead with equanimity.'

'Equanimity be damned,' Stephens said. 'I sometimes wonder if you take this seriously.'

'Oh, I do, Doctor, I do,' Phillips replied tersely, his face darkening. 'I help bankroll most of it, don't forget. Not only do I own this building, but without my money you'd still be grubbing about performing illegal abortions to finance yourself, with the police forever breathing down your fucking neck.'

'They might be doing that soon enough as it is,' Stephens said. 'I knew that hotel wasn't secure. Derelict or not, someone was bound to break in sooner or later. We should have had someone there all the time.'

'Gentlemen,' Wellington intervened, 'there's no need to squabble. We all appreciate how indebted we are to Conrad. If not for his East European contacts, not to mention his money, we would never have got as far as we have. Nor without your own medical skills, Doctor.'

A huge explosion, so close to the building it shook the walls, interrupted the conversation.

Though startled, Phillips reacted quickly. Even before the reverberation had begun to die down, he pushed Janice ahead of them into the room, then turned to the others, his face determined.

'Lock them in while we find out what the hell is going on,' he said.

A second explosion made them glance towards the stairs, where several people were shouting. A strong smell of petrol wafted towards them from below.

Hurriedly, the boy's guards bundled him into the room, then slammed the door. Janice heard a key being turned in the lock and the muffled sounds of Phillips' voice as he barked a tirade of orders on his way down the stairs. Unable to take in what was happening, except that she and the youth were alone, Janice stared at the boy. Wearing a dressing gown similar to her own, he looked more dead than alive. Yet his red-raw eyes returned her look with such intensity it took an effort of will to stop herself from turning away. It was not the look of a teenage boy. Nor anyone else she had ever seen. It worried and disturbed her. His face was expressionless except for a hint of hunger, understandable for someone as emaciated as him. Almost purple, his lips were more like lines drawn around the edges of his mouth; crevice-like wrinkles radiated from them, giving him a pinched, dried-up look, like an old man hidden inside a young man's face.

Janice tried to clear her throat to speak to him, but her vocal cords were frozen. Even the muscles of her neck were paralysed.

Gingerly at first, the boy moved forwards. His bare feet slid with faltering steps across the floorboards.

Janice felt a chill through the air as if there wasn't a degree of warmth in his body. When she saw his hands, Janice was shocked at the grey darkness of his nails. It was as if they had begun to decay underneath. Even the ends of his fingers, up to his knuckles, were blackened.

'What have they done to you?' Janice finally managed to say, though her voice sounded strangled. She felt pity for the boy's condition. At the same time, she felt afraid of him as he slowly bridged the gap between them.

He started to raise his arms as if he wanted to cling to her, to support him on his stick-like legs or to throw his arms around her in some sort of embrace. Despite her sense of pity for him, Janice was repulsed by him too. A part of her wanted to rebuke herself for it, but she was queasy at the look in his eyes and the repulsive way in which he had begun to open and close his lips.

'Don't,' she whispered, huskily, shaking her head. 'Please.' Though what it was she wanted him not to do she wasn't sure.

The boy moved nearer. The movements of his lips were more pronounced now, like some kind of fish.

Janice held one hand in front of her to stop him coming any nearer. His chest felt ice cold to her touch as he pressed against it. Immediately one of his hands moved towards her arm and she almost screamed when she felt the frigidity of his fingers as they closed around her wrist. They tightened with a strength she would never have expected the boy to have.

Frightened now, she tried to prise his hand from hers, but his other hand grasped her free wrist, pulling it towards him with frightening ease, and spreading her arms on either side as he moved in closer.

'No!' Janice shouted, terrified. 'No!'

There was a thump at the door.

A voice called: '*Janice!*'

The boy's face was only inches from her own – so near she choked on the rancid stink of his breath. His eyes were hypnotic as she stared into them. Responding to the voice outside, Janice cried: '*Here!*'

There was a second resounding bang on the door, accompanied by the sound of splintering as the lock gave way. Janice tried to force the youth away from her, when there was a third, louder bang and the door burst inwards. It crashed against the wall, where it hung off its hinges. Its lock had been ripped free and clattered to the floor.

Jimmy pushed past it, his face dishevelled. Soot and blood were daubed across his forehead and he looked in pain.

He moved jerkily, pumped with adrenalin, seeming to take in what was happening with a glance, though his eyes opened in astonishment when he saw the boy.

With two quick strides he was across the room. The already bloodied barrel of his gun whipped across the boy's head, spinning him sideways.

Jimmy grabbed hold of Janice's shoulders as she slumped in a faint.

'We've no time for that,' he said, his voice harsh from the smoke he'd inhaled. He slapped her cheeks to revive her. 'We have to get out of here fast.'

Which was when he felt nails sink into his leg.

40

The seafront of Morecambe, with so many businesses closed behind galvanised shutters, some of them so long they'd had posters pasted across them for events that had come and gone years ago, depressed DS McKenna as they drove along it. He recognised the thirties-style Midland Grand Hotel, out near the beach. He last saw it in an episode of *Poirot* on TV years ago. It had been recently renovated and looked brand new, its art deco walls glowing against the pale grey clouds above the sea.

'Wish the rest of the bloody town would follow suit,' Detective Sergeant Mason from the local police told him when he caught sight of his companion staring at the hotel. 'Though they've been saying that for years and it doesn't seem to have got much better.'

'Bloody shame,' McKenna said.

'The whole town is a bloody shame these days. If something's not done in the next few years, it'll be on its last legs. If it isn't already. The trouble is it tried to compete with Blackpool. This is what results from coming a poor second. Winner takes all, lock, stock and barrel.'

They pulled up a few minutes later. Mason guided McKenna away from the Promenade onto a cramped side street. Tape still sealed the area around the blackened front of the gutted building. A uniformed policeman stood guard outside, looking cold and bored.

'Another of the resort's hotels bites the dust,' McKenna said.

'Hardly the same class as the Grand, I'm afraid.'

'Hardly. Still, it'll leave an ugly gap.'

'It was an ugly gap before it burned, believe me. It was run into the ground years ago. Mismanagement, laziness, lack of money, from what I can gather all compounded to make this an eyesore for far too long.'

'Not as if you haven't enough already,' McKenna said. 'If you don't mind me saying.'

'Don't worry about hurting my feelings. You can't say anything I haven't said dozens of times already till my wife's grown sick of hearing me go on about it. And in stronger language too, I'd add.'

'Was the building insured?'

'We're trying to find out. The owner lives in your neck of the woods. We've been trying to contact the solicitor who dealt with the probate – it changed hands a year or so back after the previous owner, his mother died – but we've not been able to track him down. His staff keep saying he's out.'

'Do you think he's trying to avoid us?' McKenna asked.

'Doubt it. He's well established. We'll get hold of him, don't you worry. Though it might take time.'

McKenna gazed towards the seafront. 'Look's as if there's a storm brewing.'

'Heavy rain's forecast for tonight. For once I think they're right.' Mason glanced at his wristwatch. 'It's nearly six. There's not much more we can do today. It'll be dark soon. What do you say to a pint and a bite?'

'I think I'd say yes.' McKenna grinned. 'It was a bit of a rush getting here. I couldn't manage to get more than a cheese sandwich on the train.'

Mason drove them to a pub halfway between Morecambe and Lancaster which served food all day long, mainly to families from what McKenna could see, with a fake Olde Worlde look to it. It was large but discrete enough for them to sit down and enjoy a meal and a couple of drinks and talk shop in privacy. Mason was interested in hearing everything McKenna could tell him about the murders in London.

'Do you think there's much of a case against Legg?' the sergeant asked when McKenna had almost exhausted the subject and paused to take a drink of his beer.

'It's circumstantial at the moment. DNA tests might clinch it. Our problem was we didn't have any suspects before. At least we've a chance if Legg's our man.'

'You've doubts?'

'Only because of this business in Morecambe. If he wanted to disappear without drawing attention to himself setting fire to the hotel would be the last thing he'd do. It doesn't make sense.'

'For the insurance perhaps – if he did it, of course.'

'But why? If he wanted a low profile, at least till any bruises from his battering in London had cleared, that would be the last thing he'd want to do.'

'Desperation?'

'Financial? I didn't think things were that bad for him. He's a reasonably successful business in London. Not as big as he had at one time, but growing.'

'Of course we're missing a crucial fact.'

'Which is?'

'If he is the strangler, he's off his head. You don't go around doing that sort of thing if you're operating off a full six-pack.'

'Good point,' McKenna said, before Mason's mobile started to beep.

Answering it, the policeman nodded his head to whoever was speaking on the other end, then said: 'Righto. We'll be on our way.' He looked up at McKenna. 'I don't know whether this is anything to do with our man, but we've just had word about explosions and sounds of gunfire not far from here. A Tactical Aid Squad's on its way. There's a police helicopter already there.'

Leaving their drinks, Mason settled their bill at the bar, then they hurried outside to his car. 'I've a couple of bullet proof vests in the boot. I put them there as soon as I heard Legg had a gun on him.'

'Either of them XXL?' McKenna asked, patting his stomach.

41

'What the fucking hell is he?'

Jimmy grabbed hold of the boy's wrists, wrenching his fingers from his leg. He grunted at the pain as nail after nail was extracted from the muscles of his calf. He could scarcely believe how much strength he had to exert to do it. The boy's fingernails had dug deep and he could feel blood trickle down his leg even as he forced him away. With a final effort he pushed the boy backwards so hard that he fell against the wall. Jimmy reached for the gun he'd discarded in order to free himself from his grip. It had seemed an easy matter, otherwise he would have been tempted to pound the boy about the head with the gun instead or used his knife, but the skinny-looking youth had not looked strong. Staring at him in disbelief, Jimmy was sure there was no way those fleshless arms should have had any strength in them at all, let alone the brute power he'd felt.

Janice called out a warning. Jimmy barely had time in which to turn and fire at the man who launched himself from the doorway.

One more fucking bullet wasted, Jimmy thought, as the man fell to the floor with a wound that took away half the top of his skull. Janice vomited as blood and brains sprayed across the room behind him.

'Never mind that.' Jimmy grabbed her arm. 'Let's get out of here before any more of the fuckers appear.'

'What about the boy?' Janice asked, still shaken, her face deathly white.

Jimmy looked at her incredulously. 'Fuck him. Why should we bother about that mad bastard?'

'Look at him, Jimmy.' Janice pointed. The boy's dressing gown had fallen open across his chest. Sharp mounds where his ribs thrust through parsimonious layers of flesh were etched with cuts, some of them so old they were scars. Others looked raw where scabs had recently pealed from them.

Jimmy aimed the gun in the youth's direction. The boy had begun to pick himself up off the floor, his legs moving into a crouch that Jimmy could tell was intended to help him spring at him. Perhaps recognising the stopping power of the gun, the boy stared warily, tensed but still.

'He's a victim, Jimmy. Like me. And you, if they ever get their hands on you.'

'What do you want me to do? Let him hang on my back with those fucking nails while we dash out of here?' He shook his head. 'It's you – alone. I'm not sinking our chances for some half-crazed lad, whoever's fault it is he's gone insane.'

There was another explosion, and Jimmy guessed the blaze must have spread to more of the vehicles.

'That'll give us a few minutes,' he said. 'We'd be idiots to waste them.' He tightened his grip on Janice's arm and pulled her towards him, the gun still trained on the feral youth. For a moment she tried to resist, but she knew he was right. They might not have much chance of getting out – with the boy they would probably have none. However much she wanted to help the youth, she knew that Jimmy was right.

Stumbling past the body of the man Jimmy had shot, they hurried through the doorway. The boy's mouth opened wider, and Janice saw rows of jagged teeth inside. They no longer looked human, more like those of some undersea beast.

'Keep moving,' Jimmy said. 'If he comes for us I'll have to shoot him.'

The bottom of the stairs was hidden by smoke. Jimmy wondered if the wind had changed direction and begun to blow from the blazing vehicles towards the barn. Which would increase their chances of getting past the rest of the men. Most of them would be outside now, away from the fumes that were filling this end of the barn. Perhaps some had decided to cut and run before the police arrived, which they certainly would in the next few minutes.

Trying to breathe as little of the smoke as he could, Jimmy guided Janice through the building, away from the worst of it. The noxious fumes were choking them, and he knew they couldn't breathe them for long. Already he could feel a racking cough deep in his lungs, while his throat and lips were beginning to burn. Though dim, what light there was had become even gloomier as more clouds of smoke billowed from the car park. When he looked back Jimmy had the bizarre impression he glimpsed something leap through the fumes, but he couldn't be sure. Not only was the visibility bad but the smoke was starting to sting his eyes, making them run.

It only took a couple of minutes to reach the far end of the barn. Jimmy recognised the wooden door that led outside. He had seen it earlier when he skirted the building, looking for a way in, but had not been able to open it. Now he could see it was locked by a heavy iron bar on the inside, which he slid to one side. The next moment they were in the open. With a sense of relief, he breathed in the rain-filled air, away from the smoke. For a few long seconds he allowed Janice the luxury of filling her lungs, then said: 'We have to keep moving. They'll soon find out you've gone.' He pointed to the farmhouse. 'Over there. That's our way out of here.'

Janice nodded. Though exhausted, with no shoes on her feet or wearing only a dressing gown, she was ready to keep going.

The blazing cars made the gloom at the far end of the barn even darker as they darted towards the farmhouse. From there they ran across the short patch of meadowland to where Jimmy had made a gap in the hedgerow. Despite the darkness, it only took them a few minutes to find it by touch. Conscious of Janice's flimsier clothing, he pushed as many of the branches to one side as he could for her to squeeze past. Before following her, he glanced at the farmhouse. For a moment he thought someone must have unleashed a dog, though he hadn't heard it bark, sure he saw something large, the size of a hound lope towards them. Quickly, Jimmy closed the gap in the hedgerow, then dug up the strands of barbed wire from where he'd forced them into the ground. Hoping they would be strong enough to block the gap, he turned, took Janice by one arm and guided her towards the road. The flames from the vehicles were burning fiercely, and Jimmy was sure no one near any of the cars would be able to see what was going on at the hedge. Not until they headed down the road to where he'd hidden the car would there be any risk of being seen. Even then he hoped the men would be too distracted by the fires to pay attention to what was happening outside.

A distant, resonant thrumming noise from high in the sky to the south drew Jimmy's attention as they clambered over the five-bar gate.

'A helicopter?' Janice asked.

'Probably the police. Come to see what's going on,' he said, dryly. He helped Janice down. Her feet were thick with mud and she moved slowly as stones in the ground dug into them. 'We're going to have to hurry,' he told her. 'Are you up to it?'

Janice was tempted to say he could leave her now. Once the police arrived she would be safe. Unlike Jimmy she had no reason to be on the run. But she held her tongue, uncertain how he would take the suggestion. After how he deserted her in the hotel, he could hardly accuse her of doing the same. Though whether he would look at it the same way she was far from sure. And, whatever his reasons might be, he had come to rescue her.

They had only gone a short distance down the road when Janice had to hobble. The soles of her feet felt flayed by the rough ground. Tucking the gun into a pocket of his coat, Jimmy swung one arm around her, helping to take some of the weight off her feet.

'Quickly. It's not far now,' he said.

There were shouts from the fires. To Janice they sounded as if someone had spotted them, but she knew this was probably her imagination. It was so dark along the road they could hardly be seen.

But there was a presence. A presence behind them. It was not something she could hear but something she sensed, like a shiver running down the centre of her spine.

Janice tugged herself free from Jimmy's arm.

'Back there,' she said.

Jimmy turned. His hand automatically reached for the gun when he saw the boy heading towards them.

'What the fuck is he doing?'

Down on all fours like a strange, misshapen beast, the youth was loping across the ground. Hung from one arm, he dragged his dressing gown behind him, the rest of his body exposed. It was thin and white, skeletal in the darkness.

Jimmy felt his hair rise as he watched him. The boy was unnatural, as if whatever had been done to him had stripped away his humanity. Jimmy tugged out the gun, reluctant to waste one of the last two bullets on the boy. Yet he looked so loathsome, so vile, so disgustingly grotesque. Jimmy gritted his teeth and took aim.

'No, Jimmy, *no!*'

He glared at Janice.

'We haven't time for this shit,' he said. Yet, as the boy closed the gap with quick, jerky, spastic movements, Jimmy took his finger off the trigger. At the last possible moment, he swung the gun at the boy's head, hitting him squarely between the eyes, hoping it would knock him out.

The boy collapsed onto the ground.

Whether he was dead or alive, Jimmy neither knew nor cared.

'Let's get out of here before anyone else comes after us,' he said. 'Another few yards and we'll be at the car.'

Janice nodded, though she stared at the boy's body, unsure if he was breathing or not.

'Now,' Jimmy told her. 'Janice!'

'The boy,' Janice said. 'We can't leave him.'

'What?' Jimmy was incredulous. 'Why the fuck not? You've seen him. He's gone completely mad.'

'He's a boy. They tortured him.'

'They did something to him.' Jimmy stared at the crumpled body. 'Though he might be useful,' he added as an afterthought. 'A bargaining chip. If things turn sour.'

'What do you mean?'

'Never mind.' Jimmy hoisted the boy over his shoulder, hardly noticing the weight. He couldn't have weighed more than a couple of stones. 'Now move. If a police car comes down the road, the sight of you in your dressing gown and me with this creep over my shoulder will be sure to catch their attention.'

They ran towards the lane. As they neared it, Janice managed to ignore the pain in her feet, while Jimmy was barely slowed by the boy's body.

The moment they reached the car, Jimmy unlocked the boot.

'No arguing,' he said, when Janice started to protest as he bundled the boy into it, though he carefully arranged an oil-stained blanket into a makeshift pillow beneath his head. 'I can't risk him coming to in the car and going berserk. You saw how violent he is. Would you like to tackle him while I'm driving?'

He found an old length of towrope, which he tied around the boy's wrists and ankles, then slammed the lid shut. Seconds later they drove away, heading back towards Morecambe. Barely a mile down the road a fire engine passed in the opposite direction, its lights flashing. This was followed seconds later by a line of police cars and more fire engines.

'Looks like things will be heating up for our friends back there,' Jimmy said.

When Janice looked at him she saw he was grinning.

42

'Where's Stephens?' the man who had called himself Conrad Phillips asked as Wellington strode in, his face blotched with soot.

'Dead. Some bastard shot him.'

'Shit!' Phillips turned on his heel, taking in the bedlam all around them. Three of the vehicles were still ablaze.

'Who do you think did it?' Wellington asked.

'God knows. MI5. The Yanks. The fucking Russians.'

Wellington shook his head.

'I don't think so. We'd be dead if it was. Or trussed like fucking Christmas turkeys on our way to be interrogated.'

Phillips nodded his agreement. 'Which narrows it down,' he said angrily.

'Narrows it down to one. It must be Legg. Who else could it be?'

'I knew we should have finished him off in the hotel. It was a mistake to let him go.'

'Who'd have thought he'd have the balls to do something like this.'

'Or be able to find out where we are.'

'How the hell could he?'

'There's only one way,' Phillips said. 'Maitland. There's no one else he'd have any connection with who knows us. Maitland handled the hotel for Legg. He's the one he must have gone to. Somehow he made him talk.'

A short, heavily built man with Slavonic features ran over, coughing from the fumes. 'The boy is gone,' he told the men in stilted English.

'You sure?' Phillips asked.

'*Da*. Grigor dead. Shot. No one there now. No boy. No girl. *Nichevo*.'

'It has to have been Legg,' Wellington said. 'Who else would have taken the girl?'

Phillips looked at the sky. In the distance he could see the lights of an approaching helicopter. It was still several miles away, but nearing quickly.

'Time we were away from here. The place will be swarming

with police in another few minutes.'

Wellington agreed. 'I've set the detonators. As soon as we leave it'll go up in smoke. Nothing left to link any of us to it.'

'Nor me either. Fortunately, the registered owner is a fake company I set up years ago. The trail dies there. And soon, so will Legg.'

43

'Where are we off to?' Janice asked as Jimmy drove.

'Somewhere temporary, so I can get rid of anything that links us to this. Some clothes for you. Men's, I'm afraid, but they'll have to do till we can get something different. Some food and drink. Then away.'

'Where to? I know we can't go on the run forever, but those men back there, they know who I am, where I live. They know about you.'

Jimmy glanced at her, his face inscrutable in the dark.

'I couldn't help it, Jimmy. I thought I was going to end up like the boy.'

'You probably would have.' He shook his head angrily. 'It's not your fault,' he said, gruffly. 'I shouldn't have left you with them.'

'Was there any choice?'

He shrugged. 'Maybe not.'

Jimmy lapsed into silence as he headed to Maitland's house. It was not long before he had parked down the cul-de-sac again. This time he turned into Maitland's drive. Although it was quiet, he wanted to minimise any chance of Janice or the boy being seen in their dressing gowns by any of the neighbours.

Jimmy climbed out first to unlock the front door and make sure Maitland was still tied up. In the event, though the solicitor had regained consciousness, all he had been able to do was wriggle across the floor to the edge of the sofa. When he saw Jimmy stride into the room, his eyes stared up in alarm, flinching as Jimmy checked his bonds. Once he was satisfied they were secure, Jimmy patted Maitland on the head, then returned to the car, where he helped Janice out and directed her to the front door, before stepping to the boot. While Janice hobbled towards the house, Jimmy pulled the gun from his pocket, keeping his finger away from the trigger. If the boy was awake and tried to attack him, he knew he could subdue him without having to use the gun other than as a club. The boy might be stronger than he looked, but Jimmy was confident he was more than capable of dealing with him. Even so, he found himself holding his breath when he unlocked the boot. As he tugged it open he took a step back and tightened his grip on the gun, raised, ready to swing at the boy.

Inside the boot the boy was unconscious. A line of blood had trickled from his head where Jimmy hit him. It looked black in the gloom. With a satisfied grunt, Jimmy rolled the boy over, gripped him tightly and pulled him up. He barely moved as Jimmy carried him down the drive into the house, where Janice was waiting for him.

Jimmy stepped past her into the living room, where he lowered the boy onto the carpet. Maitland stiffened when he saw him. Agitated, the man shook his head from side to side, struggling with the gag Jimmy had tied across his mouth. The fear in his eyes didn't need any words to elaborate. His terror of the boy was all too obvious. Jimmy smiled down at him, tempted to move the boy nearer. At the same time, he wondered what it was about him that scared Maitland so much.

But there would be time to find out later. In the meantime, he decided to leave Maitland to his terrors to soften him up.

Jimmy returned to the hallway, taking Janice upstairs where he showed her into Maitland's bedroom.

'He's about your size, so help yourself to any of his clothes. Don't worry about taking them. He's one of the bastards who had you carted to the barn. It's through him I found out where you were.'

Back downstairs, Jimmy went into the kitchen. Inside the freezer he found a couple of pizzas, which he put in the oven. Quarter of an hour later they would be ready. Which, he expected, would be just about the time when Janice finally found something to wear from Maitland's wardrobe.

As it happened, he had only just taken the pizzas out of the oven and put them on the kitchen table when he heard her come downstairs.

'Something smells delicious,' she said as she stepped into the kitchen.

Jimmy was surprised how quickly she seemed to have recovered, though he knew this could be deceptive. She'd had time to wash her face and brush her hair, as well as put on a pair of cream-coloured slacks, which fitted her slim figure almost perfectly. With a thick jumper and a pair of Maitland's socks and shoes on her feet, she did not look as odd as Jimmy had expected, and he smiled appreciatively.

'Perhaps I'm going a bit strange,' he said, 'but you look fetching in that outfit.'

Janice smiled, though the action felt strained. And she could not help wondering what Jimmy's definition of 'a bit strange' was. But the appetising smell of pepperoni pizzas and mugs of coffee claimed priority. She felt as if she hadn't eaten in weeks – and wasn't even sure if one pizza would be enough.

As if reading her thoughts, Jimmy said: 'There's plenty of bread if you want some. Our friend in there doesn't skimp on food. Though it's mostly ready meals. I don't think he's much of a chef.'

As soon as they'd finished, Jimmy put aside his emptied mug and said he would have a few more words with Maitland.

Janice insisted that she went with him. Though she did not look forward to seeing Jimmy's interrogation methods, she didn't want to miss finding out what was going on.

By the time they walked into the living room, Maitland seemed to have worked himself up into a state verging on blind panic. The boy was awake again and was staring at the solicitor with wide, blood-shot eyes that never blinked, as if he was trying to hypnotise the man.

'Well, well, well,' Jimmy said with mock amusement as he looked down at them. 'I see you've been getting acquainted with each other. Or is that re-acquainted?' he added sarcastically. He bent down and tugged Maitland's gag from his mouth, none too gently.

The solicitor spluttered as he spat out shreds of material he'd chewed in an effort to rid himself of it.

'You're mad bringing that thing here,' Maitland managed to blurt out at last, his voice cracking.

'That *thing*?' Jimmy tutted solicitously. 'I thought you and your colleagues were responsible for what's happened to the boy. Now you call him 'that thing'?'

'I don't know everything about him. What I do is enough for me not to want that creature anywhere near me.'

'I bet you do,' Jimmy said. 'And I bet you've a pair of sharp little ears. Just so long as you do some talking, you might be able to keep them,' he added, extracting a knife from his coat pocket. There was still blood on it.

Maitland nodded energetically. 'Whatever you want to know.'

Jimmy chuckled, though there was no humour in the sound. 'For a start off, Maitland, why are you frightened of him? He's only a boy. For God's sake, I could lift him with one hand after the way you and your friends have starved him.'

'He's not been starved. He's like he is because that's his natural state.'

'His natural state?'

'It's hard to explain. And I don't know all of it. It goes back years ago in Romania. In the late eighties. The final years of Caeusescu, before his fall. There was an institute run by the *Securitati*, the secret police. During a raid in a remote village in one of the mountain ranges something was discovered that had always been thought a myth, a superstition. No one realised what they had found at first. They knew soon enough.'

'Which was?'

'A vampire,' Maitland said, matter-of-factly, perhaps to add credibility to his words.

'*A vampire?*' Jimmy exploded with laughter. 'Are you trying to tell me all of this has something to do with Vlad the Impaler and all that shit?'

Maitland shook his head vigorously. 'Not vampires like that. Not supernatural. But what the myths are based on. The reality. The nitty gritty. The facts.'

'You're saying this boy has something to do with that?' Janice asked.

'This 'boy',' Maitland said, with emphasis, 'is everything to do with that. After Caeusescu was shot, things went to shit. Anyone connected with the secret police had to look to their own future. Some ended up in the Romanian mafia. Others got out of there. Those who'd less to hide about their pasts ended up in the new security services.'

'And your pals?' Jimmy asked.

'Some of them decided to go into business for themselves. They provided much of the money. And know how.'

'Know how about what?'

'About vampires.'

Jimmy exploded with laughter again. 'Now I know you're trying to take the piss.' He leaned forward, tilting the point of the knife towards Maitland's face. 'Much though you're giving me lots of amusement, it's facts, not bullshit, I want.'

'This isn't bullshit,' Maitland insisted, his eyes desperate as he stared at the knife. 'Somehow, in some way, they discovered there's a virus. It comes through the blood. A bite, mixing blood and saliva, is enough. Once it's in the bloodstream, it destroys the upper functions of the brain. Those affected are reliant on the primitive parts, the amygdala, the reptile brain, which is where our instinctive reactions come from. But it does more than that. It compensates the body with greater powers of regeneration. You've seen the cuts on the boy's body. How old do you think they are?'

Jimmy shook his head, uncertain whether Maitland was telling him lies – and whether he should end them now by giving him a taste of the knife just to set him back on course.

'None of them are more than a few days old. What look like scars are the oldest. In a few days they'll have gone. You could stab him now and in a few hours the wound will have started to heal. Inside a week you wouldn't be able to find any trace of it.'

'But why?' Janice asked, more willing than Jimmy to accept at face value what he was saying.

'It's a modern day plague. It would destroy society from within with anarchy,' Maitland said. 'Things were getting desperate for the Reds by the mid eighties. The writing was on the wall. The West was winning. After running Romania for twenty odd years Caeusescu wasn't going to give up without a fight. Perhaps he had an idea what his fate would be if he fell. This was just one of many wild schemes being dreamt up then to cause havoc in the West. They hoped to be able to refine the virus so it would spread like wildfire, turning its victims into mindless, ravenous, blood-sucking maniacs – maniacs that would infect every victim they bit, spreading their sickness more rapidly than any plague in history. And with maniacs it would be hard to kill, whose wounds would heal. It was calculated that if enough people were initially infected, it could spiral out of control within days, wrecking the infrastructure of any country struck by it. Britain, France, Germany – even the US – would collapse within weeks. Some even suggested Caeusescu was tempted to use it on the Soviets. They'd become less friendly under Gorbachev and were letting him down. Before any of these countries could know what kind of threat had hit them, they would be weakened disastrously. Only Romania, knowing exactly how to deal with these things, would remain unscathed, unweakened. Not only this, but the Romanian people, seeing their country miraculously protected against something that was destroying the rest of the world, would regard Caeusescu as their saviour, strengthening his position even further.'

'But Ceausescu's downfall came before any of this could be done?' Jimmy asked.

'The experiments were finished. The refinements ready. But time ran out. The next thing Caeusescu knew he and his charming wife, Elena, were being shoved in front of a firing squad.'

'And good riddance to them,' Janice said, 'if that was what they were planning to do.'

'*If*,' Jimmy added, far from convinced. 'That's a fucking good word: *if*. I like it.'

'There is no 'if',' Maitland said with a mixture of exasperation and fear.

'So you claim.' Jimmy relaxed a little, leaning back. 'But why torture the boy? And why do it inside my hotel?'

'Where better than a down-at-heel seaside resort in a closed hotel? The boy was a runaway. No one, not even his own mother, knows or cares where he is or what's happened to him.'

'Why torture him?' Janice said.

'He wasn't tortured. As such. The treatment was all but ready. All that was needed was someone in whom it could take root. Tests had to be made. I've told you about the regenerative powers of the infection. They had to make sure these worked. And lasted. The next stage was to make sure the infection could be spread by him. And to see how rapidly it would take to have an effect.'

'And that would have been me?' Janice asked.

'If not you, another runaway would have been enticed to the hotel. Your presence saved them that trouble – though it did lose us the use of the place. We couldn't risk anyone finding out what was going on after you left it,' Maitland said with a nod at Jimmy. 'Everyone expected you to be caught by the police and were certain you wouldn't hesitate telling them what happened to your girlfriend. And what you'd seen.'

'So you're telling us the boy's been infected by this vampire virus?' Jimmy asked, sceptically. 'That he's a vampire himself?'

Maitland nodded.

'And it's affected his brain?' Janice said, horrified at what Maitland claimed.

'It's part of the process. His higher brain, the parts that are used for logical thinking, are killed by the virus – or damaged beyond use – I don't know for sure. No one explained that to me. All I know is those parts are not used or useable again. Which is why the savage, primitive part takes over, with just its base instincts.'

Janice glanced at the boy. He was so still, crouched there with the ropes around his wrists and ankles, it was difficult for her to see anything truly savage or violent in him, even though she could remember the bizarre loping with which he pursued them along the road before launching himself at Jimmy. Only his eyes disturbed her, steadily fixed on the Maitland's face. And perhaps his mouth; she remembered the odd way in which he opened and shut it, and the jagged rows of teeth.

'I think you're telling us a load of shit,' Jimmy said, finally.

'It's the truth,' Maitland insisted, sweating again. 'Why do you think I reacted like I did when you dumped the brute so close to me?'

'Because you were frightened he'd crawl over and bite through his gag – then bite you too?' Jimmy smiled slowly. It was a smile that sent a shiver down Janice's spine. It appeared to have the same affect on Maitland too, who squirmed uncomfortably within the limits of the ropes binding him.

'What are you thinking of doing, Jimmy?' Janice asked.

He glanced at her, shrugged, then looked at Maitland.

'There's one way you could convince me this bullshit is true.'

Maitland's face trembled. 'Don't be a fool. You don't know what you'd be tampering with.'

'I think I do,' Jimmy said.

Janice laid a hand on Jimmy's arm. 'What are you thinking of?'

'Finding out whether this vampire crap is true or not, that's all.' There was a gleam in his eyes that showed how much he was enjoying himself. The more frightened Maitland looked the more pleasure he seemed to feel. With slow deliberation Jimmy rose, then stepped towards the boy. For an instant the youth's eyes turned from Maitland and looked at Jimmy, and Janice was certain she could see a smile spread across the boy's face beneath the gag.

'Do you think this is a good idea?' Janice asked, feeling anxious.

Jimmy ignored her question. Instead he reached behind the boy's head and untied the gag. It fell away, sodden with saliva and a streak of blood. Janice saw once more the small, sharp, nasty-looking teeth that reminded her of the mouth of a piranha.

'Nasty looking set of gnashers, hasn't he?' Jimmy said, as if he was amused by them. He turned towards Maitland. 'Vampire teeth?' he asked. 'I thought they had fangs, not fuckin' coffin nails like these.'

'You know nothing about it.' Maitland sounded even more desperate now; his face was streaked with beads of sweat. 'I don't know much, but I know enough not to mess with him. Not like this. Not just the three of us.'

'Do you think he might be too much of a handful for me to cope with?' Jimmy asked.

'If you knew more about him you wouldn't ask.'

'Jimmy,' Janice said. She touched his arm once more to restrain him, but he shrugged her off, saying: 'Leave it to me. I can handle this.'

'No,' Maitland said.

Jimmy reached for the boy. Taking a hold of him round the waist, he effortlessly lifted him from the floor at arms length.

'Look, Mr Legg,' Maitland stuttered; his body strained against his bonds, 'there's money in all of this. Lots of money. More money than you could ever dream of.'

'What money? And why? From having this boy at a freak show? I didn't know there was anything to be made these days in that sort of thing. Didn't that go out with the Elephant Man?'

'Not a freak show. Nothing like that. It's the plague. The destruction it can cause. There are people – countries, *foreign* governments, terrorists – who would pay a fortune for this. It's like nothing anyone's ever seen before. More destructive than a nuclear bomb. And easier to set off. All we need is get the infection into a country, make sure enough people are given it and let loose hell. What do you think the North Koreans would pay to be able to unleash something like this on the United States? Or Al-Qaida? Or Iran? Or Syria? There are countries that would dearly love to use a weapon like this, especially when no one would know who to blame.'

'Is that what you and your pals are planning? To sell this as a fucking weapon? To kill thousands? Hundreds of thousands? Millions, perhaps?' Jimmy whistled appreciatively. 'Puts what some people suspect me of doing into perspective, doesn't it, Janice? Somewhat, at least.' His smile twisted wryly. His humourless eyes stared down at Maitland. 'What use would all that money be to me? Your pals wouldn't split it. I'd be lucky if they didn't pump a few grams of the shit into me. Rot my brain and set me free. Janice, too. Though, likely, we'd end up with bullets in our heads.' Jimmy's voice deepened as he lowered the boy onto the carpet close to Maitland, who jerked away from him, his eyes starting from his head as he stared at the boy's mouth. His lips opened slightly to reveal his teeth. Small and sharp, like thick, white, odd-sized needles. Saliva and blood drooled from them to drip down the narrow edges of his jaw.

'Jimmy!' Janice's voice cracked with fear and nausea. 'You can't!'

'Can't I?' He looked at her with a look of disdain.

Which was when the rope he had fastened about the boy's wrists snapped.

'Doesn't look like this has anything to do with your suspect,' Detective Sergeant Mason said when he returned to McKenna. There was still so much smoke in the air breathing was unpleasant and McKenna found himself having to suppress a coughing fit. Most of what had once been a barn was now no more than smouldering timbers. Clouds of smoke were still pouring out of the roof and windows of a nearby farmhouse, though the fire engines surrounding it had managed to dampen the flames that had still been raging when the policemen arrived a short while ago.

'Will they save much of it; do you think?' McKenna asked.

Mason shook his head dourly. 'Whoever started these fires made a good job of it.'

'What about witnesses? There were reports of gunfire.'

'Which is certain. One report was from a local farmer. He's a shotgun licence and does a bit of target practice with a rifle at the local gun club, so he knows what he's talking about. He says what he heard was one clear shot outside and a second, more muffled shot a few minutes later, possibly inside the barn. He doesn't think they came from a shotgun or a rifle. From what he remembers he reckons it sounded like a pistol.'

'Which could make it Legg. A handgun was used in London.'

'But what would he have to do with this place? Burning down his hotel for the insurance, that makes some sort of sense. But, unless he owns any of these as well, what would he have to gain?'

McKenna admitted this puzzled him. 'You're probably right. It probably hasn't got anything at all to do with him.'

McKenna stared about the desolated area, with its burned out cars and gutted buildings, the smell of burnt petrol still strong in the air, along with falling flakes of ash. He did not know why, but somehow he could sense Legg here. Contrary to evidence and commonsense, he couldn't dismiss the thought that this second act of arson within twenty-four hours was connected with him.

But how?

And why?

Crammed in one car, the five men were grim-faced and tense as they drove at speed through the dark. All were armed with 9mm Glock 18 pistols which most of them had been trained to use in the nineteen eighties when the Securitati still ran the show in Romania. Now they were here, scurrying about the backwoods in rural Lancashire, their plans for wealth beyond their wildest dreams snatched away by the antics of one man. There was a stony determination in their faces as they stared into the night.

Conrad Phillips drove the car with calculated speed. Real name Cornel Pavlenco, former major in the Romanian secret police, he knew there was still a chance of redeeming everything if they acted fast. If that wretched, money-grubbing solicitor they brought in to their operation was the link that allowed Legg to find their base two things could be solved in one blow: the elimination of Maitland and their reliance on him, and a chance to snatch the boy back from Legg. There was still a possibility that Legg might have returned to Maitland's house. If he had and they got there in time everything could be salvaged. And Pavlenco relished the opportunity of settling accounts. It was too many years since he last felt the satisfaction of terminating an enemy the way he preferred. Before this night was out he was sure he would feel it again.

The sudden speed with which the boy moved forwards caught Jimmy by surprise. One of the youth's skinny arms pushed him with such incredible force he was catapulted backwards off his feet and thrown against Janice, causing the two of them to tumble in a heap on the floor. The next moment, even though Jimmy desperately managed to scramble back onto his knees and grasp the gun in his pocket, a high-pitched scream made him freeze. His first thought was that Maitland was in agony. When he looked at the man, he could see the solicitor was too frightened to make any sound, cowering as far as he could against the sofa, his bound hands thrust in front of his face. Which was when Jimmy realised the ear-splitting shriek came from the boy, his mouth open wider than Jimmy would have ever thought physically possible. His lips were drawn into thin lines from his teeth, baring their gums. For a moment he was poised in a crouch like a misshapen beast of prey, then he lunged forwards. As if shot from a catapult he was on top of Maitland, burrowing his mouth deep into the side of the solicitor's head. For a moment he writhed back and forth, grunting horribly like a pig with its snout dug deep in the trough, before finally he pushed himself away. Gore covered his face as he spat out an ear.

His face drenched in his own blood, Maitland screamed before the boy pounced back again, his mouth to the blood that flooded from the massive wound he'd torn in the solicitor's face.

Even though he felt stunned, Jimmy recovered quickly. Raising the gun, he brought it down with as much force as he could on the back of the boy's head. It was a blow that would have killed most men. Which is what he thought he had probably done when he felt bone give way beneath him, crushed into shards, as the boy slumped forwards.

Maitland stared at him. His pupils had shrunk with terror, while his arms were beginning to shake uncontrollably. Jimmy wondered if the man was going into shock or some kind of trauma from loss of blood.

'Oh my God,' Janice stuttered. She looked to Jimmy as if she was about to gag at the sight of so much blood. 'Is the boy dead?'

Jimmy slid a finger over the trigger of the gun as he knelt beside the boy. With his free hand he felt the side of his neck. Though faint, he detected a pulse of sorts. It was weak, fluttering, like someone blowing against a membrane of skin. But it was steady. Which surprised him, sure the degree to which he had caved the boy's head in should have been enough to kill him, especially as this was the second time he'd hit him on the head tonight.

'He might survive,' Jimmy said. For the first time he wondered how much truth there was in what Maitland had said. He stared at the boy's face. His mouth was still open, and Jimmy could see the jagged rows of teeth inside. And the blood the boy had been gorging on when he'd gnawed the solicitor's ear.

Maitland groaned.

Jimmy gripped his shoulder.

'Can you hear me?' he asked.

Maitland's eyes tried to focus on his face. 'Legg?' His eyes flickered past him to where the boy still lay on the floor. 'He bit me,' Maitland said, his voice no more than a croak. 'The bastard bit me.' Jimmy could hardly fail to recognise the devastation in Maitland's voice.

'You'll survive.'

As if he'd not heard him, Maitland went on, as if to himself: 'The bastard bit me.' This time his words dissolved into a wracking sob. 'You don't realise what that means,' Maitland moaned. 'The contagion. The contagion's been passed on to me.'

'If you get to a hospital – '

'There's no fucking hospital on earth can save me now. Don't you realise that? He's bitten me! *The fucking bastard's bitten me.*'

Jimmy frowned. 'What do you think that means? That you'll turn into some kind of vampire?' Jimmy laughed, still unable to accept the idea. 'How long do you think that will take? A few hours? A few days? Several weeks?'

Maitland sobbed. 'I don't know. They never said. They'd only just finished testing his regenerative powers.'

'And how good are they?'

Maitland shook his head. 'I don't know. For God's sake, Legg, I don't know.'

'Jimmy!' Janice pointed at the boy. Already he was beginning to move, his mouth slowly opening and shutting as he started to suck some of the globules of blood still streaked across it.

Jimmy scowled. He wondered whether he should finish the job off. No matter how good his regenerative powers might be he was sure they couldn't cope with having every bone in his head crushed flat and what was left of his brains ground into mush.

But before he could act, Jimmy heard a car pull up at the end of Maitland's drive. Seconds later doors slammed shut and several pairs of feet could be heard hurrying towards the door.

'Damnation!' Jimmy rushed into the hallway, where he shot the bolts at the top and bottom of the door. Seconds later someone tried the handle.

Quietly, Jimmy leaned against it and listened.

Which was when someone fired through the door.

47

The sound was minimal. And Jimmy knew whoever shot him must have used a silencer. Even so, the pain made him gasp, though the bullet only grazed his side.

In retaliation, Jimmy pushed his gun through the letterbox and fired blindly. The percussion almost shattered his eardrums in the close confines of the hallway.

Outside, a man cried out in pain, then he heard footsteps scrambling back from the door and back down the drive.

Someone fired back at him, a quiet *phut, phut,* and two large holes appeared in the door only feet away from him. Jimmy retreated quickly. He had fired his last bullet, though they wouldn't realise that yet – which he hoped would give him time enough to do something. Though what, he had no idea.

In the living room Janice confronted him.

'Is it them?'

Jimmy nodded. 'It must be. If it was the police, they would have called a warning and ordered us out before firing. Besides, I'm sure the police don't use silencers.'

'How long do you think we have?'

'Not long. That was my last bullet. As soon as they realise I'm out of ammunition they'll be back with a vengeance. That door won't hold them long. Besides, they can't afford to wait. They have to finish what they've come here for before someone calls the police.'

Something broke in the kitchen.

It sounded like glass. A bottle, perhaps, hitting the floor and shattering.

Jimmy did not pause. Instantly, he rushed towards the back of the house. The outside door to the kitchen, which he had earlier forced to break into the house, was ajar once more when he peered inside. In the gloom he could see someone halfway across the room, their silhouette no more than a shadow against the lighter darkness of the open door behind them. Jimmy guessed whoever it was must have brushed against the table and knocked something onto the floor. Probably a ketchup bottle, Jimmy thought, remembering they had left one on the table. Despite this blunder and the silence of Jimmy's approach, the man seemed aware that someone was there. Already he was aiming a gun in Jimmy's direction.

Jimmy ducked to the floor as a light percussion, the familiar *phut* of a silencer, told him the gun had been fired. Almost simultaneously, there was a louder crack against the wall behind him as the bullet impacted hard against it, shattering plaster. Instantly, Jimmy launched himself forwards, one of the knives he had brought from Maitland's house ahead of him. He knew that what happened during the next few seconds was more luck than judgement. Despite the training the man must have had in urban combat, nothing could have prepared him for a knifepoint aimed in the right direction at the right time in the dark. The next instant Jimmy felt the knife strike home. It sank in heavily straight to the hilt, a full six inches from its point. Blood gushed across his hand. Gurgling, as he choked on his own blood, the man he had attacked stumbled forwards. The knife was stuck in his throat, jammed in the vertebrae at the back of the neck. Overbalanced by the momentum of the man's body, there was nothing Jimmy could do to stop himself from being pushed off his feet. Although he tried to keep his grip on the knife, it was wrenched from his hand, spraining his wrist. But the man was on;y seconds from death by the time they hit the floor. Thick-set and heavy, with broad shoulders, it took Jimmy more time than he knew he could spare to roll the body over and reclaim the knife, its hilt too slick with blood to grasp tightly.

He wiped the knife on the man's clothes as he stared through the open door into the back garden, tensed for another of the men to appear. A couple of minutes later, though, he knew the man must have been alone. The rest had to be at the front of the house, probably one near the car in case the police turned up. How many more would there be? If there was only one carload, there were probably no more than three, he supposed. Jimmy shook his head, as he cursed himself for failing to realise how determined they would be to get the boy back. He should have known they would realise he must have seen Maitland to find out about their place in the country. There was no other way he could have found out about it. He should never have lingered here – or have returned here at all. But it was too late now. As he stared into the darkness, all that had happened over the past few days seemed to unravel before him, one event leading to another, out of control.

'Jimmy?'

It was Janice. She stood in the doorway.

'Are you all right?'

He pushed himself away from the body and struggled to his feet.

'As right as I can be.' He kicked the body contemptuously. 'At least that's one less to worry about.' He stepped across the kitchen and shut the outside door, before pushing the kitchen table against it. He knew this wouldn't hinder anyone for more than a few seconds. But seconds counted. At the moment that was all they seemed to have.

'Is anything going on out front?' he asked.

Janice shook her head. 'They seem to be waiting.'

'Yeah. For their mate here to pump a few bullets into us.' Which was when he felt like thumping his forehead. 'You stupid bastard,' he grunted to himself. He turned and crouched by the body again. Feeling in the dark, he grabbed hold of the man's right hand. It was still gripped tight about the gun he had fired. Effortlessly, Jimmy prised the dead man's fingers from it.

The gun felt heavy when he rose to his feet, its balance spoiled by the silencer.

'It looks like our dead friend might have given us a lifeline,' Jimmy said.

Janice glanced at the body on the floor, appalled, yet at the same time impressed by the ease with which Jimmy seemed able to deal out death. It didn't appear to trouble him at all, as if none of it mattered. Perhaps it didn't, she thought as they hurried back to the living room.

'He seems to be recovering from his wounds,' Jimmy said. He nodded towards the boy, whose head wounds had already stopped bleeding. His breathing sounded normal now. While Maitland looked as if he had passed out. Even on him, the bleeding from the remnants of his torn ear had stopped.

Maitland's telephone rang, startling them both.

Jimmy reached out for it, then hesitated, uncertain.

'It'll be them,' Janice said. 'It must be.'

With a grimace, Jimmy picked up the phone and waited for someone to speak.

He did not have to wait for long.

'Is that Mr Legg?'

The voice was recognisably that of the dark haired man he remembered from the hotel.

'You should have rung a few minutes earlier,' Jimmy said. 'You might have distracted me long enough for your pal to shoot me in the back.'

There was the merest of pauses. 'I assumed he must have failed. Otherwise he would have answered the call.' If the man was concerned at what might have happened, there was no hint in his voice.

'He failed all right. Miserably. I took him down like I'll take down the rest of you.'

'Neither of us has time to bullshit, Mr Legg. You're trapped and you know it. You have the boy and, presumably, Maitland. You need to get out. We want your hostages. And both of us need to leave before the police get here and we are all arrested. That sums it up, I think.'

'What are you offering?' Jimmy asked.

'Your lives. Isn't that enough after all you've done?'

'No filthy lucre? I'm not ashamed to take money as well. I'm sure you've more than enough to spare.'

'How much were you thinking?'

'How much are they worth?'

'Don't play games. We haven't all night.'

'Would five hundred thousand pounds sound reasonable?'

'Don't make me laugh.'

'The Koreans or Al-Quaida would pay a damn sight more than that if what I've heard about this thing is true. A mindless, rampaging plague of psychopaths – or vampires or whatever you want to call them? Capable of destroying the infrastructure of a country within weeks? Half a million's nothing compared to what you know you'll get for something like this.'

'And how would we pay you? We couldn't raise a thousandth of that tonight. Cash machines don't pay out that kind of money. And we don't have suitcases of the stuff stashed away.'

'Then you'd better back off till you can raise it. Otherwise the place goes up in flames. We're getting a bit used to arson these days. And I'll bet even your boy's regenerative abilities won't help him if he's burnt to a crisp.'

'Neither of us can afford to hang around here. Someone's certain to become concerned about Maitland if he doesn't turn up at his office soon.'

'Don't worry about that,' Jimmy said. 'I'll get him to phone his staff. He can tell them he's been called away on urgent business. He'll do what I tell him to do. I can guarantee that.'

'I'm certain you can. Even so, with all that's been going on – the shots that have been fired tonight – all this activity – someone will eventually call the police, if they haven't already.'

'You'll have to risk it.' Jimmy's voice was insistent. 'There's no way I'm leaving empty handed. If you want the boy and Maitland, you'll raise the money. You'll have to make sure you do it fast.' Jimmy glanced at his wristwatch. 'It's midnight now. By midday I expect you back – alone – with the cash. Otherwise I'll do what I say. This place goes up in flames. And Maitland and the boy will die.'

'And you'll never get out of that house if you do. You know that, don't you? Some of my men will be at the end of this cul-de-sac, waiting for you. And they'll have more than handguns.'

'I'll take my chances. I might even risk calling the police. I'm sure the security services would be more than interested in looking at what you've been doing to the boy, especially if this virus crap is true. Might even be enough to buy me my freedom. Or cut a bloody great chunk off whatever time I have to serve if things go wrong. Hey, what have I got to lose?'

'You're playing a dangerous game.'

'I've been playing one of those for some time. Nothing's changed. Except you've made it a lot more interesting.' Jimmy smiled to himself, his emotions churning between excitement and anger.

'By ten,' Pavlenco, aka Phillips, said. 'I will be back by then.'

'With the cash?'

'With the cash.'

The line went dead, and Jimmy placed it back on its cradle.

He turned to Janice. 'Looks like we're out of here in the morning. And rich.'

'And the boy? Will you really hand him over to them?'

'What choice do we have? You've seen what he's like. We can't take someone as dangerous as him with us, especially if there's anything in this vampire shit. Besides, how else do you think we'll get out of here? They'll be waiting for us to try something stupid like making a break for it. He said they had other weapons besides handguns. I imagine they have. Probably something with enough fire power to tear us to pieces if we try to get away.'

'We sit here and wait?'

'And have something to eat. I don't know about you but I'm starving.'

'How can you think about food after what we've seen tonight, after what you've had to do?'

'What I did, I had to do. Either that or one of us would have been a guinea pig for those bastards to play with. I don't suppose you'd fancy having your brains scrambled like that kid's.'

'And Maitland?'

'We'll wait and see about him. If it's true about the virus he'll start to change, become as mad as the boy. Thinking about which,' he went on, 'it might be an idea to put some more rope around their wrists. Young Dracula there snapped the ones I tied him with too easily before.'

While Janice stayed in the living room, watching for signs of activity outside, Jimmy went for some more rope. A few minutes later he retied the boy's wrists. As if demonstrating the truth of what they had been told about the regenerative powers of the virus, his head wounds were already beginning to heal. Jimmy felt at the back of his skull. Amazingly, the soft texture of the multiple fractures his blows had inflicted had begun to solidify. Already it felt as firm as a normal skull. Disturbed, Jimmy went on to take a look at Maitland's wounds. The bite to his ear had removed most of it but the blood had stopped flowing a while ago. Oddly, the wound itself looked as if it was starting to knit. Where there had been a bloody gash, it looked more like a raw lump. Were these regenerative powers so good, Jimmy wondered, that Maitland's ear might grow again?

Puzzled, he returned to Janice at the bay window. She had pulled the curtain back a little so she could see out.

'I think they've driven away,' she said, her voice low.

'They won't have gone far. Probably no further than the road at the end of the cul-de-sac. From there they can get away from here if the police arrive. At the same time, they can make sure we don't make an attempt to drive off.'

213

'Do you think they'll get the money?'

'Sure. If they don't, they know I might do what I've threatened. Especially after the way I've dealt with them already.' He chuckled quietly. 'The guy I spoke to will be on his mobile now, getting it sorted. It'll be interesting to see what half a million in notes looks like. Do you think they'll need more than one suitcase to pack them in?'

Janice shook her head numbly, certain that things were far from settled, that it could only get more violent. Whether either of them would survive, she was far from sure. She had seen more of the men they were up against than Jimmy. They would never let them go, whatever deals they might concoct.

Even so, despite all her anxieties, as the long hours passed she began to doze. She tried to keep her eyes open, worried the men would return and try to sneak to the house, but it was so dark outside her eyes had nothing to focus on other than a few street lights high above the branches of the trees, and it was not long before her head began to nod.

After making them some sandwiches and coffee in the hope of helping to keep them awake, Jimmy slumped on the sofa. His fingers still curled around its butt, the pistol rested on his lap. But he was beginning to doze too. It had been a long night and they were both more exhausted than they had ever been in their lives. In the silence of the living room, with the gentle hiss of the gas fire and the heavy, regular breathing of the boy and Maitland, it was difficult for either of them to keep awake, however much danger they knew they were in. Taut nerves and over-exhausted muscles melded together in the small hours of the night to make both of them fall asleep.

Asleep with their nightmares.

It was from one such nightmare – in which decaying zombies were crawling on all fours over the streets outside her flat in South London, searching for her – that Janice awoke to see Maitland staring at her.

48

The solicitor's eyes didn't blink. They could have been the eyes of an exceptionally realistic shop window dummy or a Tussauds' waxwork. Their lids were wide open as he stared at her. Large and black, button-sized circles, his pupils seemed to see straight through her outer being and deep into her soul. They were the most terrifying eyes Janice had ever seen in her life. And she could not turn her own eyes from them. It was as if she had no choice. Her heart fluttering on the verge of panic, she held her breath, unable to function on an automatic level any more, as if whatever part of her mind coped with functions like this had been paralysed. Tensely, her hands growing cramped on her lap, she waited, simultaneously impatient for something to happen, to break the impasse, at the same time dreading what would happen next.

Nearby, she heard Jimmy stir. And for a moment she hoped he would do something to interrupt what was happening. But the slight movements he made were only from whatever nightmares he was dreaming, and a few seconds later he sank even deeper into dreamless sleep once more.

In the meantime, in the lamp-lit gloom of the living room, Maitland moved. His hands slid with a strange fluidity, emerging from the ropes that Jimmy had fastened them with. It was as if the internal skeletal structure of his hands had softened into something not much different from rubber. Caught only by her peripheral vision as she stared, enraptured by Maitland's eyes, Janice saw his hands slide from the ropes, which he laid on the carpet, before reaching down for the ropes about his ankles.

Internally, Janice's mind screamed at her to do something: to move or shout or scream or grab hold of Jimmy's shoulder and shake him awake, anything other than keep on sitting there, mesmerised. It was as if her body had been separated from her consciousness. She could barely even feel it now, as if she existed on a different plane, above and beyond her physical presence. She knew this was ridiculous, that if Maitland attacked her she would feel whatever he did to her just as much as she would ever have done. But it did no good. She could no more move her arms and legs or any other part of her body than she could those of another human being. It was impossible to do anything except stare at the man.

Quietly, Maitland rose to his feet. In the half-light she could see the terrible wound on the side of his head where his ear had been torn from him. It glistened like melted wax. It looked larger now, as if it was beginning to swell – to reform. And she remembered what had been claimed about the virus's regenerative powers. Which was when she realised Maitland must have been infected by the bite, that whatever had taken possession of the boy's body had seized him too.

As she stared at the solicitor's eyes Janice felt so frightened she began to feel physically sick. Bile began to rise in her throat and she knew she would vomit. There was no way she could control her body or attempt to restrain it. Fear and nausea were building up inside her to such a pitch she knew her reaction was inevitable. Which was when she realised the boy had woken too. Her first awareness of this was when she heard something fall to the floor behind her. Then a floorboard creaked. It was only quiet, but in the near silence of the room, only feet from her, it was unmistakeable. Then she saw him, vague in the corner of her eye. His dressing gown had fallen to the floor, along with the ropes, and his naked flesh shone with a pallid lustre in the gloom.

The explosion of vomit which surged up her throat a moment later jerked Janice out of her lethargy and she was able to push herself back across the room away from Maitland and the boy, and stumble behind the settee.

*

Startled awake by the sound of Janice's vomiting and by the acidic stench that filled the air, Jimmy lumbered to his feet, aware that something had happened.

He glanced at the silent figures as Janice was racked by further spasms of nausea.

For a moment events seemed to have taken both Maitland and the boy by surprise – or for what passed as surprise in their raddled brains. The first to move was Maitland, perhaps because his injuries were superficial compared to the compound fractures of the boy. He turned and started to stare at Jimmy just as he had at Janice a few seconds ago. But his face was in shadow, the single light source, a standard lamp with a forty-watt bulb, being behind him against the wall. Unable to see his eyes in the shadows, they had no effect on Jimmy now. All he could see was that the solicitor looked as if he was ready to attack. Which was when he raised the gun to Maitland's head and fired point blank at the bridge of his nose.

Maitland's eyes and the whole of the top of his skull disappeared in a spray of blood, bones and fleshy tissue, lifted by the explosive impact of the bullet and flung in fragments against the curtains behind him. What was left looked barely human. And, though for a moment he still stood upright, Maitland collapsed a second later in a lifeless heap.

At which point Jimmy turned the gun towards the boy, warningly.

'One move,' he said, his voice resonating in a harsh whisper, 'one fucking move and your head goes the way of his.'

Whether the boy understood or not, something inside his consciousness seemed to warn him of the threat, and he stood stock-still.

'Janice!'

The girl wiped her mouth with the back of her hands. Her throat felt raw. It took her a few seconds to recover enough to reply.

'Jimmy?'

'You all right?'

'I think so. I couldn't move when he stared at me. It was as if I was being hypnotised.'

Jimmy grunted, though he carefully averted his eyes from the boy's. Just in case, he thought, even though he felt confident it would take more than a bit of hypnotism to immobilise him.

'How the hell did they get those ropes off themselves?' he asked. 'I tied them tight enough to draw blood.'

'Maitland's hands seemed to slide out of them as if he was double-jointed or something. It was weird.'

Jimmy grunted again. Weird was becoming commonplace.

He gestured with the gun for the boy to sit down. For a moment there was a look of incomprehension on the youth's face. Then he slowly started to falter backwards, till he bumped into an armchair and fell down on it, though his eyes did not waver in their cold stare in Jimmy's direction. It was a predatory stare and Jimmy felt his flesh crawl when he glanced at it.

'There's no point in tying him up if he can get out of his bonds as easily as that,' he said, his voice gruff as if to compensate for the unsettling effect of the boy's eyes. 'Would you see if there's some place we could lock him up? A cupboard maybe. Something we could secure from the outside. If I turn my eyes from him for more than a few seconds I'm sure the bastard'll take a chance on attacking me. And we've a long night ahead of us yet.'

Janice moved away, glad for something to do. And to have Jimmy awake. Though his moods seemed unpredictable, with swings to violence, she had an odd feeling of confidence in him. Like a pet dog you know would bite anyone else but not you. Though she knew that even the best of these did turn on their owners sometimes.

A few minutes later she returned to the living room.

'There's a pantry in the kitchen. It only has a vacuum cleaner, some brushes and a mop inside it. I've taken them out. There's a flimsy bolt on the door, but we could always jam a chair against it. And at least we wouldn't have to try and avoid his eyes.'

'That'll do.' Taking care, Jimmy stepped to one side, then jabbed his gun at the boy, indicating for him to get up and head for the hallway. Janice moved behind as Jimmy goaded the boy towards the kitchen. There was a growing confidence in the boy that worried Jimmy, and he knew that if it wasn't for the gun he would be fighting for his life. And though the boy's lack of any kind of flesh was even more obvious now in his nakedness, Jimmy no longer underestimated the unnatural strength of his thin muscles.

Janice had left the kitchen light on. The pantry door stood open in a corner of the room beside a Welsh dresser.

'In there!' Jimmy ordered, uncertain how much the boy understood. He prodded him in the back of the neck with the gun.

But the boy wouldn't move. Instead, he planted his feet on the kitchen floor and stood immobile.

'Move!' Jimmy ordered. There was an edge of anger in his voice. Short fused, his temper was close to erupting and Janice was certain he would shoot the boy in the back of the head. She tensed, moving her hands to her ears.

Jimmy snapped. He gave the boy a shove in the middle of the back. However much strength there might have been in those shrunken limbs, there was little weight in him. Kinetic energy sent the youth sprawling ahead of Jimmy towards the pantry, so hard he had to lunge with both hands to prevent himself from colliding with the wall inside. Even so, he was able to spin around with incredible speed, his mouth open so wide every jagged tooth in his head was visible. A high-pitched snakelike hiss issued from the back of his throat, whether from anger or a warning Jimmy could not tell.

There was a metallic click as Jimmy jammed the pistol into the boy's face, cocking it, ready to fire.

'Back off,' Jimmy whispered.

To Janice he seemed to move almost as fast as the boy. There was a desperate standoff between them, hatred and violence vibrating through the air, scaring her. She wanted to scream but she couldn't, even more scared of distracting Jimmy.

Jimmy's breath came in short, angry bursts, his shoulders tensed as he held the gun poised before him.

'Back off,' he repeated, 'or I'll fucking well blow your head off your shoulders.'

Janice wanted to close her eyes, but dared not. Half of her wished that Jimmy would finish things now with one clean shot, even though she knew they might need the boy to get out of here, that if they killed him they would be killed by Conrad Phillips and the rest of the gang.

The boy's eyes stared up at Jimmy's face. Though he was four or five inches shorter than the man's six foot, there was a lethal menace in his gaunt body that belied the death-camp look of his physique so that it was as if, bizarrely, it was Jimmy who was at risk in a physical confrontation between them, not the boy. And Janice could truly believe he was what Conrad Phillips had called him, a living vampire. What humanity he might have once possessed seemed to have been drained from him – or poisoned by the virus that had been pumped into his veins, so that he was something that Janice could barely recognise.

Then the boy, giving way suddenly, backed into the pantry. At the same time, he closed his mouth, though it was with what seemed like a look of contempt, and just as slowly relaxed the tension in his limbs, as if he accepted that the pistol aimed between his eyes only momentarily held an advantage over him.

Immediately, Jimmy stepped back, kicked the door shut in the boy's face, then shot the tiny bolt by its latch, even though the slightest pressure from inside would easily tear its screws from the wooden panels. Only a few feet away stood a six-foot fridge freezer, a massive brute, American style, with a crushed ice dispenser at the front. After pushing the gun into one of his pockets, Jimmy grabbed hold of the fridge with both hands.

'Give me a lift,' he told Janice as he manhandled it in front of the pantry door, moving it urgently, as if he knew any moment it could burst open.

The fridge's feet screeched over the quarry tiles on the kitchen floor till it was jammed in front of the pantry door, blocking it. Panting from exertion, and with a look of relief on his face, Jimmy shoved other pieces of furniture next to the fridge, then placed several glass tumblers on the edge of them.

'If he tries to push the door open these will fall onto the floor. They'll warn us he's out.'

'How much time do you think that will give us?' Janice asked.

'Not much. With his strength and the kind of speed he's capable of, he could be out of there in seconds if he thought he could get away with it. Anything, though, is better than nothing.'

For the first time Janice could see that Jimmy was beginning to look genuinely exhausted, not only physically but mentally too as he sank onto one of the kitchen chairs, his shoulders slumped.

'We're a long way from getting out of this mess,' he said, quietly.

Janice replied that she knew.

He looked up at her. 'It's not often I apologise,' he said. 'It's not a word that's in my vocabulary,' he added with a rueful attempt at a smile. 'But I'm sorry, Janice, for dragging you into this pile of shit. I should have left you in London. It wasn't fair. You don't deserve it.'

Janice shrugged.

'A lot of people don't deserve what happens to them,' she said, wondering if he ever equated this idea with the women he had attacked and killed.

But his eyes betrayed nothing. And she was sure, in some way, that he didn't. That this side of him was never even remotely explored by the rest of him.

Janice went to the sink and poured herself a glass of water.

There were still a few hours before morning. And as she drank the water, cleansing the taste of vomit from her mouth, she was far from certain if either of them would see it.

49

Detective Sergeant McKenna had rarely had such a good breakfast. Perhaps Mason was trying to impress him. Though it was more than likely his wife, Julia, who had that intention after toiling in the kitchen for the best part of an hour getting everything ready. Either way, he was more than satisfied with the outcome, however much it might have dented his attempts to diet.

When he'd finished, it was with a deep feeling of satisfaction that he laid aside his knife and fork on his plate and reached for the cup of freshly ground coffee that Julia had placed on the table beside him.

'I shouldn't say it but I think Julia could give my wife a few tips on how to prepare a man for a day's work,' McKenna said as he looked over the remains of the breakfast: the emptied bowls of porridge and honey, the toast and marmalade, and the eggs, bacon, liver, sausage and fried tomatoes that had collectively verged on the sublime in his gourmet's mind.

'Would you like me to pass that comment onto your wife for you?' Mason asked with a self-satisfied grin.

'Hardly! Don't get me wrong. My wife's a damned fine cook in her own right. But today's banquet comes under a five-star classification, in my mind at least.'

'And mine,' Mason added. 'Though,' he went on in a quieter voice, even though his wife could hear him, 'between you and me and the gatepost, it's a bit more special than usual. Don't think I get pampered like this every day. Besides, a sergeant's pay wouldn't be enough to cover it seven days a week.'

'I don't suppose your waistline would stand it either. Though I've room to talk!'

Excellent though the breakfast was, neither of them had much more time in which to linger. Despite a late night at the arson attack on the farmhouse and barn, there was a heavy schedule ahead of them today. McKenna had to report back to his governor in London on what progress he was making, while last night's fire was going to take up much of Mason's day.

'I'd still like to have a word with that solicitor of Legg's mother to see what he knows about the insurance details on the hotel,' McKenna said as they were putting on their coats to go.

McKenna had already tried calling Maitland's office but his receptionist had been vague about where he was. 'He's not called in. He might be at home,' she'd admitted after he identified himself. 'He sometimes has a heavy night, if you know what I mean, and doesn't come in till afternoon. We handle things for him till then.'

Which made McKenna wonder just what sort of business he ran. 'Dodgy,' had been Mason's reply, touching the side of his nose. 'Definitely dodgy.'

'I don't think I'll be able to spare the time to go round with you to see Maitland,' Mason said, regretfully. 'We're short handed and up to the gills with work.'

'Is there any chance I could borrow a car to drive to see Maitland by myself?'

'No problem,' Mason said. 'You could borrow the wife's. I know she's nothing planned today. Just put in some petrol, if you wouldn't mind. It'll keep her happy.'

So it was that half an hour later, McKenna drove Julia Mason's Peugeot 206 to the offices of Christopher Maitland Solicitors. If the man wasn't in, he would find out where he lived and try there, he decided, Julia Mason's ample breakfast making him feel at peace with the world as he drove. Last night's clouds had lifted and it looked as if it was going to be one of those glorious spring-like days that heralded a taste of what was still to come.

50

The air in the living room had begun to smell grungy. Janice looked at where Maitland had collapsed on the floor, his knees pointing forwards, his feet tucked unnaturally beneath them as if he'd fallen while praying. She averted her eyes from looking further at the corpse. She had only seen what was left of his head once. And she had no intention of looking at it again if she could help it. She had never seen anything so repulsive in her life compared to what the bullet had done to him. She had expected a neat hole. Perhaps the bullets in the gun that Jimmy had taken from the intruder, whose body still lay at the back of the kitchen in a crumpled heap, had some kind of explosive charge inside them. Either that or the close proximity of the gun when Jimmy fired it accounted for the damage.

Janice shuddered as she hugged her arms about herself, feeling cold and frightened. The house looked like a morgue, she thought with a feeling not all that far from horror as she wondered what the police would make of the place when they eventually forced their way in. Or what they would make of the boy they had locked inside the cupboard, if he was still there when they got here.

'There's light in the sky,' Jimmy said suddenly from his seat by the window, the pistol on his lap.

Which made Janice wonder what arrangements they would have to make with Phillips and the rest of the men when they returned with the cash. She could not believe they would allow them to get away with that kind of money. Nor with what they knew about the virus. Somehow she doubted even Jimmy would be able to think up a plan that would give them a chance of getting out of here alive. Not against those men. They were ruthless professionals. Only men like that could create something as dangerous and evil as the thing they had turned that poor runaway into and have the ability to control it.

'Where would you fancy going with all that money?' Jimmy asked suddenly.

Janice shrugged, her doubts about their ability to get out of here alive, never mind the money, too strong to give her any faith in it all. 'You want me to go with you?' she asked finally.

'Wouldn't you stand a better chance of getting away by yourself, without me holding you back?'

'Maybe,' he said. 'But it can get lonely sometimes when you've no one to talk to, no one whose views you like to hear, whose voice you like to listen to. It's not often you come across someone you genuinely don't feel lonely with. Someone whose company you value. Who means something to you.'

'You're beginning to sound almost poetic, Jimmy Legg,' she said. 'I didn't know you had it in you.'

'Just a gruff, brutal, selfish bastard with none of the finer points in me, is that what you mean?' He laughed, quietly. 'That's me all right. That's the real me, I suppose,' he added, reflectively.

There wasn't consciousness as such. There was an awareness of being. But there were no thoughts. None that would be recognisable to any human being. That the rest of its brain had been destroyed did not affect the amygdala, the reptile brain that co-exists within every human skull, nestled within the temporal lobes, always there, always active, alive with emotions and primal instincts, safe from logic and any of the higher thought functions. Changes wrought by the invading virus had lessened some aspects and increased others, warping and twisting what was left into a coherent whole, as alien from what had existed before as the brain of a man is alien to that of a serpent.

The extreme damage that the bullet had inflicted on the rest of the brain had accelerated some changes. As had the need to repair some of its primary sensors. Sight had been destroyed. But the surviving brain instinctively knew that sight was essential for its survival. Basic, at first, a form of sight was retrieved through the existence of several damaged nerve endings, blood vessels and other fleshy sensory matter.

During the long, dark hours towards the end of the night tendrils of fibrous tissue grew, melded and continued to work, rebuilding a crude approximation of what had been damaged – crude but workable.

Which was all that it needed.

At ten o'clock the telephone rang.

They were waiting for it. A couple of hours earlier, Jimmy had prepared breakfast as the night drew to a close and they could see the first hints of dawn. It had been almost as lavish as that enjoyed by Detective Sergeant Ian McKenna, but the mood was gloomier. At first, Janice was not even sure she could eat anything at all in this house and had taken her plate into the dining room to avoid having to look at a corpse at the same time as she ate. She had seen so much violent death in the last twenty-four hours she had almost grown used to it, but not so she could dine in its presence.

Jimmy pushed himself up from the sofa and picked up the phone. Janice listened intently, knowing he had still no plan of action.

'We'll have to play it by ear,' he told her earlier when they discussed what to do.

Phillips was on the other end of the line.

'We've raised the money.'

'That was quick of you,' Jimmy said, matter of factly.

'We had to call in a few favours to get it. Fortunately, someone had a sizeable amount of cash they wanted to launder. Used notes, various denominations. Just what you'd prefer, I imagine.'

'Couldn't be better. How bulky is it?'

'We managed to cram it into two suitcases. How you transport it is your problem, not ours. All we want are the boy and Maitland.'

'There's been a problem with Maitland,' Jimmy said.

'Problem? What do you mean?'

'The boy bit him. He became infected. He tried to attack me and I had to kill him.'

'You still have the body?'

'Where else do you think it'd be? We've not been in a position to go out and dispose of it.'

There was a slight pause, and Jimmy had the impression Phillips had either covered the mouthpiece or put it on mute and was talking to someone else.

'Leave Maitland's body where it is,' Phillips said finally. 'We'll arrange what to do with it.'

'Suits me. Couldn't stand the bastard before he became infected. Believe me, he was fucking worse afterwards.'

'Have there been any other problems?'

'Apart from having to lock the boy in a cupboard to stop that antisocial problem of his from getting out of hand, no.'

'You have a bizarre sense of humour, Mr Legg.'

'Which is getting more bizarre by the minute. Events are having that effect on me.'

Phillips ignored the comment, saying: 'One of my colleagues will visit you in a few minutes. He'll have one of the suitcases of money with him. While at the house he'll check everything you say is correct. He will also have a Taser. This is not to be used against you, so don't worry when you see it. You can have your gun trained on him while he is with you to make sure he doesn't try anything. That won't trouble him. The Taser is for use on the boy. Practice has shown this is the most effective way of neutralising the threat he poses without killing him.'

'I'll have my gun trained on him while he's here all right, whether he's got a Taser or not. Just make sure he knows if he even so much as points that fucker anywhere near where I'm stood, he's liable to have his brains splattered across the wall.'

Jimmy put down the phone. Turning towards Janice, he said: 'It's starting.'

Janice shivered. 'It's how this mess is going to finish that worries me.'

Jimmy walked over to her. 'Me too, if I'm being honest about it, Jan. Me too.'

If they had expected to be given time to brood about this, they were wrong. A few minutes later a car pulled up at the end of the drive and a man got out of the passenger side, a heavy suitcase in one hand. Janice recognised him as the fair-haired man who had called himself Kingsley Wellington, a ludicrous pseudonym she hadn't believed at the time. Wellington glanced at the house as the car reversed up the street, leaving him alone. Janice thought there was a look of apprehension on his face. Something bulky in a dark plastic case was hung from a strap over his shoulder. He hugged it to him as he heaved the suitcase towards the house.

A few seconds later he was at the front door and Jimmy opened it to him, his pistol pointed at the man's stomach. He carefully backed away as the Wellington stepped inside the hallway.

'Leave the suitcase by the coat stand,' Jimmy said. 'I don't want to have to drag it any further when we get out of here. Though we'll look inside first – just to make sure it's not been packed with old newspapers. They don't spend well.' He called Janice over as Wellington unclipped the suitcase's fasteners and opened it. True to their word, it was filled with bundles of used notes. 'Check a few of the bundles just to be sure,' Jimmy told her.

'They're kosher,' Wellington said. 'Two hundred and twenty thousand in this bag. The remainder in the next. After I've verified the boy is undamaged you can have the rest and leave.'

Jimmy laughed. 'He's a bit damaged,' he said. 'I had to give him a few hard knocks to stop him from spreading his infection to the two of us. But you'd understand that, I'm sure. Still, he looked to be recovering well enough the last time I checked.'

'Which is why I brought this,' Wellington said, indicating the bag over his shoulder. 'Do you mind?' His fingers touched the strap at the front.

'Be my guest,' Jimmy said. 'Just be sure to keep it pointed away from me. I can be a bit jumpy when people aim weapons in my direction.'

Wellington smiled thinly as he unfastened the bag and took out the Taser. The gun was bulky, with yellow flaps at the front of its black plastic barrel.

'This will subdue him without causing damage.'

'I hope it works quick for your sake. He moves like lightning.'

'It's quick all right,' Wellington said.

Jimmy nodded towards the back of the house. 'He's in there. Locked in a cupboard.'

As they stepped into the kitchen, the man glanced at his dead colleague. His body still lay on the floor where Jimmy had shot him. Then Wellington looked at the line of furniture crammed against one wall. Carefully, he began to move them to one side till he reached the fridge, then he checked the Taser, and looked at Jimmy.

'Put that thing away for a second and I'll give you a lift,' Jimmy said. 'But I'm not taking my eyes off you.'

Together they shuffled the fridge away from the pantry door. They had hardly cleared it when the door burst open.

Immediately, as if he had expected it, Wellington reached for the Taser. Knowing the threat from the boy was too real to be used as a ruse, Jimmy stepped back as Wellington aimed. A second later the boy burst out. His skin looked like a semi-transparent sheen of wax. His eyes were huge as he stared at them, thin networks of veins spread over their whites. When he opened his mouth even Jimmy shuddered at the rows of teeth. The next instant Wellington fired and two darts hit the youth on the chest and stomach. Fifty thousand volts surged into him, knocking the boy off his feet, so that he lay curled up on the floor like a grotesque foetus, shuddering.

'That will keep him out of action for at least ten minutes,' Wellington said, briskly. He stepped over to boy, retrieved the darts, then pulled out two pairs of stainless steel handcuffs from the bag he'd stored the Taser in, fastening them about the boy's wrists and ankles. 'He'll not work his way out of these,' he said, straightening up with military brusqueness.

Impressed, Jimmy said. 'I'll feel better when that Taser's back in its bag and you can't be tempted to use it on me.'

Wellington smiled. 'Anything to oblige,' he said. 'You only have to ask.' He carefully fastened the bag shut. 'Okay?'

'For now.' Jimmy followed him as they returned to the hallway.

'I'll take a look at Maitland,' Wellington said.

Jimmy pointed into the living room. 'He's where I left him. I had to blow half his head away.'

Wellington glanced at the body. A large pool of blood had spread across the carpet from the gaping wound across the crown of Maitland's head.

'No half measures,' Wellington said, though he stepped no closer than a few yards from it.

'If you've seen enough, perhaps we could make arrangements for Janice and me to get out of here. I can't see any point in lingering. With all this activity I don't give it long before someone rings the police.'

Wellington nodded his agreement. 'I'll have to phone and let everyone know everything is satisfactory.' With Jimmy's approval, he lowered the shoulder bag onto the floor and reached inside his jacket for his mobile. Stepping nearer the window, Wellington dialled.

'No problems,' he said into the phone a moment later. 'The boy's cuffed. We shouldn't have any trouble when he comes round. Otherwise there's Legg and the girl to make arrangements for.'

Which was when he ducked behind the furniture in the bay window as a cloud of smoke exploded from the shoulder bag. The room was instantly filled with it. Janice screamed, her eyes stinging from the acrid smoke as she glimpsed Wellington strap a pair of goggles to his eyes, before crawling behind the furniture.

Squinting fiercely through the smoke, Jimmy tried to make out where Wellington was, when the door burst open and two men shouldered their way into the room, military-style gas masks on their faces. Despite the masks and the blistering smoke that burned her eyes, Janice recognised Conrad Phillips. She could not mistake his black, slicked-back hair. The other was a portly East European she remembered from the barn in a leather jacket and jeans. Both held handguns with silencers. Both were pointed at Jimmy Legg.

Phillips reached for and grasped the barrel of Jimmy's gun, taking it from him.

'Very wise,' Phillips said, his voice distorted by the gas mask as he tucked Jimmy's gun into one of his pockets and gestured for him and Janice to step into the hallway. 'Hands behind your necks,' he said sternly.

They had no sooner stepped out of the room than someone screamed.

It was a man.

In agony.

In *extreme* agony.

The scream rose into a crescendo.

Despite the acidic smoke that had reduced his vision to a tear-filled, agonising slit, Jimmy was shocked to see Maitland's body move. The corpse seemed to be trying to roll over and straighten its legs, its motions jerky. At the same its arms had reached beyond the gory crater of its cranium to grasp hold of

Wellington, who was trying to climb out from behind the sofa. At the same time, it spat out a chunk of what looked like human flesh, perhaps a mangled thumb, which it had bitten from Wellington's hand. Its own hands gripped the man's lapels as it dragged his face towards its own with irresistible strength. Blood sprayed between them as Maitland's head lunged forward, burying itself in Wellington's face. The man flailed at the creature but could do nothing to keep it off him, his actions more frantic as pain took over and he lost all sense of reason.

Acting on impulse, Phillips turned and fired three shots into Maitland's back, but the bullets appeared to make little impression. The greasy dome of the corpse's skull, where some sort of reconstruction seemed to have taken place, bobbed back and forth as it bit and tore at Wellington regardless of the bullets pumped into it. For a moment it lifted its head from the strips of flesh that were all that remained of Wellington's face and stared at them with the opaque globe of what looked like a crude human eye, a gristly structure that had grown from the tissues of its exposed brain. It blinked before its mouth opened, exposing its teeth.

In that moment of distraction, as the rest of them stared at the abomination, Jimmy slammed his fist into Phillips's companion. Unprepared for the blow, the man doubled up in agony, which was when Jimmy brought his elbow down against his temple in a hard, bone-crunching jab that floored him. Even as the man collapsed, already unconscious, perhaps even dead, Jimmy knelt and tugged the gun from his hand. But Phillips had seen him. Turning, he fired. Jimmy felt the impact of the bullet as it struck his side, as if a white-hot poker had been plunged into him. It took away his breath, and for a moment he felt as if the world had tilted to one side and his sense of balance deserted him.

You idiot, Jimmy thought to himself as he gritted his teeth against the pain, his mouth grimacing.

He looked up in time to see Maitland's reanimated corpse toss what was left of Wellington's head to one side, then jump to its feet. A good third of its head had been blasted from it and its face was the colour of curdled milk, bespattered with blood. But what was left of Maitland seemed to have almost superhuman strength. Blood drooled from its mouth as it turned its head towards Phillips, who fired at it again, shearing lumps of flesh and bone from the side of its face in bloody swathes. None of this seemed to deter the creature, as if it had passed through pain and fleshy concerns, as if none of these mattered any more. Perhaps the damage Jimmy's bullet had done to what was left of Maitland's brain had sent it insane – even by vampiric standards – and turned it into something even more ferocious than the boy.

As if he sensed this too, Phillips backed away from the creature as he fired again, exploding more of Maitland's skull as the solicitor rushed across the room towards him.

Jimmy felt Janice's hands on his arms as she tugged him away from the struggle.

'You're hurt,' she said urgently, concerned.

Jimmy grunted, in too much pain to speak.

Phillip's gun fired again – the familiar *phut* – and Jimmy saw more of Maitland's head disappear in a cloud of blood and bones. Then Maitland was on him. Phillips beat at the unrecognisable mess of the head with his gun as the creature gripped him by his shoulders.

The front door was blocked as the two struggled in the hallway, Phillips's gas mask ripped to one side as Maitland's shattered mouth tried to fasten itself to him in an ugly, tooth-filled grimace.

'The back door,' Jimmy managed to grunt.

Janice helped him to his feet. Blood was pouring from the wound in his side, and his trousers were already sodden with it. No wonder he felt so weak, he thought. He knew he had to get a grip of himself, but the pain and blood loss were sapping him, making his thoughts fuzzy. But he had to think. There was more to be done if the two of them were to get out of here alive.

Despite the pain, Jimmy clasped one hand on Janice's arm.

'We have to kill them,' he managed to say to her. 'Both of them back there. Maitland will infect him. Then Phillips will attack us. Shoot them both. In the head.'

'But that didn't kill Maitland. He still came back,' Janice said, sounding more concerned about Jimmy's blood loss than the possibility of Conrad Phillips being turned into a vampire.

'I think I know why.' Jimmy stopped for a moment as he almost blacked out. 'They said most of the brain is destroyed by the virus. Only a part of it survives. The reptile brain. Is that right?'

Janice nodded. 'He called it the amygdala. Or something like that.'

'Perhaps I missed hitting that. Perhaps that survived when I shot Maitland.'

'My God, Jimmy, what are you asking me to do? Shoot till there's nothing left of their heads?' She shuddered, sounding sick. 'I couldn't do it, Jimmy. I don't even know if I could shoot them at all, even if they attacked me.'

Jimmy leaned against the wall. At the end of the passage there was a scream – it was a mixture of pain and horror. Looking back, Jimmy saw that Maitland had finally forced his mouth to Phillips's neck. Blood gushed from the bite. Phillips struggled to free himself, but it was obvious from the look on his face he knew it was too late, the thing had infected him. That he was doomed.

'Kill me!' Phillips cried as he desperately forced his head round to stare towards Jimmy. 'For Christ's sake, kill me!'

Jimmy's mouth twisted at the irony. As if Phillips – or whatever the bastard was called – deserved any sympathy from him when he had been prepared to infect whole countries with the virus if the money was right.

'I'll kill you all right,' Jimmy muttered. 'But it won't be to save you. It'll be to save us from what you'll become.'

Despite the nausea that was overcoming him, Jimmy took a firm grip on the gun still held in one hand. 'Help me,' he said to Janice, his teeth clenched. 'Support my arm when I raise it.'

Janice put her hands to his arm as he aimed at Maitland. As if the creature sensed what was happening, it unclenched its teeth from Phillips's neck, its mouth dribbling blood, and turned to face them. Which was when Jimmy fired. The recoil seemed to tear through his insides where the bullet that hit him had already ripped him apart, and he cried out in pain. But his aim was good. The back of Maitland's head exploded. This time the amygdala too had been hit, he knew it. For a second Maitland jerked upright, then collapsed to the floor. Freed from the creature's grasp Phillips stared at it as blood pulsed from his throat, then he raised his own gun up to his mouth, jammed the silencer deep inside and pulled the trigger.

'Let's get out of here,' Jimmy said.

'What if there are any more of Phillips's men outside?'

'If there are, we've had it. But I don't think there will be. He wouldn't have burst in with just one backup if there'd been more.' Stumbling, Jimmy led them to the front door. As they passed the bodies of Maitland and Phillips it was obvious they were dead – permanently dead. Phillips must have known exactly where he needed to shoot himself – and made a professional job of it.

Janice grimaced as she averted her eyes from the blood and brains strewn over the walls and carpet.

Jimmy stopped at the door, gasping for breath.

'You go, Janice,' he said.

'But you need help.'

'I think I'm past that now.'

'You could go to hospital? Get patched up.'

'For what? To be ready for prison? I'm not going to spend the rest of my life inside.'

'After what you've done, stopping Phillips and all the rest of them, surely that would count?'

'For fuck all, Janice. You know that. Besides...' He paused to catch his breath and steel himself against the pain. 'I don't think this is a minor scratch. It'll take more than a plaster to put it right.' He coughed, tasting blood. 'I'm going back inside. Finish the boy off. You should get out of here. Take the car. Drive away. Forget what you've seen.' He looked down the hallway. 'I'll start another fire when I'm done. Destroy any connection you might have with this place.' He tried to smile, but he couldn't manage it. 'Get going, Jan. Please.'

With hesitant steps, Janice opened the front door.

'Jimmy...'

'Please!'

She turned, stifling tears, then ran towards the car.

53

Jimmy watched her climb into the Fiesta, reverse through the open gate onto the road. He saw her look back at him, and he waved, though it was an effort that made blotches of darkness form before his eyes. Then she was gone. And there was a silence.

Like the grave, he thought.

Slowly, Jimmy pushed the door shut, locked it behind him, then turned and headed down the hallway, his feet so heavy he could barely lift them as he leaned against the wall for support. He felt dizzy and he knew he would have to act fast. But it seemed such a long way to the kitchen. Too long. An eternity.

And he needed to rest…

Time to rest later, he told himself as harshly as he could. There's work to be done. Work that has to be done.

And now.

Jimmy reached for the doorframe to steady himself as he stepped into the kitchen. Instinctively, he tightened his grip on the gun even though it felt so heavy he wasn't sure if he could raise it anymore. Ahead of him something moved. One shot, he thought. That was all it would need. One shot to the head. But the shape moved fast. Too fast. He could barely follow it with his blood-drained eyes, his brain too fuzzy to concentrate even when he saw the boy's eyes stare into his with a look of hunger.

54

Janice drove fast. Whatever Jimmy said, she was not going to give up on him. He might be a murderer but she was not going to desert him now.

A short way down the road she spotted the very thing she had been looking for.

Slamming on the brakes, she drew up beside the telephone box, jumped out and ran into it.

There would still be time for an ambulance to take Jimmy to hospital. He might not want to spend the rest of his life in prison. But she could not leave him to die in that house alone. No one deserved to die like that.

Detective Sergeant Ian McKenna never even glanced at the pale cream Fiesta or the girl stood in the telephone box as he drove towards Maitland's house. Fifteen minutes at the solicitor's office had been more than enough to convince him he was on the right trail and he was impatient to see the man. Even so, he had been diligent enough to make sure he called to tell Mason where he was going.

'Let me know how you get on,' Mason said. 'Gut instincts are sometimes right.'

Which was all it was, Ian knew. Nevertheless, he felt confident that Maitland had something to do with Legg, though how or why, other than his involvement with the mother's will, he was far from sure.

A few minutes later he saw the sign for Harper's Close. Number eleven, at the end of the cul-de-sac was Maitland's house according to the directions he'd been given by the solicitor's receptionist. As he drew up outside its wrought iron gates Ian noted they were open and that Maitland's Alfa Romeo was parked on the drive.

Bingo, he thought. The bugger's in. Which put a smile on his face as he pulled himself out of the car. For a moment he tucked his shirt back under the overstrained waistband of his trousers, not helped by Julia Mason's generous breakfast this morning, then plodded up the drive. After ringing the doorbell for several minutes and hammering on its panels, he walked to the side of the house. A couple of times he called out Maitland's name, his voice sounding husky from exertion as he marched down the concrete path to the back of the house. Authoritatively, he rapped his knuckles on the kitchen door, then pushed it open, interested to find it had already been forced.

'Maitland, are you in? It's the police,' he called out again, before entering the kitchen.

At first the upheaval inside the room hardly surprised him. A kitchen table stood across the middle of the room as if it had been violently pushed to one side, perhaps in a struggle, and there was a huge, American-style fridge – the very thing his wife had been nagging about getting for the past six months – stood next to it, its electric cable stretched to its limit from its socket on the wall.

It was then Ian saw the body sprawled on the floor. He did not need to examine it to realise the man had been killed by a gunshot wound to the chest. Blood had settled in a broad pool across the quarry tiles. Its colour showed several hours had passed since the man was shot. Was the body Maitland's? Carefully, mindful of his arthritic knees, Ian knelt beside the body to get a clearer view of the face. Which was when he heard something move behind him.

His spine tingled with apprehension as he turned.

Hidden from sight by the furniture when he entered the room, another body lay on the floor. Someone was crouched above it, small in stature, glisteningly pale – and naked. Ian recognised the body as Jimmy Legg's, though his upturned face was expressionless. Blood oozed from a wound to the side of the man's neck where he had been bitten. The other figure, though, was odd, so odd, in fact, that Ian could not for a moment take in what he was looking at. It was thin and white, with eyes that stared with a strange luminescence in the gloom. And for the first time Ian felt afraid, unsure if the creature was animal or human. Or neither. His heart pounded so hard he had serious concerns he was about to have a heart attack as he rose and started to step away from it, when he saw the handcuffs fastened around the creature's wrists.

What the hell had been going on here?

'Who are you?' Ian asked, his voice shaking. But the creature didn't seem to understand his words. Instead, its mouth opened wide with an explosive hiss, exposing the jagged teeth inside.

Then it leapt.

Epilogue

After making her phone call, Janice returned to the Fiesta, uncertain what to do next. Although Jimmy had told her to keep away, that he would make sure there was nothing to link her to what had happened at the house, that he would destroy all the evidence with fire, she could not abandon him. Somehow, in some way she had to help him. If not, she was sure the truth would be buried behind the sensationalism of whatever else he had been guilty of doing, bad though that was.

Janice felt torn in her loyalties. She despised what she knew Jimmy had done. At the same time, she knew he had risked his life to save her.

Despite the urgency of her call, it was half an hour before the first police car arrived. In its wake more vehicles, including an ambulance, were there minutes later. When the last had gone by and the road was quiet again, Janice drove towards Maitland's house.

She pulled up a short distance from the close, climbed out and walked towards it.

*

Detective Sergeant Mason was the first to arrive. He recognised his wife's car parked outside the house at the bottom of the cul-de-sac.

'Ian!' he called as he rapped on the front door, which was still locked shut. When there was no answer, he told the uniformed policemen who had accompanied him to force the door open. Within seconds it had been pounded in – and Mason saw the bodies inside.

*

Janice did not go down the close. She would wait, then go and see whoever was in charge as soon as she managed to get her thoughts together again, and do what she could to help Jimmy.

Which was when she saw him.

At first she thought she was hallucinating. Somehow Jimmy

240

must have escaped from the house before the police arrived at it and made his way to the road, because there he was no more than a block away from her. She could not mistake that unruly shock of jet-black hair. She waved to him as he stood by the roadside. He turned and saw her and started to run towards her. Janice realised that the gunshot wound in his side must not have been as serious as he thought, because it didn't seem to bother him now, even though his trousers were soaked in blood.

As he neared her, though, Janice was sure there was too much blood on his clothes, that it was a wonder he hadn't collapsed. But he was running towards her as if he had not been hurt at all.

It was not till he made his final sprint towards her, so fast she had no time in which to scream before his hands were clasped around her throat, that she saw the glassy, death-like look in his eyes.

As Jimmy crashed into her with all the momentum of his racing body, further along the street a naked boy with manacled wrists and an overweight man, his shirt hanging out and soaked with blood, picked their way towards the nearest houses…

Parallel Universe Publications

CLASSIC WEIRD 2 selected by David A. Riley
ISBN: 978-0-9932888-4-5

OTHER VISIONS OF HEAVEN AND HELL by Jessica Palmer
ISBN: 978-0-9935742-1-4

A SAUCERFUL OF SECRETS by Andrew Darlington
ISBN: 978-0-9935742-0-7

THE WINTER HUNT AND OTHER STORIES
by Steve Lockley & Paul Lewis
ISBN: 978-0-9932888-9-0

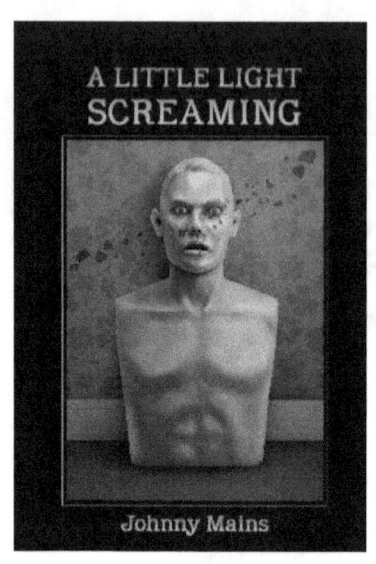

A LITTLE LIGHT SCREAMING by Johnny Mains
ISBN: 978-0-9932888-5-2

ENGLAND 'B': 90 MINUTES OF HELL by Richard Staines
ISBN: 978-0-9932888-7-6

AND NOBODY LIVED HAPPILY EVER AFTER by Kate Farrell
ISBN: 978-0-9932888-8-3

FISHHEAD; THE DARKER TALES OF IRVIN S. COBB
ISBN: 978-0-9935742-4-5

KITCHEN SINK GOTHIC: Selected by David and Linden Riley
ISBN: 978-0-9932888-3-8

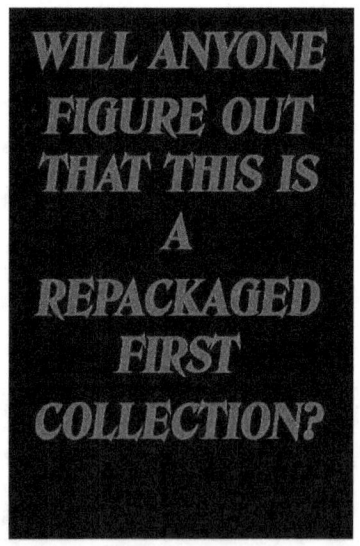

WILL ANYONE FIGURE OUT THAT THIS IS A REPACKAGED FIRST
COLLECTION? by Johnny Mains
ISBN: 978-0-9574535-7-9

BLACK CEREMONIES by Charles Black
ISBN: 978-0-9574535-5-5

HIS OWN MAD DEMONS:
DARK TALES FROM DAVID A. RILEY
ISBN: 978-0-9574535-8-6

THEIR CRAMPED DARK WORLD by David A. Riley
ISBN: 978-0-9574535-9-3

THE HEAVEN MAKER AND OTHER GRUESOME TALES
by Craig Herbertson
ISBN: 978-0-9932888-2-1

GOBLIN MIRE by David A. Riley
ISBN: 978-0-9574535-4-8

THINGS THAT GO BUMP IN THE NIGHT
selected by Douglas Draa and David A. Riley
ISBN: 978-0-9574535-6-2

CLASSIC WEIRD selected David A. Riley
ISBN: 978-0-9574535-3-1

MOLOCH'S CHILDREN by David A. Riley
ISBN: 978-0-9932888-1-4

Check our website:

http://paralleluniversepublications.blogspot.co.uk/